Adeline Sergeant, Jules Lermina

The Chase

A Tale of the Southern States

Adeline Sergeant, Jules Lermina

The Chase
A Tale of the Southern States

ISBN/EAN: 9783337004170

Printed in Europe, USA, Canada, Australia, Japan

Cover: Foto ©Andreas Hilbeck / pixelio.de

More available books at **www.hansebooks.com**

THE CHASE

A TALE OF THE SOUTHERN STATES

From the French of Jules Lermina

BY

ADELINE SERGEANT

ONLY TRANSLATION SANCTIONED BY THE AUTHOR AND BY THE
INTERNATIONAL LITERARY ASSOCIATION

LONDON
J. C. NIMMO & BAIN
14 KING WILLIAM STREET, STRAND, W.C.
1880

CONTENTS.

PROLOGUE.

	PAGE
I. THE THUNDERBOLT	I
II. THE WOMAN WITH AN IRON WILL	17

CHAP.

I. ON THE BANKS OF THE MISSISSIPPI	26
II. THE BLUE HILLS	34
III. SAMBO	49
IV. THE BATTLE FIELD TRAGEDY	64
V. THE DETECTIVE	82
VI. THE DANGERS OF MIMICRY	95
VII. A WANDERER	110
VIII. ANOTHER ADVENTURE	132
IX. THE PURSUIT	147
X. INDIANS AND SNAKES	154

CONTENTS.

CHAP.   PAGE

   XI. NED BARK'S PREDICTION 173

  XII. EUSÈBE AS CAPTAIN 190

 XIII. AT ANASTASIA 207

 XIV. THE REVELATION 222

  XV. THE CRUSTACEAN 235

 XVI. THE MYSTERY OF DEVIL'S ROCK . . 247

 XVII. THE RETURN 259

XVIII. RED RALPH'S FOREFATHERS . . . 273

 XIX. A CAPTURE 287

  XX. THE END APPROACHES 302

 XXI. PUNISHMENT 320

 XXII. ALL'S WELL THAT ENDS WELL . . 337

THE CHASE.

PROLOGUE.

I.

THE THUNDERBOLT.

A FINE autumn evening; purple clouds still glowing on the horizon; the warm air heavy with fragrance; the dark foliage of the Bois de Boulogne softly shadowed forth in outline against a clear sky; the measured fall of horses' hoofs advancing at a foot-pace towards the city: so much for the picturesque aspect of the scene.

A few words were now and then softly interchanged between two of the riders, one of whom was a lively, handsome young man; the other, a girl, whose long fair hair fell over her graceful shoulders and slender figure like a mantle.

"Dear Alice! how happy I am! If you knew how much I love you!"

"Do you think that you will always care for me?"

"Always; I swear it."

So much for the sentimental side of the picture.

Finally, at some distance behind the two lovers, could be seen a fantastic and pretentious-looking individual of foppish appearance, equipped from head to foot in the height of fashion, to a degree which can be imagined rather than described: a young exquisite whose sole occupation was to fidget in his saddle and suck the handle of his riding-whip.

So much for the absurd side of it.

Let us introduce our characters more in detail, and satisfy the natural curiosity of our readers by beginning with Alice Lodier. She was twenty years of age: a fair and lovely girl, with dark-grey eyes. The child of creole parents, she had been orphaned since her infancy, together with her brother, the young man who took the third place in the opening list of our *dramatis personæ*. She had been educated by her maternal aunt, Madame Longpré, a woman of the most rigid principles and of iron will,—so, at least, she used to say,—characteristics which did not prevent her from yielding a profound submission to all Alice's caprices.

They were very innocent caprices, however. Alice was one of the purest and sweetest of girls, although she possessed a somewhat mutinous disposition 'which did not love restraint. In spite of her delicate appearance, she was strong and energetic. She loved fresh air and liberty; her greatest delights were to gallop in the face of a high wind, to swim against the stream, to draw in great breaths of air and life. Her moral was like her physical nature. She reached out enthusiastically after all that was noble and true—after justice, devotion, and earnest striving for the right.

Good Madame Longpré often called her Donna Quixote. And indeed there was no class of evil-doers or misbelievers with whom she was not ready to break a lance. Add to these qualities an inexhaustible fund of sympathy with the weak and kindness for the suffering; and even the most sceptical of readers will admit that Alice was worthy of the admiring epithets which we have—only too sparingly—bestowed upon her.

One day in Alice's life a new prospect suddenly opened out before her. Young men of high rank and good breeding had often already fluttered round the heiress, who, they knew, would have many thousands for her marriage portion. But as yet Alice might have placed her hand upon her heart and answered in the historic words—

"It beats no faster than usual!"

When suddenly a warning throb surprised and half dismayed her.

Six months had passed since this phenomenon was first produced. One fine evening, a servant at the door of Madame Longpré's drawing-room had announced M. Charles Valville, and a young man of high stature and dark complexion, with frank, clear eyes and smiling mouth, had bowed to the old lady and said—

"Madame, my father, M. Valville, of New Orleans,

made me venture to hope that for his sake you would kindly receive his son."

And while the worthy aunt, with the assistance of her spectacles, deciphered the foreign handwriting, and then cried out that M. Valville had been an old friend of M. Lodier's, and that she was delighted to receive his son, Alice's heart throbbed faster still—so fast and so loud that Charles must surely have heard it beat, for he glanced at the girl and blushed like a child, while she only turned a little pale.

Her brother was also present, and, with the tact that characterised him, lisped out—

" What a funny idea! He's from America!"

Charles looked at the young exquisite, with his tiny coat, and hair fresh from the curling-irons, and repressed a smile as he assured himself by unmistakable points of resemblance that this little product of civilisation was really the young lady's brother.

Eusèbe Lodier had not a bad disposition ; he was not even without intelligence ; but he was utterly given over to foppery, affectation, and love of fashion. He was constantly to be seen in the green-rooms of the theatres of the Variétés, or of the Palais Royal ; and thought it the height of wit to imitate the dress and manners of his favourite actors, Lassouche and Priston ; above all, the height of good taste to turn everything into ridicule.

To Eusèbe, patriotism, love, devotion, passion of what kind soever—political, artistic, or scientific—was nothing but mere 'stuff and nonsense.' He was well versed in slang, and used it not a little. Certainly it would have been useless to talk sentiment to him. He repeated continually that he was a practical man, a man of the world and not behind the times—not he !

It was Eusèbe who followed in the wake of Alice and Charles as they re-entered Paris after a long ride by way of the Champs Elysées, passing slowly along the avenue in the light of the setting sun.

The two young people loved each other, and seemed never weary of telling each other of their love. Their engagement had been sanctioned by Madame Longpré, who, in spite of her iron will, made not the slightest opposition to the proposed union of the young couple.

As for Eusèbe, on his way to the woods with Alice and Charles he had begun to say that they were becoming quite wearisome with their billing and cooing, and that they touched the light guitar rather too frequently. He consoled himself by humming comic songs beneath his breath. It was his sole revenge. He did condescend now and then to sing a comic song.

"What are you going to do this evening?" Alice was asking of her lover.

"Oh, I am going to pay my respects to Madame Longpré."

"I should hope so," said Alice, smiling. "But I meant to say, where are you dining, and with whom?"

"I will give you a faithful account of myself, my dear wife," replied Valville gaily. "One of my friends from New Orleans, Doctor Freedy, a Franco-American, came to France about a fortnight ago. At first he only passed through Paris, as he was obliged to go south immediately.

But this morning he telegraphed to me that he was on his way back, and that we would dine together this evening at the Maison d'Or."

" Doctor Freedy—was it not he who . . ."

" Who saved my life? Yes, indeed! One day when I was walking on the banks of the Mississippi I slipped and fell in. Certainly the Father of Waters meant to hold fast his prey . . ."

" When Doctor Freedy threw himself into the current upon some logs of wood . . ."

" And drew me out of the water—restored a citizen to his country."

" I love him already!"

" And so do I, for without him I should never have known you, Alice."

" Hush, flatterer! Then you are going to dine with him?"

" And, if you will allow me, with the fair Eusèbe."

Hearing his own name, the brother approached them.

"Oh, you have come down from the clouds, have you?" he said. "Got down to earth at last? Well, take care you don't hurt yourselves."

Charles slightly shrugged his shoulders, and said with some abruptness—

" Will you dine with me and one of my friends to-night at the Maison d'Or?"

" Wherever you please; I don't mind."

" Thanks."

Then leaning towards Alice, he added in a lower tone:

" Dr. Freedy must have seen my father and my sisters

before he left home. Perhaps my letter had already reached them, and he has brought me good news!"

"I shall be so glad if your sisters like me already, without knowing me, as I like them."

"A liking which they deserve. Lucile and Jeanne are worthy of you; and if I were not afraid of repeating such a worn-out bit of commonplace, I should say that my sisters were two angels. And when you are my wife, Alice, you will come with me to ask for my father's blessing, will you not?"

"Have I not promised? Do you doubt my word?"

Let us discreetly refrain from listening to their parting words, uttered as they reached a small house in the Avenue d'Antin, when Alice gave her lover's hand a last pressure, and bestowed upon him one of those beautiful smiles which were as tender and as well worthy of remembrance as a kiss of love.

"I will leave my horse at the stable," said Eusèbe to Charles, "and shall see you at your place presently, shall I not?"

"As you please, my dear fellow," said Charles.

Glad of these few moments of solitude, the young American bent his steps towards the Rue de Miroménil, where he occupied a bachelor's suite of rooms, which he had furnished with the fastidious taste of an artist and a traveller.

His groom took his horse to the stables, and Charles, after completing a hasty toilet, threw himself into an arm-chair to dream a while of his present happiness and of his hopes for the future.

Charles had lost his mother at an early age, but his father had proved a loving and devoted protector to his three children. He was one of the richest planters in Louisiana, a just and honest man, who had been amongst the first to proclaim the emancipation of the slaves, a circumstance which had procured for him the enmity of the Southerners, whose efforts he had refused to aid during the so-called war of secession. He possessed a considerable fortune, but he maintained as a principle that men should be valued only by what they know and by what they do. Charles received, therefore, a remarkably good education; and, as he possessed good abilities, he profited by his opportunities. His father then sent him to Europe in order that he might be thoroughly inoculated with that social and moral culture, which, he believed, the Latin races have done more than any other to initiate and to propagate.

Of French origin, M. Valville still nourished a profound affection for his fatherland; and upon the death of his wife he nearly quitted America for ever. But the care of his own interests forbade him to put this resolution into practice. It was, however, with sincere delight that he received from his son the lengthy letters which told him once again of France, of her brave struggles and her reconquered greatness.

His two daughters, Lucile, who was older than Charles, and Jeanne, who was younger, were at once his consolation and his pride. No family was ever more closely united, or more deserved the esteem of all who knew it.

Yet M. Valville did not hide from himself that around

him, in that same Louisiana, which was still writhing in its defeat, subjected by the United Northern States, but not subdued, and ready still, perhaps, to uplift the standard of revolt against the Union, his own belief in the equality of both races, black and white, and the bold application which he had made of the law of emancipation, had raised against him a sentiment of deep hostility which waited only for a fit occasion to declare itself. His son had begged him hundreds of times to realise his property and return to Europe, to his native country. Certain in his own mind of his father's consent to his marriage with Alice Lodier, whose father Valville had long known and loved, Charles said to himself that when they went to Louisiana they would triumph together over his lingering indecision.

So Charles rejoiced in the contemplation of a happiness that satisfied both his conscience and his heart.

"Hop! Let's be off," said Eusèbe, entering hurriedly.

Awaking from his dream, Charles took his hat and followed the young man.

"I suppose double harness will suit you," said Eusèbe, with his irritating drawl. "As for me, I won't be dragged into such a snare just yet, I can tell you."

In Valville's humour at that moment he could not but feel displeased at Eusèbe's tone, and he answered coldly—

"Listen, my good fellow. You are quite at liberty to think just what you please for yourself, but, once for all, when we are speaking of your sister, whom I love and esteem—when we speak of my wife, in fact—I beg that you will make no more of these jokes, which may be very witty, no doubt, but which are insults to the purest and worthiest of feelings."

Eusèbe, whose assurance was more apparent than real, showed that he was a little embarrassed.

"You know," he said, "I make fun of it, but . . ."

"But you don't believe a word you say," interrupted Charles, touched by his confusion. "I do not set myself up as a judge, but since we have mentioned the subject, let me say that it is a foolish pride which plays at scepticism and want of feeling—and, besides!" he added laughing, "you will be in love yourself some day."

"As for that . . ."

"And some day you will be more enthusiastic and Quixotic than we are ourselves!"

"Come!" said Eusèbe, struggling with himself, "when you see me caught, times will have changed indeed."

Charles took his arm.

"Look here," he said in his friend's ear, "I will simply put a possible case before you : nobody can hear us, so just answer frankly. What would you do if some ruffian offered any insult to your sister?"

Eusèbe started, and for a second his whole countenance changed. But suddenly obstinacy resumed her sway, and he merely hummed the refrain of a song—

> "I would draw my sword, my sword, my sword,
> I would draw my father's sword."

"I understand you," said Charles. "You are a brave fellow, Eusèbe."

"Not at all; not a bit of it," cried the young man. "I am not such an ass as to go in for high tragedy."

"Oh no: we understand; you are as hard as iron, of course. In the meantime, here we are at the Maison d'Or. Let us see if Freedy has come. And then, to dinner!"

"Not any too soon!" laughed the lad. "I am quite exhausted with listening to your sermon."

Doctor Freedy had not yet arrived. The telegram had mentioned seven as the time of meeting, and it wanted still a few minutes to that hour.

Charles entered a small drawing-room, and ordered some Madeira.

"Eusèbe," he said, as he filled the two glasses, "here's to your future exploits—the Coming Knight!"

"Ah! only give me the chance, and then you'll see!" replied that amiable young man as he tossed off his glass with a scientific jerk of the elbow, that a jockey might have envied him.

At that moment the door opened, and Dr. Freedy presented himself.

"At last!" cried Charles, as he rushed to greet him.

Edward Freedy was the perfect type of an English gentleman, according to the French idea. He was of middle height, pale and clean-shaven. He seldom laughed; he was never excited. His voice was cold and monotonous. His movements were as regular as those of an automaton. He was impassible in every sense.

Nevertheless, the story went that in India he had fought like a lion to save certain of his countrymen whose lives were in danger by a revolt of the natives. In Ireland, it was said that he had once saved a child who had fallen into a torrent. Indeed, rumour went so far as to accuse him of having, in the space of four-and-twenty hours, encountered and killed four duelling opponents, for behaving with gross insolence to a lady in Germany.

"How glad I am to see you, Freedy!" cried Charles, who was anything but impassible himself. "Come, let us sit down and have two good hours' chat over the present, past, and future."

He noticed that Freedy's calm expressionless gaze was fixed attentively upon the little fop, who, in honour of the event, had donned a costume of the highest fashion—baggy trousers, pilot coat, with enormous sleeves, and collar open at the throat—which somehow recalled to mind the fantastic attire of a learned monkey. Charles could not quite suppress a sigh as he regarded him.

"M. Eusèbe Lodier," said he, "my future brother-in-law."

Freedy bowed. But Eusèbe held out his hand.

"Shake hands," he said. "The friends of our friends, you know, etcetera!"

Not the faintest sign of surprise could be seen in Freedy's face. They shook hands.

Dinner was served, and the repast began immediately.

"Forgive me my selfishness," said Charles, "but first of all, tell me whether you have seen my dear father and sisters."

"I was at Battle Field Plantation on the fourteenth

of September," was the answer. "I saw M. Valville. He was in excellent health, and sent his love. Miss Lucile and Miss Jeanne were as pretty as ever. Kind messages from them too."

"Nothing more?"

"Really, I think not."

"Had not my father received a letter from me?—an urgent letter about most important matters, upon which my whole future depends?"

"I do not know what you are alluding to, my dear boy," replied Freedy. "But I remember that Mr. Valville said to me, just as I was setting off, 'I will write to my son by the next post, and he will be quite satisfied with what I say.'"

"My dear, good father!" cried Charles. "And you think that that is nothing, Freedy? Why, my whole happiness depends on what you have told me!"

"I am very glad to hear it," said Freedy.

"These philosophers!" said Charles, laughing; "anything human is quite out of their way. Here's a man who feels nothing! Really, Freedy, when I look at you, I ask myself if it is indeed you who surrendered your whole fortune to save a ruined brother: if it really is you who have risked your life for your fellow-creatures twenty times or more?"

"Quite so," murmured Eusèbe. "Another fool!"

Freedy looked at him coldly, without any expression of annoyance. Then he addressed himself to Charles.

"My dear fellow," he said gently, "the organisation of the human frame is very delicate. One should not squander its resources. You are constantly expending yourself, like a true Frenchman, in ready money, and some day you will find that you have exhausted your capital."

"A pretty metaphor . . ."

"It is the truth. Why do you excite yourself about everything? Why should you laugh at what is not amusing?" and he glanced at Eusèbe: "why should you weep over what is not sad? Smiles and tears, enthusiasm and energy, are precious gifts of which one should be sparing, and of which you emotional men are much too lavish."

"Yes, I know how philosophic you are. By the by, tell me, if you please, you who go by clockwork, why you were six minutes behind your time in coming here? yes, six minutes! High treason against all punctuality!"

"I have accused myself, it seems," said Freedy, "but I must excuse myself also. When I arrived in Paris from Marseilles, I went home to get my letters. But my servant was out and had taken the key, so that I lost six minutes in waiting for him."

"Six minutes' lost time!"

"Almost. Except for one point. I left word where I was, in order that he should bring me my letters here."

"See what it is to be a man of business!"

As he said these words, a knock was heard at the door, and a man-servant of most correct appearance presented himself.

It was Jack, Doctor Freedy's servant. In noticing the exactitude with which he copied the doctor's manner, one might have been reminded of the proverb—"Like master, like man."

"Any letters?" Freedy asked.

"Yes, sir."

"Give them to me, and wait outside. I will see if I have any orders for you."

"Yes, sir."

His correspondence consisted of some half-dozen letters. Freedy was interested in several industrial undertakings, for which he had supplied the machinery.

"Allow me," he said to his two companions.

"Pray, do as you would at home," said Eusèbe, while Charles merely responded by a slight movement of his head.

Freedy took his knife, cut open all the envelopes and placed them beside him, one by one. Then he drew out each letter, read it, folded it up, and replaced it in its envelope before passing on to another.

He held the last in his hand.

Suddenly an almost imperceptible change came over his features. He half closed his eyes, and then began to read once more. His gaze became fixed, as though he could not comprehend the meaning of those lines, over which, nevertheless, he continued to pore most earnestly.

Charles noticed these signs of emotion, so rare in a man of his phlegmatic temperament, but he did not venture to question him on the subject.

Freedy looked at his friend, and passed his hand over his forehead.

"What can be the matter?" cried Charles at last, carried away by sudden anxiety. "Has some misfortune happened to you?"

Freedy's lips moved, but no sound issued from them. It seemed as if the strong man must be suffering indescribable agony, for beads of perspiration stood on his pale forehead.

"For Heaven's sake, Freedy, speak! You frighten me!"

"My friend," said Freedy, in a deep, hoarse voice, "this letter is from Mr. Thompson, a millowner at Algiers.* He is a trustworthy man, who would deceive no one willingly, who would never give ear to a report unless he could ascertain its truth. I must mention these facts before I tell you why he has written to me."

"How strange you look! You really alarm me!"

"Be as brave as you can. Read!"

With a quick gesture he held out to Charles the open letter.

Charles dared not look at it.

"Read it!" repeated Freedy.

Suddenly a terrible cry, a sort of convulsive sob, escaped from the young man's breast.

For this was what he read:

"Mr. Valville's plantation at Battle Field has been burnt down and plundered. Mr. Valville was murdered, and his two daughters have disappeared."

* A town on the Mississippi, exactly opposite New Orleans.

II.

WHEN Valville, true to his word, appeared at ten o'clock that evening in Madame Longpré's drawing-room, he looked so pale that Alice, seized by a presentiment of misfortune, rose abruptly and advanced to meet him with outstretched hands.

"What is the matter?" she exclaimed.

Eusèbe, in great fear of any manifestation of violent feeling, was trying to hide his embarrassment at a side-table covered with albums. Charles could not speak; but Alice saw that the tears trembled in his eyes, and were ready to fall.

Without waiting for an answer—suddenly possessed by a feeling of terror that made her dumb—she drew Charles forward to a sofa. He sank down upon it with fixed eyes and trembling lips.

Madame Longpré was lying back in an arm-chair fast asleep. Alice touched her arm and drew her attention to Valville, placing her finger on her lips at the same time.

By a mighty effort Valville spoke at last in a hoarse voice.

"A terrible misfortune! My father! my dear, good father!"

"Yes?"

"Murdered! and my two sisters gone . . . disappeared . . . carried off!"

Alice uttered a cry. In reality she did not seem able to understand what he had told her. She asked herself if she were not the victim of some dreadful nightmare. Only a few hours had passed since she had quitted Charles, happy in an avowed affection, full of confidence in the future!—and could a frightful catastrophe have fallen upon him so suddenly? No, it was impossible!

. It seemed as though Valville could read the thoughts of the heart which belonged to him so entirely, for he continued with greater firmness of tone.

"I cannot doubt it; you need not doubt it yourself. It is impossible for you, in the midst of your Parisian civilisation, to understand how such crimes should be committed. You do not know what fierce hatreds still linger in our country, so lately devastated by civil war."

Then, rising to his full height, he added—

"Father, I will avenge you!—And you, dear sisters, if it be true that you have fallen into the robbers' hands, —as my grief and hate foretell—I swear to take no rest— nay, not for a single hour—until the wretches have suffered for their crimes!"

"But how can these horrible tidings have reached your ears?"

Charles replied briefly to this question. Doubt was unfortunately impossible. Scarcely had Freedy communicated to him the contents of his letter before Charles, in spite of the lateness of the hour, rushed off to his banker's, whither his letters were always sent. He had delayed calling there for several days, with the natural carelessness of a happy man; but now he found that there was a letter for him from his American banker, whose words confirmed the fearful intelligence.

Charles raised his head at last, and passed his nervous fingers through his black locks.

"You understand me, Alice, do you not? The reason why I am here to-night is to bid you a last farewell."

The young girl shuddered: a marble pallor overspread her countenance, and her eyes for a moment closed.

Charles continued—

"Words cannot tell you how much I suffer. Alice, you know how I loved my father. He had the noblest heart, the purest conscience that ever deserved a son's respect. When he fell beneath the blows of his murderers, I know, I feel, that one word only burst from his lips. He called me to his help! And that last cry— I hear it!—it breaks my heart. Yes, father, I am ready! I am ready!"

With arms wildly extended, and face as white as death, Valville seemed to bend before a phantom form which he alone could see.

"You are going?" said Alice faintly.

"To-morrow; as early as possible. It seems as though everything conspired against me, perhaps to punish me for my cruel negligence. No steamer leaves

Havre for five days; but the day after to-morrow one starts from Liverpool, bound for New Orleans. Although it is a longer voyage, I shall reach my destination sooner in this manner than by waiting, and in twelve days or a fortnight I shall set foot in Louisiana. Then let those who struck the blow beware! Let traitors and cowards beware!"

A long silence followed the last threatening words, words which to Alice were resonant with the brave and generous emotion of the man she loved.

She mused deeply, with her head leaning on her hand.

Suddenly she raised her face, and looked with a sweet but penetrating gaze into the young man's eyes.

"Listen to me," she said very seriously, "and answer my questions as if your father himself could hear."

He looked at her in his turn, and a quiver of anguish convulsed his features. He had loved her so much! In a few weeks they would have been united—would have set off to Louisiana together, in order to bring back with them the father whose blessing could never now be theirs! And he had not even the right—so fate decreed —to weep for his vanished happiness.

Lost in thought, Alice stood before him.

"Charles," she said in her deep, low tones, "was it from your heart and with your whole soul that you asked me to become your wife?"

"Do you doubt it, Alice? My life belongs to you."

"Well then, in my turn, I may tell you, Charles, that I accepted you as my husband of my own will, and with all the tenderness of a loving heart, and I will prove this to you in the hour of trial."

Charles looked at her. She seemed to him like a vision of light appearing in the midst of the charnel-house into which he felt as if he had suddenly been plunged.

He seized her hand, but she drew it gently away, and, turning to her aunt, knelt down at the old lady's side.

"You have been a mother to me," she said. "You gave me your loving care when I was a child, and I have told you the inmost thoughts of my heart. Now answer me in your turn. When he whom I love is overwhelmed with bitter suffering, have I a right to abandon him?"

Madame Longpré was fond of advancing her claim, which was innocent enough, or at least inoffensive, to the possession of an iron will which nothing in the world— no, nothing!—could subjugate. Therefore, as she had hitherto assisted merely as a passive spectator of the scene before her, she now began to realise that the time had come when she could prove "that she was not a cipher in the family," which was also one of her favourite expressions.

So, lifting her hands to her white hair—she had the kindest and gentlest long-featured old face that one can well imagine,—she cried—

"Pray, what do you mean by that, Mademoiselle? I really cannot understand!"

This title of Mademoiselle was only employed on the great occasions when she wanted to make manifest her iron will. Perhaps it frightened Alice, for she threw her arms round old Madame Longpré's neck, and murmured in an entreating tone—

"Aunt! my dear aunt!"

"No aunt would hear of such a thing!" exclaimed her worthy relative. "Explain what you mean! Do you imagine that I can look upon you as his wife before you are his wife? Nobody pities M. Valville for his misfortunes more than I do, but I have my own duties to fulfil, and"—here her voice rose—"I will fulfil them!"

"But, dearest aunt."

"Do not attempt to bias me," said Madame Longpré. "Your words, Mademoiselle Lodier"—and the use of Alice's surname denoted with the old lady the height of displeasure,—"your words are an insult to my authority."

Alice hung her head.

"They are a complete denial of my duty to you. What! do you imagine that, much as I like and esteem M. Valville, I could allow you before your marriage to accompany him to Louisiana?"

"But, dear aunt! . . ."

"To quit your home . . ."

"I assure you . . ."

"To give to the world the revolting sight—yes, I say revolting!—of a girl casting in her lot in so unconventional a manner with that of a gentleman,—for whom, nevertheless, I have the greatest respect!"

Utterly exasperated, she sank back in her chair, her eyes ablaze with anger.

Valville thought that he ought to interfere.

"Madame," he said, "you may be sure that I shall always treasure in my heart the remembrance of your great kindness to me. Sweet as it has been to me to hear of Alice's project, I know as well as you do that it would be impossible for her to put it into execution . . ."

"Thank Heaven!" muttered Madame Longpré.

"I bow to my destiny, although my happiness is gone for ever," he continued in a broken voice. "She is . . . she has been the hope of my whole life. I must renounce it all."

"But you will come back!" cried Madame Longpré.

"Madame," said Valville sternly, "you are a European. You cannot understand our struggles and our hatreds. Certainly, since the late war, ideas of civilisation and humanity have made great progress; nevertheless, the old leaven of rebellion still remains. I hide nothing from you. I have said that I would avenge my father and my sisters. There is more than a mere personal feeling on my part—I feel that I ought to avenge the cause of civilisation, of the future, of men's outraged sense of right and wrong, which have all been attacked in us. It is a fight for life and death!"

And bowing his head, he added—

"You are right. I cannot drag her with me into the struggle. She belongs to me no longer."

"Charles!" cried Alice, "if you die, I shall die too!"

She flung herself into his arms as she spoke.

What an unpleasant position for an aunt to be in! But Madame Longpré armed herself with stoical determination, and resumed—

"I have an iron will. Where a principle is concerned, I would die in defending it, like a soldier at a post which his officer has charged him to defend!"

"It will kill me!" cried Alice.

"Courage!" murmured Charles.

"Yes, of iron!" continued Madame Longpré. "I say now—and if necessary I would say it aloud in the streets—that it is perfectly impossible for a girl to go off on a wild expedition like this, even with the best man in the world! It is wicked to have dreamt of such a thing. And it shall never be. No!" she repeated, raising her hands to heaven, "it shall never, never be!"

When Alice spoke again, it was with dignity.

"It is growing late, Charles," she said. "You must have many preparations to make for your sad voyage. It would be wrong of me to detain you longer."

She stopped short for a moment. Charles still held her in his arms, and she could feel his tears falling upon her long fair hair. Then she drew back.

"Farewell, M. Valville," she said. "Farewell! And if I die . . ."

"Alice!"

"Enough!" Madame Longpré interrupted them, in a tone which brooked no reply. "She shall never go alone to Louisiana. Her dying father's last request to me was that I would never leave her. And I never will!"

"Very well," said Alice, as she sank down upon the couch. "Then you will see me die."

"Not at all!" cried the old lady. "I tell you again,

I have a will of iron! But no, a hundred times no!
You shall not go alone to Louisiana : it would be too
unconventional, too unusual a thing to do ; besides, I
should feel that I was relinquishing the trust committed
to me by your parents, if I let you go."

"Then, Alice, good-bye," said Charles, withdrawing
his hand from the young girl's clasp.

But Alice rose, and, with the courage born of love,
advanced towards her aunt.

"Madame Longpré," she said, "you are killing him,
and yet you know I love him."

"Well," said Madame Longpré, "why don't you ask
me to go with you ? "

"Dear aunt ! Charles !"

Volleys of exclamations followed : innumerable kisses
were pressed upon the lips of this terrible aunt with her
iron will, and returned by her with wonderful complacency.

"Just so," said Eusèbe, emerging from a corner in
order to quit the room unobserved. "They are leaving
me behind. Not at all strange that they should, either—
they don't care what becomes of me !"

END OF THE PROLOGUE.

CHAPTER I.

THE great geographer, Élisée Reclus, thus briefly describes the river Mississippi, once called the Meschacebes, or Father of Waters :—

" The Mississippi presents perhaps the simplest type of a great river. It does not rise amidst the glaciers of a mountain-range, like the greater number of streams in Europe and Asia; unlike the Euphrates, the Nile, or the Rhine, it waters no countries that have been made famous by wars or great historical events. It belongs to itself alone, and owes nothing either to history or legend. . . . The river is a country in itself, living, acting, and constantly changing. Upon its tide men and ideas are borne onwards; and the deposit of sand and clay at its mouth is a symbol of the historical deposit left by successive generations of the races which have dwelt upon its banks."

We must be allowed to add a word or two to this description. The Mississippi is at once the instrument and the obstacle of civilisation in the Southern States of America. One might call it a personification of those ancient Indian races who are always struggling against the inroads of progress, and who, after each defeat, attempt to shake off the yoke which the conqueror has imposed upon them.

Such is the Mississippi : always conquered, yet unconquerable.

There are no scenes more beautiful or more striking than those presented by the banks of the great river in the State of Louisiana. Everywhere there is exuberant growth of foliage; everywhere splendid luxuriance of vegetation.

But a ceaseless combat between the river and mankind has constantly to be renewed. In vain men try to turn it back, to limit its bounds. One might think that it was angry to see in its masters' hands the wealth which its fertility had given them, and which it would gladly snatch away.

But man's perseverance is equal to its tenacity, and will ultimately triumph. It has enclosed the river in a formidable belt of dikes and embankments, which extend to a length of more than fifteen hundred miles—nearly five hundred leagues,—an enormous mass of stone, fifty million cubic feet in bulk.

More than fifteen million tons of merchandise are borne on the breast of the mighty old river, which quivers with anger beneath its weight. It uproots ancient trees, and throws them up in barriers in the midst of its course. It detaches from its banks enormous masses of earth, which it grinds and pulverises, and which, like fortifications, form obstacles to the progress of steamers which it believes to be insurmountable.   It creeps through the crevices of the banks, and transforms them into swamps; but nature brings forth from these swamps whole cypress-forests, whose interlacing roots form natural raft-like barriers. It rises up against the dikes, pierces them, overthrows them, and spreads itself abroad in a vast watery plain.

But in vain it shows itself untired.   Man also is indefatigable.   For there is no region more beautiful, no climate more delicious. The ancient enemy calls therefore to its aid a terrible auxiliary—yellow fever.   Yet even this hideous scourge is being vanquished by sanitary measures and the triumphs of science.

Even where it has ravaged, nature daily grows more lovely.

There is scarcely, perhaps, any scene more striking than that presented in October by the river-marshes, when the mist of an Indian summer, floating gently over the brown waters like a sort of mirage, transforms the vine-garlanded trunks of the trees into ruined colonnades stretching endlessly away into the distance; and around those gulfs of mud which the treacherous river is everywhere hollowing out, the palm-trees stand in groups, bound together like maypoles with streaming festoons of Spanish moss.

The river has other allies: the reptiles which twine round the branches, the alligators whose cries disturb the silence.   Sometimes one sees suspended to a network of boughs a strange mass, which is an eagle's nest; while in the distance a big owl utters his prolonged and plaintive chant.

But to these hostile voices a village-bell responds; or, from a neighbouring plantation there rings out reassuringly and consolingly some cheerful negro song.

Let us look further. Human labour boldly protests against these empty menaces. Charcoal-burners continue to throw tree after tree into their furnaces; negroes go on rolling great bales of cotton towards the wharves; your whole being is penetrated by the balmy odours exhaled from inextricable thickets of wood and fern.

It has been well said that the United States contain the only power that can fight the Mississippi, and conquer its revolts.

And this is true. To the Americans has been given a spirit so bold and so persevering that it shrinks from no effort, and is discouraged by no rebuff.

Some weeks after the scene described in our prologue, a great barge, laden with charcoal, was descending the stream of the Great River a few miles above New Orleans.

Evening was approaching. The clouds were gathering round the summits of the surrounding hills. The dark waters spread themselves out between their wide banks like the face of a mighty sea. The boats that carry on the navigation between St. Louis and New Orleans require special construction. The masses of mud which rise from the bed of the river prevent the use of deep keels: these vessels are therefore merely immense rafts, upon which formidable erections, almost like fortresses in appearance, are constructed.

The boat of which we speak was surmounted by a scaffolding composed of thick planks, which formed a vast shed, where tons of charcoal were piled.

In front, the smoke curled upwards from two chimneys, tall and black like the trunks of two poplar-trees. Above the scaffolding, a flat bridge, surrounded by a wooden gallery, and recalling to mind an Italian terrace by its form, supported a long cabin, terminating at one end in a sort of tower, upon which a sailor acted the part of watchman.

A shout was suddenly heard.

" Stop her ! Back ! A mud-bank !"

It was the captain who gave this order upon a signal from the watch. For, a few yards before them, there had all at once emerged, as if upheaved by some subterranean force, a blackish mass surmounted by a few branches of trees. It was one of those alluvial deposits which start up suddenly from the bed of the old river, as though to surprise and engulf imprudent vessels in their slimy depths.

At the captain's order, the powerful steam-engines attempted to perform their work. But the impetus already given was too great to be arrested by a single effort, and the bows of the *Black Boy*, which was the steamer's name, were already deeply embedded in the mud bank.

A storm of curses resounded from the bridge. The engines worked and the steam hissed forth more violently than ever, while the boat, with enormous force, tried to break or tear down the heavy barrier that impeded its progress. But in vain.

Fortunately the bow was caught on one side only, and the work of extrication was possible. Alas! the river succeeds in its treacherous designs only too often, and but too many vessels are engulfed in its watery depths!

There was a sudden movement on board the *Black Boy*, like that before a combat. At the captain's orders, twenty negroes threw themselves into the water and gained the bank, dragging with them enormous cables of rope and an iron chain.

As soon as they had landed, a buoy which had been thrown into the stream was drawn to the bank and hoisted up by the negroes' arms. It was a sort of block pierced with square holes, meant to serve the purpose of a windlass. Another buoy conveyed the long beams of wood which were to be fixed into the sockets prepared for them. The iron chain, bound to the fore-part of the boat, was fastened to the windlass: the men, hanging upon the beams, waited for the signal, and then, pushing vigorously, began to wind the chain round the moving block.

The Wasp—such is the nickname of the overseer whose special function it is to direct the negroes' work—stood at the distance of a few feet from his men, whom he encouraged by look and voice, and, it must needs be said, by exclamations of not the most orthodox character.

Upon the bank at this moment appeared some labourers belonging to a neighbouring farm, who looked on curiously—for there are idlers everywhere—and seemed to regard the negroes' work with great interest. One could hear the creaking of the prow as it tore down the great black mass.

Suddenly the Wasp started. A whistle, so soft that no one else seemed to notice it, had reached his ear; it died away into a sort of jerky tune.

He turned round and glanced with apparent indifference at the group beside him; then, drawing back a little, approached a man who was sitting at one end of a block of wood, with an enormous stick beside him.

" What's the matter, Jack ? " asked the Wasp in a low tone. ·

" The matter is, that the enemy's coming."

" What enemy do you mean ? "

" The one who has his father to avenge."

The Wasp could hardly repress a slight shudder.

" You are mad ! He is in Europe : he has not come to New Orleans by any steamer . . ."

" It is you who are mad ! I tell you he is here—not far off . . . He came by rail to Natchez . . . and from there he is venturing to ride, in order to conceal his arrival more completely."

" How do you know ? "

The other sneered—" Because I saw him."

" You ? "

" Yes; and he is now in the Blue Hills, and will be at Crescent City to-morrow. Wait; I have not told you everything."

" What else ? "

" He is not alone !"

"Ah! who is with him?"

"One whom you know well enough ... Doctor Freedy."

The Wasp uttered a low growl.

"Freedy! I am done for, then!"

"What a fool you are! Don't I tell you that they are going over the Blue Hills to-night?"

"To-night?"

The man reflected for a moment, then continued with a decided gesture—

"You are right. They must never reach New Orleans."

At this moment the iron chain accomplished its work with one last mighty effort, and the *Black Boy*, again at liberty, made ready to continue on its way.

The buoys were hauled up. Then the negroes, at the Wasp's command, threw themselves into the water and regained the boat.

But the Wasp himself did not follow them. And when his absence was discovered he was creeping away with his companion amongst the low brushwood and the scattered trunks of fallen trees.

CHAPTER II.

To the west of the Great River rise certain high hills, over which the heavy autumnal fogs rest long in threatening masses of sombre cloud. Exposed to the winds of the Mexican Gulf, these hills, which are constantly enveloped in a sort of bluish vapour, are ravaged at times by frightful tempests, which uproot and damage the trees to such a degree that, at the distance of only a few miles from the luxuriant vegetation of the river-banks, the scene presented is one of utter desolation.

At the very hour when the Wasp and his accomplice were exchanging mysterious confidences, five well-mounted persons were traversing one of the most sterile passes of these mountains, where a violent wind crisped the manes of the horses and played strange pranks with the cloaks of the travellers.

First of all came two ladies—one, because she was full of the rash bravery of youth; the other, because her iron will compelled her never for one moment to lose sight of her young companion.

Then came three men, one of whom was lingering far behind—being the guide!

Suddenly the young girl stopped short and uttered a low cry.

"What is the matter, Alice?" cried the other.

"Come! come!" responded Alice. "The guide has deceived us. This road leads only to a precipice."

At these words the two men spurred forward their horses, and were almost immediately at the young girl's side.

Our readers will have recognised at once the persons who thus found themselves in the Blue Hills upon the western bank of the Mississippi.

When Alice, forcing back her horse upon its haunches, uttered the cry, "We are betrayed!" Valville sprang, as we have said, to her side at once; and gazing into the dark depths below, which seemed to lose themselves in nothingness, he could not repress a shudder of horror and alarm.

Not that he feared for himself. Valville was one of those men who hold life very cheap. But, for one second, a terrible doubt of his ultimate success awoke within him. Ever since he had again set foot upon American soil he had felt that he was enveloped in a network of hatred and of treason.

The steamer in which he had embarked at Liverpool belonged to one of those American companies, who, with utter carelessness of their passengers' lives, send out vessels which are thoroughly unseaworthy, and seem to hold together only by miracle. Before a third part of the voyage was over, the engines were so much damaged that it became necessary to work the ship by means of the sails. The machinery was repaired more or less effectually; but everybody felt that another accident might happen at any moment.

And in fact a heavy sea injured the steamer so far as to destroy the greater portion of its rigging. And it was with great difficulty, after abandoning the project of coasting along Florida, that the captain managed to bring his ship as far as the mouth of the St. John's river. At this place the four passengers, exhausted by fatigue, caught a train that was on the point of starting for Louisiana.

But their troubles had only just begun.

The course of the train was interrupted between Blakely and Mobile by the breaking of a bridge. The only other way of arriving at New Orleans was by rejoining the Mobile line at Meridian, and returning to Jackson, the capital of the State of Mississippi, by a circuitous route. At Jackson they would be able to proceed by railway to their destination.

But at Mobile a singular event took place.

It is well known that Mobile is the capital of Alabama. It is a pretty town of 35,000 inhabitants—a quiet place, without much apparent commercial activity. Its chief thoroughfare, Government Street, is bordered by mansions of palatial magnificence. Beautiful gardens abound on every side, where great taste for horticulture is displayed. The foot-paths of the street are shaded by fine oak trees, and the great square between Dauphin Street and St. Francis Street is like an enormous basket of flowers beneath a dome of verdure. Everything is on a large scale—streets, shops, and buildings. The air sweeps round the place in mighty currents, without let or hindrance.

But there is no outward life, no motion, no activity. In this respect the town is like one of the ancient fishing villages on the banks of the Mississippi when the fishermen themselves are absent. Yet there is at Mobile a brisk cotton trade and an ever-flowing stream of traffic.

During the last few years a Cotton Exchange has been established, and numbers already more than one hundred acting members. The bales of cotton which annually pass through Mobile must amount to three or four hundred thousand. The greater part of this merchandise is transmitted to the foreign vessels which crowd into the Lower Bay.

Nevertheless, Mobile has lost the high commercial rank which it enjoyed in olden days. But the advantages of its fine position, and the vast resources of the State of which it is the capital, may yet restore to it its past prosperity.

Constrained by circumstances to wait several hours at Mobile, Doctor Freedy employed his enforced leisure in visiting some friends. Valville, whose impatience became more and more feverish from day to day, at first refused to go with him; but yielding at last to his solicitations, and desirous also of paying his respects to the celebrated Admiral Semmes—one of the heroes of the late civil war,—the young man decided finally to accompany his friend.

As they were crossing Dauphin Street they met a

peculiar-looking individual, who, advancing from an opposite direction, came straight upon them, and appeared to be greatly surprised at the meeting. He stared full into Doctor Freedy's face, and seemed inclined to stop, but finally resumed his onward way.

"Do you know that man?" asked Valville.

"Yes, and no."

"Which means . . .?"

"That I have met him before," said the American, in his usual phlegmatic manner; "but that I do not know him."

"Do explain yourself more clearly."

"My dear Valville, to know any one is to be ready to meet him; to go and speak to him, perhaps to shake hands with him. You understand me?"

"You mean that this man is unworthy of our interest in him?"

"A bad rendering. I would not speak to him; I would not sit down by him; I would go out of any house that I was in if he entered it; but" ... and he laid strong emphasis on the words, "I am very much interested in him."

"Really, Freedy, you speak in riddles."

"Wait: I will explain it all directly. At present, just turn round quickly and look behind you."

Valville obeyed. There, about a hundred yards behind them, in front of Barton Academy, trying to hide himself behind a willow fence which protected one of the trees, stood the man whom they had passed, gazing after them eagerly. He was taken by surprise by Valville's quick movement, and drew himself quickly into the shade. This man wore a typical costume. It consisted of a short coat of coarse cloth, torn and dirty, trousers tucked into thick-soled boots reaching to the knee, and a soft felt hat on the back of his head. As for his face, it was thin, long, and bony. A goat's beard on his chin, widening into a sort of fan-shape, completed the portrait, which was certainly not very attractive.

"That man wants to play the spy on us," said Valville. "Although I have been away from America for some years, I recognise the type of those adventurers, fortune-seekers who shrink from nothing; and I should guess that beneath the band that joins his waistcoat and his trousers there are hidden at least a revolver and a bowie-knife."

The bowie-knife is a sort of cutlass with a very sharp blade, which has played, and still plays, an important rôle in all American quarrels.

"Well guessed," said Freedy. "And during the disturbances of the Kellogg election at New Orleans, I nearly made close acquaintance with the said bowie-knife, which accounts for the great interest which he is manifesting in me."

"He tried to kill you?"

"Assuredly. But what astonishes me," added Freedy with a smile, "is that he should be still alive; for I threw him out of a window of the St. Louis Hotel, sometimes called the Capitol of New Orleans . . ."

"Good! then I don't wonder that he wants to stop and look at you," said Valville, laughing in spite of himself; "but are you not afraid that he will try to revenge himself upon you for the leap that you made him take?"

"My dear Valville, I think that you have forgotten a great deal since your departure, and that you have much to learn. Of course a 'scalawag' always tries to revenge himself. But wait a moment," added Freedy, imposing silence by a gesture upon Valville, who was about to interrupt him and to ask the meaning of the term 'scalawag;' "we must first show this honest personage that we are not afraid of him. In America, as everywhere else, assassins are always cowards. If you don't want a hyena to throw itself upon you, you must walk straight up to it."

"Do you think he would attempt anything . . . here . . . in the open street?"

"Note, if you please, that in the open street at Mobile we are more alone at midday than we should be at midnight in the obscurest corner of Paris. Follow me."

· And drawing down his elbows close to his sides, Freedy began to run in the direction of the Academy. But when they reached the tree behind which they had seen the man conceal himself, they found that he had disappeared.

"This is miraculous," cried Valville.

"No miracle at all," said Freedy coldly. "Men of this kind—bandits, to tell the truth—who have been miners at San Francisco and trappers in the Rocky Mountains, who are in the pay of the White League o-day, and will be soldiers of the Black League to-morrow,—these men have all the habits as well as all the cruelty of savages. A 'scalawag' is a sort of pariah in revolt, self-exiled from society; a guerilla chief, as the Spaniards say, who hovers upon the flanks of the great army of workers, until some of them, separated from the others and alone, fall into his ambuscades; then such a man can kill and steal at will. Having tried everything, and believing no longer in the power of work, he expects everything from chance; and it must be said that here some 'scalawags' do succeed; as soon as their travestied piracy has procured a galleon for them, or their pockets are full of dollars and bank-notes, then they lift up their heads and reclaim their places in society. You see the kind of ruffians they are: the sore spot in American society and the Southern States, where the strife that still subsists between the black and white races continually gives them fresh facilities for action. They are the brigands of ancient legend, but they do not keep to the forests like those of old. In the great towns, such as Houston, Galveston, and New Orleans, they lie in ambush, ready to profit by any sort of political skirmish or electioneering excitement; ready always and above all to provoke the troubles by which they know how to profit. It is a very army of evil, and I tell you it is a large one! . . ."

Struck by a sudden idea, Valville interrupted him.

"These are the wretches that killed my father?" . . .

"As to that," said Freedy with a mournful smile, "the case is different: and in a minute we shall hear something more about it."

"How so?"

"Let us go in," said Freedy, indicating with his hand the door of the St. Borromeo Hotel, one of those vast caravanserais beside which the Paris Grand Hotel would look, as far as size goes, like a country inn.

Here Alice and Madame Longpré, exhausted with fatigue, were snatching a few hours' rest.

The two men had scarcely passed through the immense portico, threading their way with difficulty through the piles of wooden cases and trunks that rose before them like broken fragments of Cyclopean architecture, when a negro servant approached them.

"A telegram for Doctor Freedy," he said.

The doctor took the paper that was presented to him, and drew Valville into one of the rooms on the ground-floor where several men were sitting at tables, swallowing great bumpers of whisky.

Valville was very pale. For had not Freedy told him that he was about to hear fresh news on the subject of his father's murder?

Since his departure from France, the young man had suffered terribly. Is there anything worse than to see yourself condemned to forced inaction by ignorance and impotence, to count the hours and the miles which separate you from the land where those you love have shed their blood, and to be compelled to restrain your anger and your impatience to avenge their wrongs?

Sometimes at night, when Valville stood alone upon the deck, his eyes fixed upon the dark expanse of sea that surged around him, it seemed as though he could see a spectral form rise from the waves and stretch its arms to him ; as though he could hear a voice that called him to the rescue !

But what could he do ? By what supernatural power could he have hastened the course of the vessel which bore him slowly—oh, so slowly !—to America? His sisters' voices seemed to call him also. The account received by Freedy, and partially confirmed by another vague report before Valville's departure, told only of their disappearance. But this word was more horrible, more alarming, than any other. The young man shuddered, and dared not think of it.

At Jacksonville, the port where he landed in Florida, he had thrown himself into the train which was just starting, without finding a moment's time in which to telegraph to New Orleans. By degrees a dreary torpor seemed to take possession of him. He was conscious of a sensation of indifference which resembled the fatalism of an Oriental. He was ready to let fate lead him whither it would, and felt that he could neither direct nor control it. At Mobile he was utterly depressed and disheartened. He began to fear that when he accepted the sacrifice made by Alice and her adopted mother, he had assumed a graver responsibility than he ought to have done, yet it was too late to draw back.

But Freedy was on the watch. This cold American, master of a calm energy which did not expend itself in useless outer show, had telegraphed at once to New Orleans. And he had just received the answer to his telegram.

"Read it! read it!" said Valville, whose voice trembled with feverish impatience.

"It is in cipher," said Freedy. "It will take me a few minutes to read."

He drew from his pocket a small note-book, the pages of which were covered with a network of lines, figures and letters, something like telegraphic shorthand.

Then he began to read in a low voice:—

"Mr. Valville dead. House burnt down on the night of the tenth of October. Negroes fled: some of them certainly accomplices. Valville killed by a pistol-shot on the verandah. Of the two sisters, one was found next day in a dying state on the borders of a 'bayou,' or marshy stream, with severe scalp-wound. Better now. The other sister disappeared. All search for her vain up to present date. Grave suspicions. Struggle between blacks and whites imminent. Other fires in Louisiana. Great conspiracy organised. Prudence necessary. Ned Bark takes charge of affairs. Faithful and clever. Charles Valville must not go direct to New Orleans, but to Woodman's house at Pontchartrain. This telegram will serve as introduction. There let him wait for Ned Bark. Plan will be formed. Will come myself. Beware of carpet-baggers and scalawags. Leave railway, where your arrival will be telegraphed. Once at Covington, go over Blue Hills. Five hours' ride to Woodman's house."

Valville had risen.

"Ah! you see, Freedy!" he exclaimed. "Not a minute to lose!"

Freedy remained thoughtful.

" Yes," he murmured to himself, "this seems to be the symptom of some new and terrible convulsion of our poor country. Ah, Louisiana ! those are right who call you 'Paradise Lost!' But it shall yet be 'Paradise Regained !'"

Valville repeated his appeal with impatience.

"Charles," said Freedy, "you have made a great mistake in bringing Miss Lodier and her aunt with you. We must get them to go immediately to New Orleans. There they can be received into some French family, where they will wait for you without incurring the dangers to which we are sure to be exposed. I will go and speak to the ladies, Valville, and try to obtain their consent."

Freedy pleaded his cause eloquently, but in vain. The courageous Alice, upon hearing of the perils which threatened the man who was as dear to her as a husband, was resolved to share them with him. As to Madame Longpré, she would allow nobody to dictate to her concerning her conduct. She had long passed the age for receiving advice.

She was an energetic little woman, with an extraordinary reserve of strength hidden beneath a delicate appearance. She had always loved romance, and was delighted to throw herself blindly in the way of an adventure. Moreover, Alice had said she would not be separated from Charles. And as she always appropriated Alice's decisions to herself, she was quite convinced that this one was her own, and nothing in the world could have modified what she was pleased to call her resolution, unless Alice had changed her mind.

Freedy repressed an inclination to shrug his shoulders, but accepted the inevitable.

An hour later a carriage, or sort of covered coach, was conveying the four travellers along one of the lonely roads which connect Alabama and Louisiana. In twenty hours they found themselves at the foot of the Blue Hills, a group of hills of some considerable height, which appear to be the last vestiges of those high mountains which the waters of the Mississippi have little by little undermined, and carried down to the marshes.

Here Freedy discovered, to his great regret, that the travellers would not be able to traverse these unknown mountain-paths without a guide.

At some miles' distance from Covington the carriage stopped for a time on the banks of one of those marshy creeks, which, flowing at the foot of the hills whose outlines are sharply defined against the horizon, announce the vicinity of the Mississippi.

A man was there, seemingly indifferent to everything that passed, smoking his pipe, and letting his horse drink the marshy water.

He turned his head when he heard the sound of wheels, then resumed his former immobility.

Freedy accosted him in order to ask which was the shortest way to their destination.

The man took his pipe out of his mouth and spat on the ground before he answered.

"Where are you going?" he said.

" To Pontchartrain."

" Do you think you'll get there alone ? " said the man sneeringly.

" Alone or in company, what does it matter ? Tell us the way."

" It matters a good deal if you want to get there !—The Blue Hills are not very high, but they are as dangerous as most other mountains."

The result of this colloquy was that the man proved willing to earn a few dollars by acting as guide to the travellers.

The opportuneness of his offer caused some uneasiness to Doctor Freedy. But how could it be supposed that this man was an emissary of their unknown enemies ?

As night came on, they resumed their course.

Seeing that the carriage could not be taken through the steep mountain-passes, it had been left at Covington at a very innocent-looking sort of farm, which possessed chickens, ducks, a watch-dog, and, as usual, the inevitable fan-palm with its great fronds fluttering in the wind. The four travellers then proceeded on horseback.

We have seen how Alice suddenly discovered that their guide had deceived them. The surrounding solitude was full of shadows : before them was a deep and wide crevasse, down which they had very nearly been precipitated ; and in the distance the flying hoofs of a retreating horseman could be heard. The pretended guide had taken at once to flight.

" Ruffian ! " cried Valville, discharging his revolver at hazard in the direction of the fugitive.

"The fellow is far enough away by this time," said Freedy coldly. "But he betrayed himself too soon. The night is not yet so dark but that we may succeed in regaining our way. In the first place let us turn back. You, ladies, must go in the middle: I will go first, and Valville last: eyes open, and finger on the trigger."

"Dear Alice!" Charles whispered to the girl. "Who can tell whether I am not leading you to death?"

"Must we not live and die together?" she answered gently.

Madame Longpré had bravely drawn a revolver from the little bag that hung at her waist, and brandished it in the most heroic manner.

"Forward!" said Freedy.

In a few minutes they had reascended the slope down which they had just come. The fog thickened around them like a belt of darkness as they went.

Freedy stopped. He began to see that to wander onwards in this obscurity would be madness. The man who had misled them had plotted well: the least false step might lead them to instant destruction.

"Wait for me!" cried Freedy.

And he plunged resolutely into one of the footpaths that he saw before him.

But hardly had he proceeded more than a few steps when a pistol-shot rang in his ear, and a long sharp cry resounded through the night.

Struck with alarm, Freedy turned his horse's head abruptly round, and rapidly returned to the plateau that he had just left.

CHAPTER III.

SAMBO.

DOCTOR FREEDY was not the man to be moved by idle fears. He had proved his energy and his courage a hundred times : yet when he heard that pistol-shot, followed by that hoarse shriek, his whole frame was shaken as if by fear.

The night had grown very dark.

"Courage! here I am!" cried Freedy, with his finger on the trigger of his revolver.

But at the same instant a well-known voice responded—

"Here!—to the left!"

It was Valville who spoke.

At the same time a tall, black, fantastic-looking figure rose up in front of Freedy's horse, and laid a hand upon the bridle.

Freedy resolutely covered him with his revolver.

But the glare of a lighted torch suddenly illumined the scene; and Valville, seeing Freedy's threatening gesture to the man whom he took for an enemy, dashed forward, crying—

"Don't fire, Freedy! He has saved our lives!"

"Without poor Sambo," said the unknown, who was a negro of colossal stature, "you die over the precipice."

As he spoke, Sambo—for such was the negro's name—pointed towards a depth of shadow to which Freedy, deceived by the darkness, had been rapidly directing his way at the moment when the black man's hand seized his horse's bridle.

"You are all safe and sound?" asked Freedy.

"All!" answered Valville, raising his torch, and revealing the two women, who had left their horses, and seemed to be bestowing their care upon an apparently wounded man. This man lay upon the ground at a few yards' distance from the precipice; but Freedy could not see his face.

"What has happened?" he enquired.

"Only Sambo can tell us," said Valville. "One thing is certain—that we were about to fall into a snare, and that this good fellow saved us."

"Sambo's life is yours, massa," replied the negro affectionately.

"But that man on the ground?"—

"Was simply a bandit who was waiting to fire on us, hidden in the brushwood by the pathway. But Sambo, an old servant of my father's, rose up all at once, rushed upon the wretched fellow, and, snatching his gun from him, fired, and put a bullet into his head."

Freedy sprang from his horse, and walked quickly towards the little group formed by the two women and the wounded man.

The man had received a wound upon the head, from

which the blood fell fast and formed a pool upon the ground; his eyes were shut, and a reddish foam was gathering upon his writhing lips, which trembled convulsively.

"I know this man!" cried Freedy suddenly. "It is Dick Salter, nicknamed the Wasp; a sort of overseer on board the charcoal-barges which ply between Louisville and New Orleans on the Mississippi."

Alice had been trying to bandage the wounded head, and to stop the bleeding, with all the womanly tenderness which forgets the crime of a criminal at the sight of his suffering: she now looked up and addressed herself to Freedy.

"Doctor," she said, "he will die: can you not save him?"

Freedy had also knelt down, and with skilful fingers was touching the wounded head.

"Lower the torch," he said.

For some moments he continued his examination, last of all raising the man's eyelid, so as to see the pupil of his eye.

"He is dying. The ball has penetrated his brain."

"But cannot he speak?" cried Valville. "Can he not, even at the last moment, confess his crime, and name the assassins whose tool he has surely been?"

"Perhaps," said Doctor Freedy.

He returned to his horse, and opened a little bag which hung from the saddle, and which contained a traveller's medicine-chest. From this he took a small phial, and, returning to the wounded man, forced his teeth open with the blade of his knife, and poured down his throat a few drops of some colourless liquid.

Sambo stood calmly by, with his hands crossed over the gun.

This African, whose enormous outline was clearly revealed by the yellow torchlight, was a veritable giant roughly hewn in bronze. His black woolly hair, his big lips, his glistening white teeth and bright eyes, all contributed to lend a most fantastic appearance to this strange wild being.

Who was he? How had he come to the Blue Hills? Why did he call Valville "massa," and say that his life belonged to him? All this will be presently explained.

Meanwhile the drops of liquid swallowed by the dying man, were gradually producing upon him a great effect, which every moment increased.

"Do you hear me, Dick Salter?" said Freedy; "and will you answer me?"

The name thus pronounced evidently reached the ruffian's ear, for suddenly his eyes opened and rolled wildly in their sockets, his lips moved, and, amidst half-audible oaths, the words were heard—

"Freedy! Curse you!"

"I know you," said Freedy; "you tried to kill me once before: you are in the pay of the scalawags of Louisiana. Who sent you here? Why did you wish to commit murder? Whom would you have killed?"

"You! you!" groaned the dying man, grinding his teeth; "and then the other one—Valville! After the father, the son! a cursed race!"

"You are one of my father's murderers!" cried Valville, almost beside himself. He advanced with uplifted hand, as if he could have struck the man, but Freedy arrested his arm.

"We do not punish the dead! Let him speak : and let him receive our last forgiveness!"

The miserable man writhed as he lay upon the earth.

"Die? no, no! I will not die!"

"You are condemned," said Freedy solemnly. "So, speak."

"Then . . . if I speak . . . you will save me?" he asked, digging his nails into the ground in his agony.

"No," said Freedy. "You are punished : it is all over with you; but I say to you, before you die show at least some sorrow for your crime : name your accomplices. You are only a soldier in a robber's band : name your chief."

"My chief?" moaned the man, whose voice was failing and dying away in strangled sobs of agony. "Yes, I will name him! for when you hear his name, you will know, you—you, too!—that you are condemned to death! . . ."

"His name!"

"His name is Red Ralph!"

"Red Ralph!" exclaimed Freedy.

"Yes, Red Ralph. Now you tremble, do you not, Doctor Freedy? You tremble, you, son of the planter Valville? . . . Ah, the fair Jeanne—your sister! . . ."

He could not complete his sentence. Terrible gasps

escaped his breast. His stiffened body was arched in one last convulsion, and then he fell back . . . dead !

Valville's face was livid.

"Speak ! speak again !" he cried, seizing the dead man by the arm.

"He will be silent now for ever," said Freedy solemnly.

He passed his hand over his brow, and then said energetically—

"Come ! to horse ! Let us get out of these accursed mountain-passes."

"Yes," said Sambo, who had assisted at this sad scene without betraying a single sign of emotion; "me lead you—in two hours reach Pontchartrain."

"Do you know the Woodman Plantation ?" asked Valville.

"Me come from there," said the negro.

"And we can be there in safety in two hours ?"

"Yes; me promise."

Overcome with emotion, Alice had fallen on her knees by the wayside. How courageous soever a woman may be, she is never without feeling; her very strength, when it is even most heroic, is full of gentleness.

It was the first time that Alice had witnessed a death-scene; and as she knelt beside the dead body, she gave way to a passion of mournful tears. Her aunt, not less touched, was yet outwardly much more composed.

Valville approached them, and gently begged them to mount their horses again.

Alice lifted her head and looked at him.

"What!" she said, "are we to abandon this poor man?"

"We must," replied Freedy. "Is not the high-road the robber's battle-field? There he fights and there he dies; it is only just."

It was moreover impossible for the travellers to encumber themselves with the ghastly burden. This Alice could understand; but could not the body be protected from the attacks of wild beasts?

Valville and Freedy explained to her that both time and tools were wanting to dig the man a grave, and with a deep sigh the girl turned at last to go.

"Alas!" she whispered to Valville, "may this desertion not bring misfortune upon us!"

"Are we not undertaking mortal combat?" answered Charles. "Dismiss these vain fears, dear Alice, and remember that whenever the rights of humanity speak louder than my duty, I shall be the first to respect them. But at present it is your life and that of your second mother of which we must think before everything."

The little procession then proceeded on its way.

Sambo walked first, close to Freedy, who, plunged in thought, repeated from time to time in low tones the name which the dying man had uttered.

"Red Ralph!" he murmured; "as long as that man lives we shall never be out of danger! And Valville knows nothing, for the name left him perfectly calm! Some day, however, he will have to hear the whole story."

Then addressing himself to Sambo, he said—

. "Tell me, please, how you became aware of the danger that we were incurring; and, first of all, why did you call Charles Valville your master? Do you belong to the Battle Field Plantation?"

"Yes," answered the negro; "I tell you, I would give my life for him, though I could not give it for his father."

We will not continue to place in the mouth of the negro that broken dialect of which we gave a very short specimen at the beginning of the chapter. Besides, the reader should know that the negro language—which has been too often travestied by novelists who are acquainted with it only by tradition—does not consist at all of this phonographic sort of patois. It is really a mixture of different languages, which by slow degrees is forming a new dialect, composed of English, French, Spanish, and Indian. It resembles some of the African tongues in sound.

It is easy to write " Me hab good massa!" "Little nigger do dis!" but no negro ever really talked in this way. Negro-songs, like negro-words, require faithful translation. They have a special charm and fitness which are completely lost when they pass into another language. Therefore Sambo shall henceforward speak like other people.

" You are very much attached to the Valville family?"

" Oh yes! how could I be otherwise? I owe my life to poor Mr. Valville, whom I was not able to defend."

" How was that?"

" Twenty years ago," said Sambo, " in the times of slavery—when that frightful institution which lowered us below the level of brutes had grown more oppressive and cruel than it had ever been before—I belonged to a planter at Natchez, the most ferocious master who ever tortured my brother-men; and that villain, Dick Salter, was the overseer of his negroes. Never a week passed without the death of some one of us beneath the lash, or other refinements of cruelty that those monsters loved to invent for us. My father, sir, my father"—and here the negro could scarcely restrain his tears—"my father was one day condemned by Dick Salter—that man whom the young lady regretted to surrender to the wild beasts and the crows—to receive fifty blows, not on the shoulders, but on the face and chest. Do you understand? An old man! And what had he done? what crime had he committed? Perhaps, worn out by fatigue, he had fallen asleep beneath a palm-tree : besides, do you think these men wanted motives, pretexts? No; they struck and killed because they liked to do so. And just then, too, dark rumours were current in the Southern States. The martyr John Brown had fallen at Harper's Ferry; possible revolt was contemplated, and we must be kept down by terror! In truth, it was enough to terrify the boldest! To return to my father's fate . . ."

Each time that he uttered this beloved name, the negro trembled as if he had been seized by ague.

" In vain the negroes on the plantation—even those who, by some act of cowardice or treason, had gained the master's favour—begged him to spare the old man. In vain they appealed to the pretended magistrate, the so-called syndic of the negroes, who, instead of defending or protecting them, was too often the accomplice of their executioners. The punishment was upheld, and I saw the poor trembling old man tied up in broad daylight to an oak-beam placed crosswise in the middle of the cotton-field; and Dick Salter, the wretch, was charged with the execution of the sentence. How was it that I did not spring forward and snatch him from the arms of death? Can you guess why?—My father had commanded me to live: he wished, poor martyr! that his death should be an example to us all; and with the pride of his race he defied the tormentors! The whip fell—it tore open his forehead, his eyes, his mouth, his nose—it laid bare the muscles, and crushed the flesh! At the fiftieth blow my father shouted, 'Liberty! liberty!' and died. Yes, he was free! But I was maddened—I was resolved: my father's cry was his command that I should work for the emancipation of my brothers. That very night I fled from the Natchez plantation. Where did I go? I know not: by chance, across the treacherous forest, less cruel than mankind: amongst alligators and panthers that seemed to me less terrible! but I was young then—little more than a child. I did not know what peril, what fatigue awaits the path of a runaway slave. I lost myself. Hoping to get further and further away, I doubled; and yet I was very few miles from that accursed plantation.

"On the third morning I suddenly awoke from a sleep of several hours' duration, and heard the sound of shouts and horses' hoofs which were rapidly approaching.

" I shuddered in terror : the men-hunters, Dick Salter and other ruffians, were on my track, accompanied by those horrible dogs which our persecutors had trained to hunt down human game.

" I sprang up, hoping to escape them. I tried to gain the river. There, I thought, I would throw myself into the rapid stream, and, thanks to my strength, I could fly!—fly across a marshy tract of land, broken and insecure by reason of small streams as it was ! But in vain I gathered up all my strength, in vain I exerted my muscles; every minute I stumbled and fell ; and the horses' gallop came nearer and nearer : I was surrounded by enemies on all sides. Every road, every pathway where a horse's hoof could be set, was guarded. I was hiding in a marsh where monstrous toads were creeping and serpents twining round my knees—my clothes were torn to rags upon my shoulders—and for more than thirty hours I had eaten nothing. I felt my strength failing : my temples throbbed. If I had had to fight men only ! But just behind me, a few paces off, I heard the panting breath of one of my master's dogs ! I confess it, I grew icy-cold with terror !—Oh, those dogs, those lovers of human flesh ! I had seen them at their work ! I knew what their fierceness could be like when stimulated by the fierceness of men ! The enormous animal, with bleeding muzzle, had scented me out, and for one moment I turned and saw the hideous creature, whose head crashed through the reeds behind me. I sprang forward with a cry, but in vain ! a violent shock prostrated me, a horrible feeling of hair and foam was on my breast, great crooked fangs were about to bury themselves in my neck—I was lost! With straining hands I tried to choke off the monster . . .

"Suddenly a shot was heard, and the pressure relaxed. The body of the brute grew rigid, and was shaken by a violent spasm: then it dropped dead at my feet.

"Thirty yards off a man was running towards me with a gun from which the smoke was still rising. And at the same moment Dick Salter and his men were at my side. 'Who fired? Who killed my dog?' he cried in a paroxysm of rage.

"I had instinctively flown to my protector, and bending one knee to the ground, I pressed my lips to his hand. He did not repulse me, but said loudly—

"'I killed that dog.'

"'You! very well,' cried Dick. 'Your life for his!' And he pointed his gun towards the stranger. But before he touched the trigger, a ball had shattered the weapon in his hand; and the shot had been fired with such skill that the ruffian himself was not wounded. He uttered a howl of rage, and called to his companions—

"'Fire! fire!'

"Mr. Valville—for, as you must guess, it was no other—then said quite calmly—

"'My name is Valville, and this negro belongs to me.'

"His name produced a singular effect. Dick Salter started, while the others exchanged uneasy looks. There were two causes for this sudden change. The Valville family, of French origin, having held large estates for more than a hundred years, had a reputation of which no one could be ignorant: Mr. Charles's father was particularly. noted, both for his humanity, and for the almost miraculous feats of skill and strength which were attributed to him. Also, though I did not hear of this still more powerful reason for some time afterwards, the Natchez planter owed him a considerable sum of money, and it was only through his generosity that my master had not been completely ruined long before.

" 'Dick Salter,' said Mr. Valville, 'now that you know my name, consider yourself lucky that I do not put a bullet into your head. I have told you that this negro belongs to me. See here'—and he drew a paper from his pocket-book—'this is a note of hand of your master's, due to-morrow for five thousand dollars. Bring me this evening the bill of sale for this negro, and I will remit to your master the note of hand at once.'

" I was weeping, trembling, choking with emotion. Dick Salter hesitated: not that he doubted the readiness of his master to make such a profitable bargain, but because his cruel nature regretted the loss of its dominion over me. But Mr. Valville knew how to control the wretch, who at last bowed and rode away, not without a parting glance of bitter hate at me.

" From that day forward, the Battle Field Plantation became my home—a home, oh, how happy ! until that fearful night when I had been sent by my master to New Orleans, and those assassins burnt the house and killed

Mr. Valville.   Are you surprised now that I said my life belonged to Mr. Charles?"

At this moment the little party quitted the rugged paths and emerged upon the open plain.   The faint light of dawn became visible in the east.   For the present all immediate danger was over.

"But how did you learn the plans of this wretched Dick Salter?" asked Freedy.   "How was it that you arrived in time to strike him down?"

"In this way," said the negro.   "You know that Miss Lucile—the daughter of Mr. Valville who was found wounded at some distance from the plantation—was received into the house of Mr. Woodman, the planter of Pontchartrain, who was an intimate friend of Mr. Valville.   You understand that I could not abandon my dear mistress—when I grieve so deeply for my dear master and for Miss Jeanne . . ."

"Do you think those villains have killed her?"

"Who knows?" said the negro, lifting his eyes to heaven.   "We cannot tell whether to hope or fear!"

"Go on with your story."

"Well, yesterday evening, I noticed, near one of the creeks which surround the house, a man who seemed to be proceeding towards the Blue Hills.   Now Mr. Woodman knew that you would come by that route. The man in question was soon joined by another, and they conversed together.   A ray of light that fell upon the face of one of them showed me that it was Dick Salter.   It was long since I had seen him.   My first impulse was to spring forward and kill him on the spot;

but I saw that he was taking leave of his companion, and that he then shouldered his gun and made for the hills. A sudden suspicion crossed my mind, and I put myself on his track—so carefully that he should not even guess what unseen shadow followed him! Used to the darkness, my eyes never lost sight of him for a moment: all at once I saw another man riding at full speed from the heights, who called to him: 'Quick! they are coming!' Dick Salter answered, 'I shall be there.' And he began to run, mounting the hills with great swiftness; yet still I followed. At last I saw him crouch down behind a clump of brushwood. With his finger on the trigger, there he waited. You know the rest! I saw the muzzle of his weapon pointed to the breast of Mr. Charles: I sprang upon him, and I avenged my father by saving my benefactor's son!"

"If I am not mistaken, I can see from here the outbuildings of Mr. Woodman's plantation?" asked Doctor Freedy.

Upon an affirmative sign from the negro, the doctor turned round to his friend.

"We are approaching the end of our journey, Valville," he said, as the three riders advanced.

Valville held out his hand to Sambo.

"You saved us," he said; "but remember that a terrible task still remains for us to accomplish."

Raising his hat, he added—

"Father, I swear that you shall be avenged."

Sambo ran in the direction of the plantation, beckoning to the little cavalcade to follow him.

CHAPTER IV.

THE BATTLE FIELD TRAGEDY.

Notwithstanding all their energy, Madame Longpré and Alice were completely exhausted by fatigue when, guided by Sambo, they reached the plantation.

Day had broken, but a grey fog from the lake still hung over the wide fields and covered the buildings as with a thick veil, behind which their forms could very faintly be discerned.

Upon entering one of the gates, Sambo uttered a loud whistle, and almost immediately a crowd of servants, both black and white, pressed forward to meet the travellers.

At the same moment Mr. Woodman also appeared.

He was a man of high stature, dressed in a grey suit, which fitted closely to his figure, and showed to admirable advantage the strength of his mighty limbs. As soon as his eye fell upon Valville, he advanced to meet him.

Without speaking, but recognising in Woodman a sincere and tried old friend of his father's, the young man, consumed by a fever of sorrow and anxiety, threw himself upon his neck and burst into tears.

" My father ! " he cried.   " My poor father ! "

Woodman pressed him to his breast, and spoke in a grave, kind voice.

"Take courage, my boy," he said, "do not be cast down.   Your father was a good man and a brave worker; weep for him, but remember that he has left you others to care for still."

They were approaching the house.   Just then the door opened, and a young girl appeared : a girl whose forehead was covered by a linen bandage.   A double cry resounded through the air.

" Charles ! my dear brother ! "

" My sister Lucile ! "

It was indeed Valville's elder daughter ; and the linen bandage hid from sight the mark of the horrible and mysterious wound that she had received : mysterious, we say, because that monstrous attempt to scalp her proved that there must have been found, in the ranks of the bandits, one of the miserable descendants of the great Indian race, degraded to the level of incendiaries and assassins.   Wheresoever hatred and cruelty can be found, it is there that the ' scalawags ' recruit their ranks !

Repressing the tears that filled her eyes, and withdrawing herself from her brother's arms, Lucile turned to the two ladies.   At the first glance Lucile and Alice felt that they were indeed sisters ; and as the young Parisian was pale and trembling with exhaustion, Lucile led her, with Madame Longpré, quickly towards the house.

"My dear brother," she said to Valville, "I have not forgotten the traditions of hospitality which our father left us ; you may count upon me."

"But where is Jeanne? Jeanne !" cried the young man, whose hands clenched themselves with pain as he thought of his other sister.

Lucile appeared to hesitate ; then running suddenly to his side, she put her arms round her brother's neck, and whispered in his ear :

"You will soon know all ! but just now I can only tell you that Jeanne is courageous and indomitable : and," she added more slowly, "she would prefer death to dishonour."

"Dishonour !" cried Charles. "What does that terrible word mean ?"

Lucille referred him to Mr. Woodman.

"Our friend, our kind protector will tell you all."

"Ah, come ! come !" exclaimed Valville, seizing the planter by the hand. "However horrible the story may be, promise me to hide nothing !"

And the two men moved off towards a group of palm-trees, followed by Freedy, who had been silently gazing at the graceful picture presented by Lucile as she conducted her new friends into the house.

"Now," said Woodman, " Charles Valville, listen to me, and summon all your strength ; for I have terrible things to tell you.

"I must first recal to your mind certain events which you may have forgotten, for your father kept you carefully apart from political dissensions ; but the facts to which I am about to refer, are, in my opinion, intimately connected with the horrible catastrophe which cost my poor friend Valville his life.

"You know, my dear fellow, that your father and I were ardent partisans of the cause of freedom, and that during the war we both fought boldly in the Northern army. This is enough to show you that the rights of humanity always found defenders in us, and that our opinions, whatever they might be, were based, not on prejudices which we entertained, but upon real interest in a nation which has been so long down-trodden, and which we aided to recover its liberty.

"I know that in France these facts are little known; and during your long residence on the other side of the ocean, it must no doubt have been difficult for you to form any opinion concerning the events that took place in your native country; especially in view of the contradictory accounts that the press put forward on all sides.

" But this is the truth, which I will place before you as briefly as I can.

"Among the emancipated negroes, a great number, I may say the majority, endeavour to make themselves worthy of the rights they have regained. Certainly it is very difficult for them to conquer their old idleness and natural indifference. But, little by little, good education, united with a proper sense of their own true interests, and the claims of family affection, come to our aid as we try to help the poor creatures; and I may safely affirm that on the Valville plantation, as on my own, we have reason to congratulate ourselves upon having to do with men, and not with slaves.

"In time, with perseverance, we shall arrive at the epoch of the fusion of both races; and the era of prosperity, interrupted by the war, will again begin: this time to be more durable and more complete than ever.

"But is it necessary to explain to you how this terrible war, almost unexampled in the annals of humanity, has left behind it a legacy of half-healed enmities, of desired revenge, and vengeance only adjourned and not abjured? In the opinion of the partisans of slavery, their defeat is not irremediable; and more than one amongst them longs to dismember the great Republic.

"There are even men who, irritated at the recovered glory of our old Republic, seek to drive it into anarchy, and to excite disturbances, hoping that in the hour of peril its pretended deliverers—themselves the authors of the dangers incurred—will be enabled to seize the reins of supreme power.

"These men, knowing that they are despised by the working portion of the community, dare not throw off their mask and proclaim aloud their wish to re-establish the old despotism of the white race over the black. Do you know what, in their skilled hypocrisy, they are trying to do?

"With Machiavellian astuteness, they incite the black race to every kind of excess. They appeal to the cruel and ambitious passions which cannot fail to exist in a certain portion of a population, degraded first by slavery, and then intoxicated by liberation. Of these negroes, who were formerly slaves, they are constructing unconscious instruments for the re-establishment of slavery. In one word, they wish that, disgusted by the follies, the excesses, the brutality of the negroes, the white men should again reduce them to subjection. They stimulate these unfortunates, who are more ignorant than guilty, by ceaselessly repeating that to them alone should power belong, that in their turn they ought to take office and exercise over the South an absolute dominion, and, in fact, reduce their former masters to social slavery. Who are the men who have designed this frightful scheme? Do not think that they are the merchants, the planters, the workers of the country! No: these, even if they were formerly friends of slavery, have accepted the freedom of the negroes as an established fact, and they are working with might and main to accomplish the industrial renovation under the most favourable conditions possible.

"At the head of this destructive party—the party of a secret reaction—are placed the adventurers who never possessed a foot of land in Louisiana : 'scalawags', pariahs of civilisation, who infest America throughout, in search of fortune to be gained without work : men, in fact, who are often called 'carpet-baggers.' And these persons, who come from no one knows where, make their appearance in every case of crime or disturbance—all their worldly wealth consisting in a carpet-bag and a revolver at their belt.

"Our friend here, Doctor Freedy, will confirm my words. When in September 1874, the rioters of the negro party suddenly took possession of the Capitol and claimed the civil authority by means of an armed force; when the adventurer, William Pitt Kellogg, deposed the legal governor, Warmouth, as also MacEnery and Penn, the most respected men in Louisiana, and substituted in their place the negro porter, Pinchbeck, formerly croupier at a gaming-table; when blood flowed in Canal Street, that splendid commercial artery of New Orleans; when Badger with three cannon and two hundred men of a black regiment transformed the pedestal of Henry Clay's statue into a redoubt from which the mitrailleuse swept down the disarmed citizens;—then, as Freedy can tell you, in the midst of the rioters we recognised a bandit of the Rocky Mountains, Red Ralph himself!"

"Red Ralph!" exclaimed Valville, suddenly interrupting Woodman's narrative. "I have heard that name before—and under terrible circumstances!"

Woodman imposed silence upon him by a kindly gesture.

"With this ruffian there were also Sam Dorry, once banished from New Orleans for theft; Phil Samster, the incendiary of the docks; and, stranger still, for this is an element introduced by the scalawags which I have not hitherto mentioned to you, several Redskins of the Seminole race.

"You may know that these Indians belong to the ferocious Creek tribe, and that they have been transported to the south of Florida.

"These Indians despise the blacks and hate the whites. Incapable of work, they have become a sort of mercenary troop taking pay from any adventurers who can give it them: such are the *bravi* of Louisiana. And when they have committed a crime, how can they be caught when they fly to the impenetrable and mysterious region called 'Everglad,' at the extreme south of the peninsula of Florida?

"Amongst these Seminoles was a well-known chief called Bloody Foot."

At this name Freedy looked at Woodman, and the two men exchanged a glance. But that was all.

Woodman continued:

"The men of Louisiana, daunted for a moment by this cannonade, which had broken out upon them without notice, without provocation, soon recovered their courage. Your father, Valville, and Doctor Freedy, sprang upon the barricade, at the head of the exasperated citizens. With his own hands Valville seized Red Ralph, and planting a revolver at his temples, he cried: 'Wretch! I could kill you! but the gallows are needed for a robber like you!'

"Livid and grinding his teeth, Red Ralph responded:

"'Kill me, or I will kill you!'

"But Valville was generous. He could not bring himself to kill a conquered man. He placed the brigand in the hands of the authorities. That same evening Red Ralph was free.

"What else shall I tell you, Charles? I cannot enter into the details of the combat that was then established between law and usurpation. In spite of the energy exhibited by your father and all other honest men, the elections took place beneath a reign of terror.　The Conservatives, for so we called ourselves, elected by their townsmen, were violently expelled from their seats. It was a continual strife between right and might, until the Government at Washington, opening its eyes at last, re-established some shadow of authority.

"But a terrible blow was aimed at the prosperity of Louisiana.　The State is crushed by taxes and debts. The negroes are demoralised.　The principal cities are impoverished.　The public debt amounts to twenty-two million dollars!　The public funds are diminished by thirty per cent.

"Governor Warmouth, weak and irresolute, leaves complete liberty of action to the intrigues of the black party.　The metropolitan police are in this party's hands. 'Scalawags' and 'carpet-baggers' occupy all the seats of the legislature.　Intelligent and industrious negroes keep in the background, but rascals have the power.　And without partiality, negro criminals are much worse than white ones, because they unite to their bad instincts both ignorance and a sort of savagery, stimulated by persons who have something to gain by any kind of public excitement.　We see around us open vice and organised robbery.　Everything leads us to dread new and terrible complications.　The adventurers are on the alert.　Their vengeance on the chiefs of the resistance of 1874 is carried out almost in broad daylight.　Burning plantations, and assassinated proprietors: a reign of terror extending over the entire country!

"Your father, my poor Charles, had long been one of

the intended victims. You know the rest. One dark night the robbers entered the plantation. Sambo does not doubt but that there were traitors in the place. Surprised in his sleep, your father still sold his life dearly. But a bullet laid him low; your two sisters ran to his help. What passed then, Lucile even cannot tell; surrounded by the flames, separated from her sister, she fell; and most horrible pain was inflicted upon her, for one of the assassins attempted to scalp her!"

"Horrible!" cried Charles. "I will have the ruffians' lives."

"She cannot tell why the crime was not fulfilled to the end, or how she found herself fainting on the edge of one of the streams that surround the house. She was rescued next morning. The steward of the plantation gave me all necessary information, and I flew to New Orleans, where I demanded the assistance of the police. Ah, my friend, I understood then how deep was the hatred which pursued us! My cries of anger were scarcely heeded. A formal inquiry was begun, and has naturally tended to no result. That is two months ago, Charles, and your father has not been avenged, neither has your sister reappeared. But you are here, and with Freedy's help, with your courage and my energy, which I put at your service, I swear that we will yet lay our hands upon the bandits, and dearly shall they expiate their cowardice and their crime."

Valville remained motionless. He had covered his face with his hands. Freedy and Woodman alike respected his silence.

But at last, upon a sign from Freedy, Woodman continued.

"Now, my dear boy, the time is come to take some decided measures. You will understand that I have not remained inactive. It was needful, above all, in order that our researches should not be utterly useless, to obtain the concurrence of a trustworthy man, of tried ability, who would consent to devote himself entirely to the success of our enterprise."

"And this man?" asked Charles, raising his head.

"I have found him," said Woodman. "And besides, his name is almost historical in the United States. It was he who pursued and discovered the assassin of President Lincoln; it was he who—after the great robbery of the Chicago bank of nearly a million dollars—got scent of the thieves, and delivered them up to justice. Finally, and this is the chief reason why his aid will be so precious to us, Ned Bark, for that is his name, has long lived in Louisiana, Texas, Alabama, and Florida. He knows the tricks of the scalawags as well as those of the Redskins."

"A valuable auxiliary," said Freedy. "I am personally acquainted with Ned Bark, and I am sure no one better could be found to guide us in the pursuit of the assassins."

"Now, Charles," said Woodman, "listen to me. I have taken all the necessary measures to protect the interests of the Battle Field Plantation as much as possible."

Charles made a sign of protest. What did he care for the plantation or its revenues?

"You do not understand me, my lad. Of course I know that just now all material considerations are nothing to you. But, for one thing, the plantation supports a number of black and white persons who have shown unfailing devotion to your father, and whom it is our duty not to leave without resources; also, remember, Charles, that you are not alone, and that now you are the head of the family. The estate belongs in part to your sisters, whose interests you must protect."

"You are right," said Charles. "But alas! of my two sisters one has disappeared. Shall we ever see again?"

"I hope so."

"What reason have you for your hope?"

"Lucile herself will tell you."

So saying, Woodman rose, and drawing aside the branches of the magnolias, he said:

"Look there."

At some little distance from them, beneath a magnificent cactus, whose thorny branches rose high into the air, they saw Lucile. Her forehead was hidden by a large straw hat; and she walked very slowly, with her eyes fixed upon a notebook in her hand. Beside her a greyhound ran gleefully towards a tame heron, which turned its long bill disdainfully to the graceful animal.

"Go and join your sister," said Woodman. "Freedy and I have many things to talk about; and as soon as Ned Bark, whom we expect, arrives, we will tell you."

Charles pressed his friends' hands, and approached

the young girl. She did not hear his footstep, for she was absorbed in her book.

When Charles was almost at her side, he called her softly by her name.

The girl started; then, recognising her brother, she held out her arms to him.

Lucile Valville was indeed a lovely girl. Her long chestnut hair fell over her shoulders; her refined features were moulded with exquisite delicacy. As she raised her head, her forehead could be seen, covered by the linen bandage which hid her wound and gave a strange expression to her gentle countenance.

The brother and sister conversed long together. They had many things to say; many sad reminiscences to interchange. Charles could never weary of asking questions, for his grief was augmented by the thought that he had not seen his father for so many years.

"Oh, he often spoke of you," said Lucile, "for, I may tell you now, you were his dearest. He longed for the time when you would return and settle in Louisiana— but when your last letter reached him . . . ."

Charles coloured and looked down, for the letter which Lucile mentioned was the one in which he had informed his father of his engagement to Alice Lodier.

"Yes?" he said hesitatingly.

"His plans seemed all at once to change," said Lucile.

"What do you mean?"

"Long before that, our dear father had talked of

realising his property and going to live in France. I think he then decided upon doing so."

" And my marriage—what did he say about it ? "

" Did you ever doubt his consent ? " said Lucile, softly.

" Ah, my dear father ! Why was I not there to fight or to die with him ? "

" He said, ' My Charles is an honest young man, and will have chosen one worthy of himself.' And then . . ." here it was Lucile's turn to hesitate, "someone else warmly pleaded your cause. . . ."

" Freedy, of course ? "

" Yes, Doctor Freedy himself. Father kept him for some days at the plantation. And they talked a great deal about your future—oh, about your future and about yourself."

Charles looked at her attentively. Lucile was as pale as if all her blood had receded from her cheeks to her inmost heart. A new idea flashed across the young man's mind; an idea that contained both joy and hope.

Suddenly Lucile broke the silence.

" But Jeanne ! Jeanne ! let us speak of my poor sister."

" Yes, Mr. Woodman said that perhaps you would have something to tell me."

" Mr. Woodman has spoken the truth. Perhaps the trace of her that I have discovered is very vague, but we ought to neglect nothing. Listen."

They sat down together upon a bench.

"You know that Jeanne is of an energetic disposition. She loves violent exercise, riding, swimming, shooting. Father used to call her Charles the Second—his second Charles. But at the same time she is so kind, so generous. She always loved me, and took care of me as if I were a little child. Do you remember that one day she saved me from a horrible alligator? I was walking thoughtlessly on the river-bank, when one of these terrible creatures suddenly rushed towards me. I was lost! I was frozen with terror, and did not even try to fly; when a gun was fired, and the animal uttered a hoarse cry. It was my dearest Jeanne who killed the monster."

"No, I had not forgotten it," answered Charles.

"If I recal it to your mind, it is to give you confidence in her. Yes, my sister has been snatched from us; she has fallen into the hands of ruffians. But I say to you that Jeanne is brave, and while her life remains she will struggle; and I am sure she will escape."

"But if she was struck down like you?"

"I am sure that they have not killed her. At the moment when I was knocked down by a man whose face I could not see, at the moment when the scalping-knife had touched my head, I heard one word; one only, but I have not forgotten it! A man's stern voice cried 'Back!' and the hand upon my throat relaxed its hold. I had lost consciousness, but I was not dead. I am sure that the man who saved my life would not allow my sister to be killed; and if you still doubt—well, brother, I can give you a proof. . . ."

"A proof?"

"Yes, I am certain that if I was spared it was on my sister's account; he who carried her off would not approach her with his hands red with my blood. . . ."

"Why such generosity? Were not these men vile assassins?"

"I told you that I would prove my words. Here is the proof."

And she showed him the note-book that she had been reading.

"What is that?"

"You know that many American ladies are in the habit of keeping a journal in which they write down their thoughts and the events, more or less important, of their daily life. This book contains Jeanne's journal; and if you read it carefully, you may perhaps find in it more information than even I have done. But, for the present, look at these lines and tell me what you think of them."

Charles took the book. He opened it with a feeling of profound emotion.

The writing was firm and clear, and seemed to betoken a character full of energy and courage.

Lucile pointed to one paragraph. Charles read:

"To-day, a singular adventure happened to me. At the end of the plantation, near the foot of the waterfall beside which I am so fond of sitting, a man suddenly started up before me and said roughly, 'I am your father's enemy. But I love you. Consent to follow me and you will save your father.' I thought a madman was speaking to me. I shrugged my shoulders and retreated towards the farm-buildings. He followed me for some time and added, 'Take care! Red'—here he said some name which I could not catch: Red somebody—'loves you and hates your father!' I came in and closed the gate behind me."

A little further on, the young girl had made another entry.

"That man has not reappeared, so I will not mention him to my father. Why should I disquiet him unnecessarily?"

Further still:

"I have found a note in my room; from the stranger, no doubt. Still the same words: 'I love you.' I have burnt it. I think that I really must warn my father."

Then came these concluding lines, dated the very evening before the crime itself.

"I have again seen that man, but he did not speak to me. He pointed to my father's house with a menacing gesture. Who can he be? I feel very anxious. Can it be true that some danger threatens my father's house and all those whom I love? Oh! if Charles were only here. Certainly to-morrow I will speak to my father."

"But that 'to-morrow' never came," Lucile murmured. "It was on that very night that the attack took place."

"And the man whose name Jeanne did not hear distinctly," said Charles; "I cannot doubt—I know who he is; give me the book, Lucile. Yes, you are right. The man who has carried her off loves her with a savage love ; he did not wish for your death, but he killed our father, and he must pay for his crime with his life."

At this moment Woodman was heard calling Charles.

"I must leave you, dear sister. Need I commend Madame Longpré and her niece to your tenderest care ? "

" Do I not love any one who loves you ? " said Lucile.

Charles slipped his sister's note-book into his pocket, and advanced to the spot from which Mr. Woodman had called to him.

At the same time a little, dry, wiry-looking man was seen crossing the lawn with rapid steps.

It was Ned Bark, the American detective.

CHAPTER V.

THE DETECTIVE.

MUCH has been said, and much written, about detectives: fiction has taken possession of them, and, to speak the truth, has created a somewhat fanciful type of the class. Edgar Allan Poe's Dupin and Gaboriau's Lecoq are such typical figures, which have undergone a hundred metamorphoses and are yet evermore the same. Transported to any country in the world, and disguised in any possible costume, they are everywhere identical; the Dupin or the Lecoq whom we have known so long and so well.

The American detective deserves a special place in this gallery of portraits. Some detectives have been represented as consumed by a passion for the welfare of others: all of them, by a desire for glory. But the American detective works simply and solely for money.

Besides, what different kinds of work they have to do! What are the qualities necessary to European detectives? Plenty of tact, more or less of the power of intuition, skill, and perseverance, without which nothing is possible. They keep still, they think, and they compare:

then at the precise moment they put their finger down on the right point and say: "The truth is here."

The American detective is a veritable soldier, constantly on horseback, in a railway carriage, on a steamboat; from Canada to Texas, from San Francisco to Philadelphia. He is the knight-errant of justice, the Ahasuerus of punishment. He does not content himself with receiving reports, and quietly playing the part of a man, who is solving peaceful riddles at his desk. The American detective gives himself to the service; fights, travels, fires his gun in answer to a pistol-shot, and risks his scalp in the Rocky Mountains and his health in the Mississippi swamps. He has probably neither pen nor paper about him, nor any writing materials at all; but he has powder and bullets, and a knife with a blade a foot long. He threatens and is threatened, hunts and is hunted.

For instance, Fred Hall, one of Ned Bark's colleagues, was told one day that three dangerous robbers had escaped from the Houston prison, and that they had most likely gone in the direction of the Red River. He jumped on his horse, found the three men in a wild and desolate region, killed one of them, disarmed the next, and forced him, by means of a revolver at his temples, to act as a guard over the third.

But if he is to put all his faculties into his work and stake his life upon the game, the affair must be worth a good many dollars to him. He is an adventurer of a special kind, who puts into his contest for good an activity, a courage, a dash, which others too often employ only for evil. Nevertheless he wants to make his fortune, and one day to retire to his farm, there to enjoy the fruits of his works. Like Hercules, he has accomplished his twelve labours at the command of a king; that king, the almighty dollar!

At the same time he is as honest as most other men; for his probity forms part of the resources which he puts at the disposal of those who employ him; he shrinks from no portion of the work which he undertakes, and forfeits the reward in case of failure: in fact, he works by contract.

He possesses therefore less imaginary grandeur, he is less mysterious and less stagey than the detectives of romance. But when any European detective has done his fifty miles a day on a horse bareback, when he has cheerfully sustained a three days' siege behind a block of stone, when he has seen himself twenty times at the very point of death, then he will be equal to an American detective.

Which is to say, he will then equal Ned Bark.

For it is his portrait simply that we have drawn.

He was short, muscular, thick-set, well-built either for fight or flight. Unattractive at first sight, he had the thin face of a true Yankee, with its inevitable tuft of hair like a goat's beard on the chin. He was one-eyed, having partially lost his sight in some past affray. The one remaining eye had retired beneath the bony ridges of his brow, as if it wanted to preserve itself from a like accident behind a fortification. But from the depth of this redoubt it flashed forth—to continue the comparison—with the keen brightness of some deadly weapon.

When this curious-looking individual entered the room where Woodman, Freedy, and Valville awaited him, the three men rose, and the planter gave him his hand. Ned Bark was not at all unmindful of such tokens of respect.

"Ned," said Woodman, "let me introduce Mr. Charles Valville to you, the son of the Battle Field planter, and brother of the young lady who has been carried off."

Ned looked at him, or rather fixed his eye upon Valville's face, as if he wished by one such gaze to measure the worth of a man who had his father to avenge.

Probably he was satisfied with the result of his examination, for he said, bowing—

"Your father was a brave man, sir. I guess you are worthy of him."

"I will answer for him," said Woodman, "and so will Freedy."

"Certainly," said Freedy; "and if Ned Bark has formed any such plan of action as we expect from him, he may feel sure of being well seconded."

"One moment," said Woodman, who knew the detective's habits; "let us first settle the terms of remuneration."

"My whole fortune!" exclaimed Charles with youthful ardour.

Ned Bark smiled.

"Let us have figures," he said.

"Fix your own terms," Charles began again.

But Woodman interrupted him. "Ned Bark fixes nothing. He bargains, which is much better. My dear Valville, will you let me manage this affair?"

Charles, whose French notions were somewhat shocked by this method of acting, bowed his head without reply.

Woodman continued—

"Look here, Ned Bark. Cash on account, a thousand dollars. As soon as we are on the track of the murderers, a thousand dollars. As soon as we are on the young lady's track, a thousand dollars. If successful, five thousand dollars. Will these terms suit you?"

"First-rate," said Ned Bark coolly. "One thing more. If I am killed before completion of the work, two thousand dollars to be sent to Mrs. Bark, at Chicago."

"Agreed! We will sign an agreement to that effect."

It was a regular matter of business, and, as usual, Ned Bark expected to be paid for the risk he ran.

Woodman rapidly prepared a form, which Valville signed with a sort of impatience. Not that the price of the promised help seemed too high to him, but this manner of bargaining for it displeased him. Youth is sometimes over-nice.

"Now," said Woodman, addressing himself to Ned Bark, "here are the thousand dollars in advance. Sign a receipt, if you please."

The receipt was drawn up and signed with the same coolness.

But when Ned Bark had written his name in big letters, he turned to Woodman.

" Prepare another receipt," he said.

" Eh ? "

" Certainly : read the terms of the agreement."

" But nothing, sir," exclaimed Valville, ill concealing his suppressed anger, " nothing is due to you before-hand !"

" Certainly not—but . . ."

" While Mr. Woodman is so good as to write the second receipt, I will prove that you owe me a thousand dollars."

Valville uttered a cry of surprise, and regarded Ned Bark with a much more friendly eye.

" Then I'll write," said Woodman.

" And I will speak," said the detective.

He fumbled in his pocket and produced a note-book, which he opened.

" I have ascertained," he said, " that Red Ralph was at New Orleans on the night before the crime.   In the evening he was seen at a gambling-house in Montgomery Street, and there he held a long conversation with Phil Samster, the incendiary."

" Then those two ruffians must be accomplices," said Freedy.

" But who can tell," Valville interrupted quickly, " that this conversation had anything to do with the crime ? "

" At night," continued the detective, " Red Ralph and Samster went to a certain Brown of Shell Road. This Brown is an agent and receiver of horses from the horse-stealers, who ply their trade in Texas, Alabama, and Louisiana. There Red Ralph bought six horses, good runners, strong, and able to support great fatigue . . ."

"This is all very interesting," said Woodman. "But, without inquiring where you obtained all this information, I agree with Valville in asking if you have nothing more conclusive to tell us?"

Ned, who seemed to consider these objections very natural, drew out of his note-book a paper which he handed to Woodman.

"What is this?" said the planter. "A saddler's invoice?"

"Yes, I found it in the grass near Valville's house. See what it contains."

"Sold to—a blank for the name—, a lady's saddle with its accessories."

"And on the back?"

"Sent from B. S. R.   That is, Brown, Shell Road."

"Evidently. Another thing. I am almost certain that the guilty persons are five in number. The sixth horse was destined for the use of the young lady who was carried off. We know two of them, Red Ralph the robber, and his friend, Phil Samster. Three others remain to be discovered, who are, perhaps, only inferiors, common thieves, tools belonging to Red Ralph. But look at this," said Ned, who felt in his pocket a second time, and produced a scrap of brown stuff.

Freedy uttered an exclamation.

"Ned Bark, that is a bit of Indian cloth."

"As you say. Again, the place where I found it will,

if necessary, remove any doubt that may still subsist in your mind. Upon the edge of the bayou where Miss Lucile was dragged by the bandit who meant to scalp her, there are a great many sharp and prickly briars which grow low, close to the ground. One of these briars tore off a rag of the clothing, which, according to Indian fashion, covered the man from head to foot. So we have to do with an Indian. Who is he? I am just about to tell you; and that will also instruct us as to the direction in which we must prosecute our researches."

Valville was now quite reconciled to the manners of the detective; he regretted the impatient words which had escaped him, and with a burst of that frankness which is so delightful in the young, he held out his hand and said—

"Pardon me, sir . . ."

"What for?" interrupted the detective, with well-acted surprise. Then he added, with a somewhat ironical smile, "I am earning my money, that is all. I think I can prove to you, however, that I am no soothsayer, and that I have gained my information in simple, straightforward ways. The Indian was no other than a Seminole, known by the name of Bloody Foot."

"I know him!" exclaimed Freedy.

"Then you know as I do that he owes his name to a horrible wound which deprived him of all the fore part of his right foot; a blow from an axe carried off all the toes, and mutilated it to that degree that he wears a sort of apparatus made of bound and twisted reeds, like a great horse's hoof; still, he is as agile and as ready to walk and run as ever.   Well, it was Bloody Foot who set fire to the house; for, under the charred fragments of the house, protected by small beams which crossed and recrossed each other, and were preserved as if by a miracle, I found, after the clearance of rubbish which has been going on for the last few days, undeniable traces of Bloody Foot—prints of the mocassin and the hoof.   You see," Ned Bark added, turning to Valville, "our science consists merely of memory, attention, and —luck."

"Then," said Valville, "three of the criminals are known.   As for the other two ?"

"So far I have not found any trace of them.   But I repeat, I believe they are robbers in Red Ralph's pay. There only remains now to tell you in what direction we ought to follow our pursuit."

"Take your thousand dollars," said Woodman.

"Not yet," said Ned Bark, winking slightly towards Valville.   "I should tell you first why this evening we must set off for Jacksonville . . ."

"In Florida ?" cried Freedy.

"Exactly," replied Ned Bark.   "Only what I have to say is a delicate matter—in fact, it is almost a professional secret—and I must ask you to give your word that you will tell nobody what I am about to impart to you."

"You may depend upon us," said Freedy.   "We know you too well to refuse the promise that you desire from us."

"Especially as the least imprudence might be very hurtful. You shall judge of that. Three days ago, after having considered the matter very seriously, certain reasons led me to believe that the robbers now infesting New Orleans had accomplices among the metropolitan police."

"A sad effect of our political dissensions," said Woodman, shaking his head.

"I do not say," Ned Bark continued, "that there are murderers among them; but what I am certain of is, that all these adventurers—the scalawags—have established close relations with the lowest members of the police force, and that these men help them, either by giving them hints, or warning them of the dangers that they run. Three days ago I went to the metropolitan board, at the time when all the policemen were gathered in the common room, awaiting their chief's orders. Many recognised me, and although they received me politely, their manner was exceedingly constrained. We were not on the same side, but we entered into conversation together. We had talked of many different subjects, when at last, as if by chance, I dropped these words: 'The crime of Battle Field will not long go unpunished.' A general sensation of curiosity seemed to be felt, and in answer to repeated questions I replied, 'Mr. Valville's son and Doctor Freedy have just arrived in America, and are setting to work to discover the assassins.' Then I spoke of other things. I had said quite enough."

" Especially as we were very nearly assassinated in the Blue Hills !" exclaimed Freedy.

" An attempt which cost a certain bandit his life, I know.   But, you see, gentlemen," and here Ned Bark's voice assumed a singular solemnity, " we must all risk our lives in the work upon which we are entering : do not doubt that for a single moment."

" We are ready," said Valville in a firm tone.

" The remark was made," continued Ned Bark, " with the intention of forcing Red Ralph's accomplices, should any of them be present, as I supposed, to compromise themselves ; and I must say that my hope was not disappointed.   Scarcely had I said the words, when I noticed at the end of the room a negro, attached to one of the brigades, slip away through a door behind him.   Was this chance ? or premeditation ?   I went out and saw the man running in the direction of the St. Louis Hotel.   There I saw him enter a telegraph office.   I entered it by another door at the same moment, and my negro would have been very much surprised if he had known that I was writing down in my note-book the telegram that he dictated to the clerk, for it is needless to state that he could not write."

" And this telegram ? "

" Very short, but very clear," said Ned Bark.

And he read out from his note-book—

" ' Blue. Pilatka. Mind. F. V. here. 267.' Which means—' Blue at Pilatka. Take care. Freedy and Valville are here.   Signed 267,'—the number of the policeman.

"Now," continued Ned Bark, "it is not necessary to be a great magician to understand that Blue is only a very simple blind for the word Red. As for Pilatka, you all know that it is a small town in Florida on the St. John's River. From which we draw the inference . . ."

"That Red Ralph is at Pilatka," exclaimed Valville.

"Or that his usual quarters are there ; not far from the Seminole territory, in 'Everglad.'"

Certainly Ned Bark had well earned the thousand dollars that he claimed, and which he made no further difficulty about accepting. Valville, full of admiration, wished that he could also claim at once the thousand dollars which would be due to him as soon as they were on Jeanne's track. But the detective knew nothing more.

"We cannot tell," he said, "what was the motive of the robbers in carrying off the young lady. I have every reason to believe that they have not conveyed her to the lonely place in which they seem now to be concealing themselves—with what design, I know not. Have patience: set to work, and our good cause will do the rest."

The plan of campaign was quickly decided upon.

Freedy and Valville were to set off with Ned Bark. Mr. Woodman was to stay at the plantation, in order to protect Lucile and the strangers.

For Ned Bark, who had supreme control of the expedition, flatly refused to allow Alice to join in it. In vain the girl begged Valville to let her go with him, saying that neither her strength nor her courage would fail her. In vain did Madame Longpré, with her iron will, declare that she had nqt come to Louisiana in order to remain inactive. Ned Bark was inflexible.

He could not foresee that in spite of all his prudence, Alice would soon be involved in the tragical adventures which were to follow.

The same evening the three men, well armed, set off for Jacksonville, intending to follow up the stream of the St. John's River, if it were necessary, even to the very heart of those strange and luxuriant solitudes which are known as ' Everglad.'

CHAPTER VI.

THE DANGERS OF MIMICRY.

ABOUT a week before the scene which we have just described, in which our friends decided upon the opening of their campaign, another scene, of a totally different character, was enacted at the railway station of Savannah, upon the Georgian coast.

A train from Charleston, in South Carolina, was steaming at full speed into the immense station; and from the cars a crowd of men, black, white, and brown, of all types and all origins, leaped out upon the platform; some of them hailing the negro-porters, and directing their steps to the interior of the town; others inquiring the time of departure of the next boat for Jacksonville.

One of the first party, a little man, with a little cap, a little pea-jacket, and a little leathern bag attached to a shoulder-strap, jumped out and ran, as fast as his little legs would carry him, to the luggage van.

He muttered between his teeth—

"At last! here we are! Saperlipopette! Not at all too soon!"

He planted himself before one of the officials, a man

with a goat's beard and a green cap, and held out a ticket.

"Yes!" he continued, in a mixture of French and English; "trente-trois—thirty-three—malles—trunks : à moi, comprenez ?"

The clerk, quite unmoved, walked to the end of the van and pointed to a great heap of cases, trunks, and hat-boxes—enough to furnish a trunkmaker's shop.

"Yes!" said the other. "Mais—homme—men—pour porter—to carry. . . ."

Then he began to talk in a very loud voice—

"P-o-u-r, pour, p-o-r-t-e-r, porter!—Yes! Hein! not understand?" he went on in French. "Are they idiots, then?—Black bread, va !"

This last expression had reference to the complexion of the official, who was a decided mulatto. He must most certainly have possessed the gift of tongues, for he turned to a group of negroes who were hanging about the station awaiting orders, and uttered a low whistle.

Five negroes advanced, jostling the little traveller; they received the ticket from the clerk's hands, and fell upon the pile of trunks.

"Sapristi! take care!" cried the little man in despair. "Aie—my hats—my eighteen hats! Hi! you madman, don't shake about my shirts like that—best Longueville patterns! You blackamoors! Heaven! my cravats !"

For a negro had just slipped and fallen all his length over a great box which was crushed beneath his weight.

But they lifted up the boxes and carried them off, rolling their eyes and showing their brilliant white teeth as they went.   Hither and thither they ran, everywhere pursued by the stranger, who clucked after them like a hen after her chickens.

To the first five negroes ten others had been added; and the mighty heap was levelled, the fortress of trunks was scattered abroad upon the shoulders of these fifteen blacks, who now quitted the station with many noddings of the head and calls to the owner of the luggage to follow them.

"Wait! sapristi! oh, the rascals! They remind me of Dupuis in the play of the Charbonniers!"

Then, plucking up his courage, he stood firmly upon his two little legs, which were very like sticks, supporting an extraordinary pair of trousers that widened from the knee downwards after the fashion of an elephant's foot.

"You, good negro," he said, addressing himself to a black giant who stared at him in utter bewilderment; "you, good negro, take me good hotel."

The negro's mouth widened almost to his ears, but he did not move.

"Brute!" shouted the traveller.   "Must I make you go on with a kick—à coups de bottes?"

"Bottes! Bottes!" repeated the negroes, as if struck with a new idea.

And all of them resumed their march in single file, while the word 'bottes' resounded from one end to the other of the little procession.

The traveller ran after them, stumbling over ropes and wildly seizing hold of tarred bales, slipping, jumping up again, and shouting—

"Idiots!   Fools!—Hôtel! hôtel!"

"Bottes!   Bottes!" repeated the echo.

And the thirty-three trunks, cases, and hat-boxes were carried down some steps, pushed over gangways, and finally piled up in the hold of a steamboat.

The little man meanwhile repeated his cry, 'Hôtel!' The only answer he received was the one word— 'Bottes!'

The tall negro returned and held out his hand; the little man protested. The negro tapped the leathern bag ; the little man shouted. The negro opened the bag and put in his hand ; the little man flew into a furious passion. The negro took out a handful of dollars, counted them, took five, and returned the rest to the bag.   Then, scarcely knowing how, taken off his feet and passed from hand to hand like a parcel, the traveller found himself on board the steamer: the bell rang, the engines worked, a stentorian voice shouted—"Go ahead!" and Eusèbe Lodier, exhausted and almost stupefied, sank down upon a heap of ropes, crying—

"Arrêtez! — stop! — moi — New Orleans!   Là!— Stop!"

A man attired in a sort of jersey, his trousers tucked into his boots, and a carpet-bag in his hand, approached him, and said:

"Monsieur is French?"

He spoke in French. A fellow-countryman! Eusèbe threw himself upon him, and shaking him by the buttons of his jersey, launched forth volubly—

"Ah, monsieur, listen! I won't have these tricks

played upon me!   Tell the engineer to stop! tell them to land me!   I am going to New Orleans!"

The other smiled a little drily, and said—

"New Orleans!   You are a good way off, sir."

"A good way off!   Nonsense!   You want to take me in, too, do you? very fine!   I have come from New York.   I was to go to Charleston, and then by train to New Orleans.   I was at Charleston yesterday evening, so . . ."

"Which Charleston do you mean?"

"Which?   No, no, my man; you would like to puzzle Coco, wouldn't you? but this is not play, I tell you!"

"There's Charleston in Virginia, and Charleston in Carolina."

"Virginia! Carolina!   Nothing but women's names! What's that to do with it?"

"Merely, sir, that the town you have just left is Savannah, near Charleston in Carolina; and that you have made a mistake, for your way lay through Charleston in Virginia."

Eusèbe opened his eyes in great dismay.

"But never mind!" said the man with the carpet-bag; "you are a stranger, so I will direct you."

At this point Eusèbe was attacked by sea-sickness, and retreated to the side of the boat, where, in the midst of his agonies, he asked himself repeatedly why the negroes of whom he had inquired the way to an hotel had insisted upon bringing him to a steamer.

It was a question which might easily have been answered.

What connection could possibly exist between boots and a steamer?

The fact was, that Eusèbe had a mania for imitating the actors of the Parisian theatres. In one of Offenbach's best-known comic operas, the actor Brasseur, in the person of a German shoemaker, bends over the feet of another actor on the stage, and cries out, with a strong German accent—

" Fus abelez ça tes bôtes ! c'est bas tes bôtes ! Otez ça !" (You call those things boots ! they are not boots ! Take them off !)

Accordingly Eusèbe had fallen into the habit of never pronouncing the word 'bottes' with its proper short o, but as 'bôôôtes,' with at least three circumflex accents. As he knew scarcely a word of English, the negroes whom he abused could not understand his commands at all until the monosyllable 'bôttes' fell upon their ears. Then indeed they took it for the English word 'boat,' and fully believed that the traveller was ordering them to take the luggage to the steamer. We know the rest.

As for Eusèbe, who had spoken English without knowing it, he did not comprehend for many a long day the origin of his misadventure.

For the moment he was delighted. Fancy finding some one to talk to !

Ever since his arrival in America he had been hurled from one person or place to another, like a projectile from a cannon's mouth. Therefore the man who had just presented himself to him, in spite of a somewhat unprepossessing appearance, which might have recalled to a regular theatre-goer the melodramatic villains of the stage, was placed at once by Eusèbe in the category of his most intimate friends.

Overjoyed at being able to speak and be understood, he made no secret of his history.

"How splendid this is!" he cried. "Here am I Eusèbe Lodier, the flower of the Pois-Chiches Club, hundreds of miles from the Passage Jouffroy—no, it is too awful! and you will perhaps ask me why!"

The other remained silent and motionless.

"I've nothing to hide! not I! I swear it! Here is the whole story. I have a sister—a brave creature—in love with a Louisiana man—a good fellow, though, between ourselves; he goes in for tragedy a little too much, but not a bad fellow, by any means. It seems that down there at New Orleans they have been killing all his family! So off he goes 'for vengeance,' and my sister has gone with him. Oh, quite properly, you know: old Mother Longpré has gone too: rather a queer old soul, but not bad either! and here am I after them. 'One minute,' I said to myself, 'You shan't leave Coco behind like that!' Coco—that's me. So I looked in at my tailor's—Blancgonnet: you know him? Hein! such taste in trousers: I'll give you his address. From there I ran off to my shoemaker's, my hatter's, my tailor's! What frightful haste I had to make—and then the packing! To cut it short, I was at Havre in three days. I went to the office and asked for a first-class ticket to America. Eight hundred francs! Sapristi! Luckily it was all the same to me. 'I had taken a round sum,' as Hyacinthe says in the play of Tricoche et Cacolet; and off I went! How ill I was on the way! but it was over in no time, you know. Well, at New York I booked to New Orleans. They set me down at Charleston: you know the rest. But enough of this chatter. You have a good sort of face! And you are going to take charge of me, are you? Well, between ourselves, now, tell me, like a friend, if I am really very far from Louisiana?"

The man had listened without saying a word. Only at the point where mention was made of a round sum of money, his eyes had glistened singularly, and rested with a certain sort of complacency upon the well-filled bag which the young exquisite carried at his belt.

"So you want to go to Louisiana?" he asked, in his guttural tones.

"I said so: I wait for your answer!"

"Well, nothing is more simple."

"Ah! so much the better. Your words are like balm to my fainting spirits. How long will it take?"

"Three days."

"Hum! three days' more knocking about. And what way must I take?"

"You trust me?"

"Of course I do! If it is all the same to you, let us talk while we are lunching; I feel a sort of aching void within—I suppose one can find something to peck at in this little ferry-boat?"

"Certainly."

" And you won't refuse to accept a feed?"

" Eh?"

" To lunch with me, then. It's very odd; you seem to speak French very well, but the idioms bother you sometimes!"

" I accept your invitation," said the other.

And the two descended together to the cabin.

Eusèbe felt his serenity return. He placed himself proudly at the table, and called out 'Waiter!' with the voice of a stentor.

Naturally nobody took any notice of him. But his very kind and obliging companion made a sign to the steward, who immediately approached them. He was a negro of the darkest shade, and his attentions effectually restored Eusèbe to good-humour.

"What is the menu?" said he to his companion. " Have they any game? I should very much like a bit of widgeon, or something more elaborate; a veal sweetbread with potato chips, green peas, a coffee ice or an almond pudding; but you can arrange all that."

Whereupon the other requested the steward to bring up the boat's usual supplies of roast beef, roast mutton, boiled ham, and other similar edibles of a light and refreshing nature.

When Eusèbe saw these Pelions of joints on which whole Ossas of potatoes were waiting to be piled, he uttered a cry of terror.

" Have I to eat that?" he asked in an affrighted tone.

" Yes! Unless you want to die of hunger," replied

the other, as he vigorously attacked one of the nutritious pyramids.

Well, Eusèbe had a good appetite. He heaved a sigh and resigned himself to his fate, though not without a protest against the cooking and the quality of the food.

"If the men at my club could see me devouring this!" he moaned.

At first he was much taken aback by the kind of liquor he was expected to drink. Under the name of wine they served him some highly-flavoured beverage which burnt his throat. Nevertheless, his friend added red pepper to his own glass.

Eusèbe, who wanted to be thought a man of the world, and to uphold the honour of his country, swallowed his beverage manfully, with his eyes starting and his mouth on fire. He would have given five pounds for a glass of water! but how could he ask for it? And at his third glass he had lost all sensation, both in palate and in tongue.

"Now, then," said the other; "I am quite at your disposal, and I will point out to you clearly and plainly what route you ought to take. Don't alter your course a hand's breadth from it."

"No danger," murmured Eusèbe, who could hardly speak.

"To-morrow morning the steamer will stop at Fernandina . . ."

"Another girl's name: very pretty."

"Fernandina; but wait, I will write down the names for you; that will be most convenient."

" You are quite a father to me ! "

" Drink away; you are not taking anything ! "

Eusèbe made a resigned grimace.   The conversation had caused him to hope for a truce to the drinking. But there was no help for it.

" I said Fernandina," continued the other.   " There you need not stop . . ."

" Ah, well ! go on, then."

" You will remain on board, and the steamer will take you on to Brunswick . . ."

" I knew a man of that name in Paris ! he was at all the rehearsals.   But it can't be the same . . ."

" You will stop on board . . ."

" Always ? "

" You will pass Jacksonville ; you must not get off . . ."

" Well ? "

" Till you reach Picolata . . ."

" What a name to remember ! "

" There you must stop . . ."

" None too soon ! "

" You will get off, go to the hotel, and have a rest. You will have a charming and obliging host to wait upon you . . ."

" A paradise ! How glad I am that I met you ! You will tell me your name, will you not ? "

" I am called Captain Cotraw."

One should be able to give the hoarse tones of the man's voice in order to make the reader understand how Eusèbe responded,

" Captain Queue-de-Rat ! . . . exactly ! "

The other did not wince.

"Of the Military College of the United States : an intimate friend of General Grant : and, if I may say it, one of the heroes of the late war."

Having thus conferred brevet rank on himself, Captain Cotraw called for some more whisky, tossed off a glass of it, and continued—

"Here are all the names written down; you can't make a mistake. At Picolata they will tell you the way to New Orleans. A little further on, keeping to the right . . ."

"Always to the right! What a treasure of a man! Ah! Captain Queue-de-Rat, why don't you accompany me ?"

"I cannot," said the man, speaking mysteriously into Eusèbe's ear ; "on the President's service!"

"Oh! Well, then . . ."

"Let us have a last glass, and finish our meal together."

"Willingly. But call for the bill, and I'll pay it."

The captain slightly bit his lip.

"If you like, I will save you that trouble."

"I scarcely liked to ask it of you," Eusèbe hastened to say. He was, in fact, beginning to suffer from violent headache.

He gave his leathern pouch to the captain.

That gentleman opened it dexterously, plunged his great hand down to the bottom, doubtless in order to ascertain precisely what Eusèbe meant by a good round sum, then delicately drew out a few dollars, called the steward, and paid him. Then he restored the bag to its owner.

An hour afterwards Eusèbe was sleeping so heavily—thanks to the brandied wine and the whisky—that a whole troop of imps seemed to be dancing a saraband in his brain.

Next morning he awoke with half-blinded eyes and fevered mouth.

" My head aches terribly ! " he said to himself.

But the captain was before him, with bright eyes and gleaming teeth which looked like knives freshly sharpened for the battle of another meal.

Luncheon began again ; roast beef, roast mutton, salt beef, salt mutton, wine and whisky.

If he had dared, Eusèbe would gladly have cried " Hold, enough ! " But he had not even the strength to do that, for his throat was in a raw and rasped condition, which prevented his uttering anything but inarticulate sounds, and the steamer rocked so violently that the effect upon him was anything but agreeable.

" Jacksonville ! "

The name resounded through the steamer. Eusèbe, curled up beneath a bench, between a barrel of tar and a cask of salt fish, did not care to move. Vaguely he remembered that he had been told to keep still.

Complete stupefaction had overpowered him. He had no other consciousness of his present condition than an overwhelming sensation of mingled sea-sickness and intoxication. How long this state of mind and body endured, it would have been impossible for him to say ; but at last a new cry resounded harshly in his ears—

" Picolata ! "

" Chipolata ! here it is ! " squeaked Eusèbe, stumbling to his feet.

He fell into a sitting posture, rose again, tumble against a sailor who thrust him back with an oath; but at last, he knew not how nor why, he found himself upon the gangway.

Here a sudden gleam of intelligence crossed his mind.

" Luggage !   Luggage ! " he cried.   " Thirty-three boxes ! "

Where were they? The first mate of the steamer knew a few words of French.

" Your ticket ? " he said.

" Ticket ?   Ah ! yes, true ! in my pocket."

He looked for it.

At last he found the ticket, and placed it triumphantly in the mate's hands. The mate glanced at it rapidly and handed it to a sailor, who ran to the hold. In two minutes he returned with one packet, which he placed in Eusèbe's arms.

" Come, get off ! " said the mate.

" Off ? with what ? with this thing ? "

For the packet which Eusèbe irreverently called ' this thing ' consisted of a few articles tied up in a plaid, over which were crossed an enormous gun and a stick as thick as the clubs used by the dandies in the time of the Directoire.

" That thing ? " he repeated.   " But I don't want that ! I have thirty-three boxes. Thirty-three, do you hear ? "

" Quite enough. Have you another ticket ? "

"Ticket? . . . always tickets! . . . Have I been cheated?"

And with a sort of rage he searched his pockets again and again. Nothing! nothing!

"Captain Queue-de-Rat!" he cried. "Help! You have got my ticket! Thirty-three boxes!"

"Thirty-three boxes?" said the mate impatiently. "We unloaded them . . ."

"Where? when? how?"

"At St. John's; see, here is the very ticket."

And they showed him—yes, they showed Eusèbe his ticket; his own ticket, on which the two figures, 33, stared him in the face as if they had been traced in characters of fire.

He wanted to argue, to protest; he called a hundred times for the valiant Captain Queue-de-Rat to come to his aid; but the captain seemed to have disappeared into the depths of some submarine abyss.

"Yes or no! are you going to land at Picolata?"

"Picolata! yes! . . . but . . . thirty-three cases!"

Pushed and jostled from side to side, the unfortunate Eusèbe found himself forced over the gangway, and gained the solid ground again with Captain Queue-de-Rat's luggage on his back.

He was at Picolata, in Florida.

And in the midst of his misery, which was profound, he had one consolation; and that was, that round his neck still hung the leathern wallet, still heavy, and therefore still well-filled.

CHAPTER VII.

THE author has too much confidence in his readers' intelligence to detain them in order to give any reasons for the disappearance of the excellent, amiable, and obliging Captain Queue-de-Rat.

The thirty-three cases were now upon their way by train to Jacksonville; and the moment was drawing near when, before the astonished eyes of his customers, the captain could display the admirable boots, the well-cut trousers, the hats of every kind, from the simple cap to the opera-hat, the many-coloured neckties, which constituted Eusèbe's most valued possessions !

And the bear-skin travelling-rug, the furred slippers, the silver dressing-case; all these were to travel far and wide upon the arm of the audacious thief, who, in order to keep his movements more free, had not hesitated to sacrifice his own luggage to Eusèbe.

But where was Eusèbe—with his little bag ?

Once upon a time, Buckingham Smith, secretary to the American Embassy at Madrid, was obliged to send his wife alone to St. Augustine, in Florida.

"Good-bye," he said to her. "God bless you ! You

are beginning your journey very comfortably. You will be safe as far as Picolata ; but from there—Heaven help you !"

And what Picolata was ten or twenty years ago, Picolata is now : a sort of grimy, dirty quay, on worm-eaten wooden piles, where steamboats unlade their merchandise ; so much for the outside of the town. Within, everything is different; for there is nothing to be seen at all. The sea-breeze blows in upon the traveller and chills him to the bone. Before him stands a shaky-looking sort of building of decaying wood, which serves alike for barn, mill, or anything else that may be wanted ; while the groundfloor is occupied by a grog-shop about ten feet square.

And nineteen times out of twenty the grog-shop is filled to overflowing by some dozen individuals of decidedly cut-throat appearance.

Such is the place where the excellent Captain Queue-de-Rat caused Eusèbe to land, in the belief that New Orleans was only a few steps further on—if you kept to the right.

Dismayed, unhappy, and feeling as if the earth were giving way beneath his feet, Eusèbe stood motionless on the pier. Some few suspicious-looking men came and hovered round him, like dogs that scent a meal. But it seemed as if their prey was not very tempting, for, with a mocking smile, they turned upon their heels and sought the grog-shop, where they resumed their in-terrupted game of ' Seven up.'

Yes, utterly dismayed and overwhelmed was poor

Eusèbe; and he might well have been so, even with less numerous misfortunes.

The fine 'Cocodès,' as he nicknamed himself, who, at Paris, never went a step except on horseback or in a carriage; who knew nothing of life but what could be seen in the artificial atmosphere of the green-room or the boudoir; who laughed at everything, and vowed that there was nothing serious in heaven or earth; the fastidious diner-out, the most persevering dancer of the season, found himself, at four o'clock in the evening, exposed to a bitter wind, fifteen hundred leagues from France, with his little coat splashed with black mud, his forehead scarcely covered by a tiny cap, his legs shaking, and his whole form shivering from head to foot.

Certainly, as he would have said—if he had been able to speak—it was not at all strange; oh no! And yet he must come to some decision. To stay where he then found himself was impossible. If he did, he would soon freeze to death, being destitute of the warm skin which benevolent nature has conferred upon the black bear and the white.

Already an odd tingling at the nostrils told him that he had caught a terrible cold in the head. He sneezed.

This sneeze was both a revelation and a resurrection.

It shook and awoke him, and as he looked round, he observed a grog-shop, through the windows of which a faint red light was visible.

The instinct of self-preservation sometimes does wonders. Eusèbe stood erect, and mechanically settling

Captain Queue-de-Rat's bundle on his shoulders, and allowing the gun and the stick to swing against his legs as he moved onwards, he directed his steps towards the tavern.

He was not a coward at heart. He pushed the door open and entered.

It is right to say, however, that he had just remembered the round sum which he carried in his little bag. Supposing that he were not able to explain himself in words, he could at least produce some sound arguments in his own favour in the shape of coin.

The men raised their heads and looked at him.

He went straight to the counter, presided over by a big man with a bearded face; and seeing there a bottle upon which was inscribed in gold letters the single word Rum, he said shortly—

"A glass of rum."

He knew so much English, as he had heard these words at an American buffet in Paris.

The man silently poured out a glass of rum. Eusèbe, who wanted above all to regain his courage, swallowed it at a draught. It burnt him, but the warmth thus afforded was not disagreeable, especially as he felt behind him the heat of an almost red-hot stove.

He reflected for a moment. He had nearly learnt the English pronunciation of the name New Orleans, and good Captain Cotraw had at least assisted him in this part of his education. Moreover, he knew the word 'go.' It was used on the racecourse.

Eusèbe submitted himself to a short linguistic exercise, and then said, with the audacity of a true Parisian—

"Go New Orleans."

The men looked at him in astonishment. He repeated his words in a louder key, for, like many persons in a foreign country, he seemed to imagine that he was talking to deaf men:

"Go—New—Orleans."

Then there was an explosion. The big man held his sides with his two great hands—about the size of shoulders of mutton—and burst into a loud shout of laughter, which was boisterously re-echoed on every side.

Eusèbe shouted again and again, "Niow-Orlianns!"

And as they began to persecute him with jokes of a somewhat doubtful character, which disgusted him all the more because he could not understand them, he had a sudden inspiration!

With an air of proud disdain, he raised his head, opened his bag, and, like a man who has never known fear, he placed upon the counter—a stone, which might have weighed perhaps about half a pound!

Horrible! a stone—a real stone!

As the laughter was renewed to an alarming degree, he rummaged angrily in his bag.

One stone! two stones! three stones! nothing but stones.

His round sum of money had been changed, not indeed into leaves, but into granite.

For a moment Eusèbe felt as if he had received a blow

on the head : a hundred sparks danced before his eyes. He had been robbed, shamefully, cruelly robbed! he was ruined; he had not a penny left, and he would look like a thief!

There is always some good in a man—especially when he is not worse than Eusèbe—and it was this last thought that hurt him most. The effect on him was so powerful that his memory returned, and he recollected that he had some change in his waistcoat pocket. The wretched Queue-de-Rat would probably have despised this trifle. Eusèbe was right; and his fingers closed upon the few dimes which alone remained. He extracted one of them from his pocket, and threw it down in payment for the glass of rum that he had drunk.

Then, with a certain hauteur which, under the circumstances, was not without its heroism, he passed the laughers, opened the door, and left the house.

Night was closing in. A fine rain was falling, but Eusèbe did not notice it. He marched stiffly out into the wet fog, and walked straight on, he knew not whither; himself, his gun, his stick, and the bundle gradually disappearing in the shades of evening.

He could not tell where he was going. But, still obedient to the mocking directions of Captain Queue-de-Rat, he bore instinctively to the right.

Not that he believed any longer that New Orleans was near.

He believed nothing. He was going nowhere: he was trying to get away, that was all.

He could not reason about it yet. His head was

in confusion; a tempest seemed to be raging in his brain.

But as he proceeded on his way, his ideas became more clear.   He began to talk to himself.

"Sapristi!" he said, "how stiff I am! quite knocked up, that's clear.   Where am I? where shall I go?   This sort of thing is not at all amusing."

On each side of the path which he was treading he heard strange sounds, breathings, and patterings.

"There must be some wild beasts about here," he thought.

A shiver ran down his spine at this idea.   But he shook off his alarm.

"Come, don't be afraid," he said.   "I'm in a hole, and must get out of it.   I haven't the least wish to leave my skin here; here goes!"

He began to run, and heard the stones slide from underneath his feet.

Suddenly he listened intently.

"Eh!" said he.   "That must be water.   Come, come, wherever can it be?"

As if to answer the question, through the scattered clouds a clear light fell upon the scene before him.

Eusèbe could then see that on his left rose a mighty wall of rock, and that, a few steps before him, a stream of water, as bright as silver, flowed rapidly beneath a fringe of trees and plants.

He approached the water, bent down, and plunged his hands and face into it, then, walking a little way back from the edge, he uttered a cry of admiration.

A rock rose up before him, opening out like the archway of some gigantic bridge; and a clear, pale moon threw its radiance over the topmost stones, out of a tranquil sky.

"That's in very good taste," he murmured. "It is better done than at the theatre of the Porte St. Martin! Upon my word, as a drop-scene, it's a great success."

And, placing Captain Queue-de-Rat's parcel in front of him, he took up his cane, and struck an heroic attitude before the moon.

But Eusèbe did not possess a poetical mind, and he would gladly have given all these glories of nature—mountains, rocks, valleys, and torrents—for one little corner of the Boulevard Montmartre. He preferred a society journal to the open book of the universe. Yet he was carried out of himself by admiration. He found the landscape before him 'quite a success.'

Only he wondered where he was. It is needless to say that his geographical knowledge was of the slightest, and that all the names recently heard, from Savannah to Picolata, had not awakened in him the least topographical reminiscence.

He had made one great acquisition, however. Perhaps for the first time in his life Eusèbe began to think seriously, and to understand the old proverb: "Heaven helps those who help themselves."

To help himself! So be it: he was quite ready to take an energetic resolution. But what should it be? Should he go to the right, to the left, straight forward, or back to Picolata? Back? No. He did not care to fall into the hands of the men who had laughed at him so recently. To the left there was nothing but water: that is to say, for the benefit of our readers, the St. John's river, which, swollen by the rains, did not present a very reassuring appearance. Before him—space, the Unknown, the moon! Too far off. To the right the scene was different. The rock before which Eusèbe had so resolutely placed himself, formed a sort of natural staircase, with wide landings here and there, which, illumined by the radiance of the moon, had the brilliant whiteness of polished marble.

Suddenly Eusèbe began to wonder what o'clock it was. He had walked for some time, and night appeared to have long closed in. Now Eusèbe had, or ought to have had, a watch, a fine chronometer which went for five days without winding up. But he dared not put his hand into his watch-pocket. Why should the distinguished captain have disdained this valuable ornament? If he had done so, he must have possessed very small love for the study of horology!

The real reason why Eusèbe found his precious time-keeper was simply this: in the moral and physical prostration produced by the combined effects of intoxication and sea-sickness, he had lain face downwards, and this position had saved his chronometer.

It was nine o'clock at night.

Eusèbe had not dined, and had no expectation of any breakfast next morning. These facts supplied him with many sad reflections, complicated with gentle reminders from his appetite of pressing bodily needs.

Something must be done as soon as possible.

"And I have nothing left—nothing!" he murmured.

His eyes fell upon the bundle which the captain had generously bequeathed to him. Nothing? After all, he had something; and for the first time it occurred to him that this bundle might be of use.

And the gun! That might be of incalculable value to him! And what was there in that plaid?

He must at once examine its contents, and for this purpose it would be well to make himself as comfortable as possible. Those broad marble steps offered every possible facility, and were the more tempting as Eusèbe, although he found himself in a wide open space, was not reassured by certain sounds recently heard, which proved the neighbourhood of wild animals, not always particularly friendly to mankind.

One! two! Eusèbe was young and active. With his bundle on his shoulders he jumped upon the rock, and clinging to its projections, clambered by means of hands and feet to a sort of platform about five yards square, which afforded very safe and comfortable quarters.

Once there, Eusèbe, who was quite tired out, sat down in Turk or tailor fashion, with his legs crossed beneath him, and placed before him the famous parcel, the gun, and the stick.

In spite of himself he could not help laughing, with a Frenchman's instinctive gaiety, as he exclaimed—

"This piece really bristles with improbabilities. It's a pity one gets so hungry! Let me look at the gun."

As he had been an ardent sportsman and a frequenter of shooting-galleries, Eusèbe was not without some technical knowledge of firearms. When he had carefully examined the gun, he clicked his tongue between his teeth in evident satisfaction.

"A first rate gun !" he murmured. "If only I were not so sorry about my thirty-three boxes ! For how am I to dress? I shall frighten the very sparrows."

It did not occur to him at the moment that it was not exactly with sparrows that he would have to deal.

"Let's look at the stick. Sapristi ! A regular club ! a first-class bamboo ! Ha !"

These exclamations proceeded from surprise mingled with delight. This stick was really a fishing-rod ; and upon unscrewing the handle, Eusèbe drew out successively six pieces, fitting one into the other. At the other end a movable case contained lines, hooks, and complete fishing tackle. This fishing-rod was a marvel of ingenuity. Eusèbe felt inclined to present Captain Queue-de-Rat with a vote of thanks.

Would the parcel offer him any more surprises? He opened it with a kind of timidity, and a new cry escaped his lips. In the midst of other articles which he examined afterwards, he found :

· First, a cartridge-box, full.

Secondly, a bowie-knife, big enough to kill an ox.

Thirdly, a revolver and the cartridges belonging to it.

Fourthly—and oh ! the praises of this fourth article

ought to have been chanted by Homer on his lyre!—a smoked ham! Yes, a ham that weighed about four pounds, dry as a stone, odorous as a pair of old boots, but a real ham, quite eatable for any one with good teeth, such as Eusèbe possessed, and with which he speedily made an incision into the solid food. By the help of his long knife he cut out a great piece, which tasted to him just then as delicious as the tenderest young rabbit!

To this ham was joined a not less welcome addition, in the shape of a flask, which unfortunately contained nothing but whisky. Eusèbe contented himself with a single mouthful, over which he made a frightful grimace, resolving to replace the burning liquor by the clearest water he could get.

"The coffee is wanting!" sighed Eusèbe. "However . . . !"

He resigned himself to his fate, and by the light of the accommodating moon began to examine the rest of his possessions. It was with a contemptuous curl of the lip that he surveyed a sort of jacket with large buttons. How badly it was cut!—what waste! And those trousers! and that furred greatcoat!—what a hideous shape!

"Ah, how beautifully these American tailors work!" he murmured sarcastically to himself.

Eusèbe's first impulse was to throw the horrible garments into mid-air; but his hand, raised for that purpose, was suddenly stayed. It was very cold. His pea-jacket did not keep his shoulders particularly warm. With courage unequalled by the most vaunted heroes of antiquity, he resolutely put his arms into the furred greatcoat. It was warm. It was comfortable. He sighed again, but he kept the garment.

Of the other things he made a bundle which might serve as a pillow, examined the gun, loaded and cocked it, opened the bowie-knife and placed it within reach of his hand, carefully readjusted the fishing-rod, then extended himself, or, rather, curled himself up on the cold stone, hummed to himself an air from the opera of Robert le Diable, and tried to go to sleep, repeating the motto of the ancients: 'Business can wait till to-morrow.'

But matters were not to proceed so smoothly as he had imagined.

Eusèbe was lying upon a flat rock at some unknown altitude above the level of the sea, with untrodden wilds before, behind, and around him. After having lived all his life in Paris, and having experienced no greater danger than that of a crowded thoroughfare, he found himself suddenly transported to the depths of a frightful solitude, but nevertheless, thanks to his courage or his carelessness, he began to grow a little sleepy.

All at once he found himself in a new and alarming position.

He was asleep—or, rather, he was dozing, for his brain was still troubled by remembrances of the past day, and anxieties for the morrow. In the midst of his drowsiness it seemed to him that he heard—though it must have been a dream !—a sort of step, difficult to describe. It was at once scraping and heavy: something like the advance of a tiger on polished marble or ice.

It was a rustling, mingled with a gliding sound.

Half-asleep, Eusèbe dreamed of a great machine with enormous wheels, which, fastened together, creaked like terrible jaws crunching some hard substance.

And he felt something—where was it?—on his foot, his ankle, his leg; something which halted, pressed, pinched !

He uttered a hoarse cry, and sprang to his feet. Before him, on the white stone, he saw a black blotch—a hideous thing—a creature with a double body, from which immense claws were stretched on either side.

Immense : for in the sudden confusion of waking he had lost all conception of size.

It seemed to him that this thing, this hideous, frightful, horrible thing was of gigantic form : the sinister apparition of some antediluvian creature, plesiosaurus or megatherium.

With a furious bound he seized his gun, and brandished it in the air.

It descended. . . .

Bah ! the monster had not been touched, but, alarmed by the noise of the weapon, which had struck the stone beside it, it was making off to the nearest hole with all possible speed.

"Never !" exclaimed Eusèbe.

No, indeed ! after giving him such a fright, the beast should not regain its home quite so calmly. Eusèbe was furious—partly because the very marrow of his bones had been frozen with terror, partly because he had just discovered that the monster in question was—what? —a spider !

He had a horror of spiders ! Certainly, it was not without a shudder that he would have passed at night through a garden where he might have to break through their fine webs ; but what of that ? He was now neither at Auteuil, nor in a garden of the Boulevard Malesherbes.

And then, such a spider ! It was a spider of the largest size, with a body of at least eight inches in cir-cumference, the enemy of small birds, which it attacks in their nests—a horrible creature which has several times been described as presenting in appearance the most vivid realisation of incarnate malice which can possibly be conceived ; a truly frightful insect indeed !

But, after having believed it to be of colossal propor-tions, when Eusèbe really saw what it was, it appeared to him as contemptible as he had at first thought it terrible. Heroic as a knight of the Round Table, he stooped down and lifted it by one leg.

Much surprised, the creature struggled and tried to free itself. Eusèbe seized it by the body, and, like a Titan hurling mountains at the gods, he launched the spider into space.

Only when he had done this, he felt that he was turning pale, and that his knees were knocking together, and—with all due deference to Mutius Scævola and other heroes of antiquity—he sank down upon the rock, on the point of fainting away.

But as it is true that there is no such thing as an unmitigated evil, and that the theory of compensation is not an idle dream, this great and deep emotion had the effect of making him exceedingly sleepy; and, in spite of the animals which now might wander over him at will, he slept as peacefully as Hercules on the completion of his twelve labours.

For had he not also subdued his hydra-headed monster?

When he awoke, he uttered a cry of surprise, rubbed his eyes, and sat up.

The darkness had gone. The sun was rising in radiant brightness, and from the height on which he was stationed Eusèbe beheld a glorious scene.

Below him flowed the St. John's River, tranquil enough between its two rapids; and upon the moving flood the sun was throwing a trail of gold, like a flame reflected in a mirror of steel.

A small island, crowned with green trees, looked like a vessel at anchor on the stream. In the distance a white sail could be seen.

Eusèbe asked himself at first whether he were not the sport of some delusion, or assisting at some fairy-like scene upon the stage. As memory returned to him, he was not less surprised. What! was this the same country, which at night, in the wind and rain, had seemed so frightful? He was quite sure that he had been very cold, and now a gentle warmth penetrated his whole being and comforted him. If Eusèbe had known that Florida is called an earthly paradise, he would have understood that though tempests frown sometimes, the sun yet claims his empire, and, even in winter, awakens, reanimates, consoles the land which well deserves its name of 'Everglad.'

Not concerning himself much with the why and the wherefore, however, Eusèbe rejoiced in the present; he leaned back as comfortably as a lady in her stall at the opera, and was very near bestowing a little applause upon the background which Dame Nature—equal to the best scene-painters—had prepared for his delectation. He had quite regained his usual serenity, and, suddenly struck by a new idea which caused him indescribable surprise, he exclaimed aloud,

" Dear me, I have really been thinking!"

It was true. For some minutes his brain had been working in a manner to which it was not at all accustomed. Eusèbe was trying to find some means of escape from the odd situation in which he now found himself.

"Let me see," he reflected; "there is no mistake about it. I, Eusèbe Lodier, am in the position of Robinson Crusoe. I have had my little shipwreck; I am threatened by all sorts of dangers. And there is only this to say, that if I am to get out of the scrape, I have nobody to count upon but Coco."

We know that this was Eusèbe's nickname for himself.

" And it is quite clear," he continued, " that I must become a hero. Hard work! it's not according to my habits at all; but, bah! one must get used to everything. It would have been easier if I had been brought up to the business; however, that doesn't matter.

" I've got a gun, a fishing-rod, some clothes, and a

ham—I've not got the daily papers; but one must manage as well as one can. Now I have to find New Orleans, at all risks. Not so easy, that, as to act Robinson Crusoe; still it must be possible.

"It is evident that Coco Eusèbe has lost his way in some corner or other of the world. But at any rate he is on dry land; and, unless this place turns out to be an island, there must be some roads leading from here to somewhere. It is one of these roads that I have to find. Hence I draw this conclusion, that sitting still is a very bad method of defence, and that before anything else I must go somewhere—no matter where; this 'somewhere' serving as a starting-point from which to go somewhere else."

This was all very logical, as one must needs confess: the most skilful dialectician could not have found a flaw in the argument.

The conclusion implied a resolution. Eusèbe was thinking for himself. In this, as in so many other things, the beginning was everything.

"I've begun it," he murmured to himself; "I shall go on thinking now to the end of time."

Happily it did not seem necessary to delay action for quite so long a period. Scarcely five minutes had elapsed before the gallant Eusèbe was vigorously strapping up Captain Cotraw's bundle, not before having, however, consumed a good slice of the cut ham; he then fastened the fishing-rod to the bundle, and the bundle to his shoulders, stuck the bowie-knife into his belt, and with one feverishly courageous hand seized the

American rifle, which he had already loaded. He then - began to descend the hill, quite prepared to act the part of Ahasuerus, which, as everybody knows, is the family name of the Wandering Jew.

Eusèbe had decided not to return to Picolata. Therefore his first principle was to turn his back upon the town, which he did all the more bravely because he had absolutely no idea whither the contrary direction would lead him.

But how could he be sure that he would not return to it by accident?

M. Eusèbe Lodier proved once more the value of having attended classes at college. He knew that the water before him was a river, and that all rivers flowed to the sea, as the geography books say. By going up the stream, therefore, he must be leaving Picolata behind, as the town was at the mouth of the river.

This course he pursued.

The walk was not an easy one. And how long would it last? a question impossible to answer. Eusèbe wore little boots with high heels, such as had been fashionable in Paris. Here the ground was heaped with intertwining briars, trunks of trees, branches inextricably entangled, which were like so many traps for those unfortunate heels; and at every sixth yard Eusèbe was stopped short, with a disagreeable sensation that some reptile had curled itself round his foot.

Then the effort necessary in order to disengage his foot led to a considerable loss of time, and the journey seemed likely to last for ever.

For the tenth time Eusèbe nearly fell upon his nose, an accident which afforded him many salutary meditations. Once more he thought—he could do no more—and having weighed the reasons for and against, he decided, with the fortitude of a Brutus condemning his children to death, that his heels must have their heads knocked off.

To decide was easy. To execute the sentence was more difficult. Eusèbe's notions on the subject of cobbling were exceedingly vague. Yet it must be done.

He found a palm-tree against which he could lean, and there he resolutely took off one of his boots. It was an odd sight to see this man with one stockinged foot raised a few inches from the ground, while he examined the heel of his boot with deep attention.

He shook his head over it in comical hesitation. At last he resolved to strike one great blow, and for this purpose drew from his belt the captain's mighty bowie-knife. He opened it and looked at the blade, which might have reminded him of the weapon with which De Rohan was beheaded. Then, calm as an executioner, he placed the boot against the tree, raised his arm, and struck with the aforesaid blade upon the aforesaid heel.

The knife was strong, and cut like a razor.

The nails in the heel gave way.

But at that very moment Eusèbe heard behind him a singular noise ; a crashing of trees and branches, a rapid movement over the brushwood.

He turned round and saw, not ten feet from him, red, open jaws, followed by a long, black, narrow body.

It was only a crocodile.

Let us be just. We may pretend to be strong-minded, and pass ourselves off for the "impavide" individual spoken of by Horace. Still it is none the less true that an encounter with crocodiles — unless one has been brought up in their society since childhood—has nothing in it of a particularly enlivening nature. So let the man who knows not fear be the first to cast a stone at Eusèbe, who, without waiting, started off like a rabbit, running wildly, tearing himself in the thorns, and catching his clothes in the briars, and constantly hearing behind him the approach of the reptile as it wriggled through the herbage, glad and expectant of its prey.

Eusèbe could go no more. He tried to reach the water, but he did not know how to swim. Also he thought he had heard that crocodiles are as much at home in water as on land. It was not a cheerful position.

Suddenly Eusèbe uttered a cry. He had perceived a small vessel anchored in a little bay; he ran towards it. His course could not be very rapid, for, in his fright, he had dropped his boot, and with only a sock on one foot he limped onwards in piteous fashion.

Nevertheless he reached the boat and jumped in.

With one stroke of his knife he severed the cord that had kept it fast.

The boat swung slowly round, yielding to the current, but stopped at the entrance of the bay, caught by the floating weeds.

The crocodile, evidently disappointed, was not at all

inclined to abandon the chance of the delicious meal which fate had sent him; a meal the more delicious as he had never before tasted any member of the Pois Chiches Club.

He uttered a sort of screech which indicated violent hunger, and which was also, no doubt, a cry for help; for at the moment when he was plunging into the water after the fugitive, there appeared upon the bank another crocodile—belonging probably to the fairer portion of the crocodile community, for it was accompanied by an interesting little family,—its mouth open, and its tail waving in the breeze like a plume.

Eusèbe, seated at the bottom of the boat, had seized his gun, and with watchful eye awaited the moment when he could commit crocodilicide.

As the paterfamilias of the band was now swimming vigorously towards him, Eusèbe, ready for the attack, shouldered his gun and placed his finger on the trigger.

But just then two new facts occurred. The boat, which Eusèbe had neither attempted nor desired to arrest, detached itself from the weeds which had impeded its course, and was borne onwards by the current.

Eusèbe saw before him the rapidly flowing stream.

And at the same moment there passed before his eyes, with the rapidity of an arrow from a bow, a small canoe, paddled by an Indian—a Redskin—with plumes upon his head.

CHAPTER VIII.

ANOTHER ADVENTURE.

IT was a veritable Red Indian; but, fortunately for Eusèbe, who experienced some alarm at his appearance—having never before seen so strange a personage except upon the boards of the theatre of the Porte St. Martin—he seemed to be too much occupied with the labour of guiding his canoe through the rapid current which threatened to carry it quite away, to take his eye one moment even from his paddles.

So Eusèbe remained unseen.

But there was another danger, which our friend well understood, and which, to tell the truth, did not particularly rejoice his heart either: and this lay in the fact that his own boat, caught by the reflux of the current, was turning round and round as if the thing of wood and bark were hesitating in which direction to overturn the unlucky wanderer.

Fortunately necessity is the mother of invention; and Eusèbe had pulled too often at Asnières and Argenteuil with the Rowing Club—of which he was one of the most enthusiastic members—to be ignorant of the use of the oar.

Throwing down his gun, he seized the paddle which lay at the bottom of the boat, and with hands that trembled a little, set himself to struggle as vigorously as possible against the stream. But his efforts were in vain. He felt that he was going down the current, and at a little distance he heard the rush of the rapids upon the rocks.

From crocodile to shipwreck! from Scylla to Charybdis!

And to think that at that very hour, in the fair town called Paris, quiet people were snoring peacefully in their beds, enjoying their early morning slumbers, while Eusèbe was fighting against the stream which bore him down with desperate swiftness.

But it seemed to be written in the book of fate that the rising sun should not yet shine upon the last day of Eusèbe's life.

At the very moment when a few yards only lay between him and the line of foam which marked the position of the rapids, over which the Red Indian was now skimming lightly in his canoe, the great trunk of a tree, floating like an immense black arm detached from the bank, drifted up against Eusèbe's boat. It was as though the frail vessel had been seized by a harpoon: closely riveted to the tree it began to follow it in its evolutions. By means of the current, this tree described a vast semicircle of so wide a circumference that Eusèbe suddenly felt a shock: he had been thrown against the opposite bank from the one on which he had previously been standing. The boat stopped short: it had stuck in a sort of pool of mud, which the current had deposited over a space of some ten square feet.

The situation was still not particularly attractive. But what did it matter? Eusèbe, who was young and wished to live, was much delighted to have escaped a death which had seemed to be as near as it was inevitable; and this black mud, over which were crawling slimy creatures very much like snakes and toads, looked to him as inviting as the greensward at Versailles. The boat moved no longer, for the trunk of the tree, itself entangled, pushed it deeper and further into the soft black mass. It was a new sort of anchorage.

How should he get out of it? It was a pretty country indeed! And Eusèbe was a fine traveller!— But a mode of action must speedily be decided on, whatever it might happen to be. One could not spend the whole of one's youth on board a canoe.

About three yards of mud had to be crossed. It was true that the bank itself did not present too reassuring an aspect. Of course it is needless to remark that Eusèbe, wholly uninformed on the subject of the American flora, was quite incapable of distinguishing pines from sugar-canes, or magnolia shrubs from the long trails of magnificent creeping tropical bindweed. And amidst the inextricable network of foliage could be heard strange crackings and glidings that were most certainly of evil omen.

But the perpetual spring of gaiety in Eusèbe's heart soon rose again to the surface. He exclaimed, quaintly enough :—

" It's a foot-bath of black mustard, that's all ! "

Experience had made him prudent.   He tied his bundle carefully on his shoulders, fastened the gun to his strap, and held in his hand only the fishing-rod which was to serve both as a support and a sounding-line ; then he rose up in his boat, ready to undertake the work of wading to the shore.

Before venturing forth, he plunged his stick into the mud.   By good luck it was not more than six inches deep, and the depth seemed to be nowhere greater, although he sounded it at several points.   There was solid ground beneath the mud : so far, so good.   One last thought occurred to him : a thought of pity for the poor boot that remained upon his foot, and for his baggy trousers.   He carefully removed the boot and stuffed it into his pocket with his socks, then he tucked up his trousers to the knee.

Thus prepared, and exclaiming, " The entertainment is now about to begin ! " he plunged resolutely into the mud.   How cold, how sickening, how repulsive it was ! But one must take things as they come !   He floundered on heroically ; he stretched his little legs in gigantic strides, and reached the bank without a pause in four steps.   There he slid forward between two long black points of mud ; and—oh, joy !—found himself on a piece of meadow-land covered with green grass, and which had hitherto been hidden from him by a veil of leaves and branches.

He was on a sort of island formed by the river and fertilised by successive inundations.

Upon the sudden invasion of a human being, whole flocks of birds of the most brilliant colours rose up and fluttered overhead. Eusèbe stood still in mute delight. But presently his eyes sought his feet, and he exclaimed,

"This comes of being in America! What negro feet I have got!"

For certainly his feet might well have rivalled well-brushed boots in blackness.

We must do him the justice to say that, accustomed as he was to the most exquisite neatness, and generally passing two hours a day at his toilet, Eusèbe felt a thrill of disgust, and his first thought was that of repairing this disaster at any cost.

A return to the river was not to be dreamed of: one might as well have plunged into a mud-bath ; he therefore walked straight ahead, and in a few minutes observed with pleasure that his instinct had not deceived him.

The river below the rapids was divided by the island into two streams, of which one speedily regained its level and was soon lost to view, while the other fell over a height of some thirty feet into a narrow channel, and was thus conducted to the main stream, which it there peaceably rejoined.

At the foot of this cascade were some flat stones, supporting some fallen trees, which formed a sort of natural bridge, and which rendered the smooth shallow pond below fairly easy of access.

This was the very place—he could not have dreamed

of a better.   It was a bathing-room, already fitted up for him !

So thought Eusèbe at once.   It was to this place that he would direct his steps.   But he prudently saw that before adventuring himself upon the trunks of the trees it would be better to take all precautions for his safety : so he laid down his burden.   Then, thinking that the fishing-rod might serve him for a balancing-pole, he drew out its various pieces and put them together.

All this was not ill imagined, and showed that necessity was, indeed, the mother of invention !

He descended by a rocky path to the foot of the cascade, whose waters almost deafened him by their roar, and there he discovered that he could speedily attain a smooth pool where he might perform all necessary ablutions.

The passage across the stream was not a very easy one.   But Eusèbe had seen far more difficult ones traversed at the circus.   He set boldly out upon his way, venturing on the strongest trunks.

But scarcely had he achieved more than a third part of his perilous transit than he felt himself glued to the place by an emotion half of amazement and half of fantastic terror.

You are perhaps acquainted with a story by Edgar Allan Poe called William Wilson.   It is the history of a person who is constantly encountering through life his double, his second self.

Now—hard as it is to believe—below him, in the calm expanse of water that was flowing gently towards the main stream, Eusèbe caught sight of an individual precisely similar to himself, or, at any rate, seemingly so at that distance.

He wore a little hat and coat, and, stranger still, had a fishing-rod in his hand! And this man, with his trousers tucked up, was crossing the stream in an opposite direction from the one which Eusèbe had meant to follow.

Eusèbe stood so still that he might well have served as a model for a statue of Surprise.

Who was this man? A friend or an enemy? Some Captain Cotraw, or, by chance, an ally? And how could he find out? If Eusèbe crossed the river, he ran the risk of losing sight of the stranger. All things considered, it was better to venture something and discover the truth as quickly as possible.

So Eusèbe, still on his pedestal of trees and stone, made a speaking-trumpet of his hands, and shouted,

"Ohé!"

The wind blew with such strength in Eusèbe's face that his voice did not seem at first to be heard. He repeated his call with all the force of his lungs.

"Ohé! Monsieur! Gentleman! ohé!"

The man had crossed the ford, and was now at the foot of the rock where Eusèbe was standing.

When there, he jumped upon a stone, and maintaining his balance with remarkable ease, turned quickly to Eusèbe, who, determined to enter into some sort of conversation with him, now began a most expressive system of telegraphic pantomime.

The man put down his line, as well as a sort of box

that he was carrying. He then deliberately took a revolver from his belt, and screwing up one eye—for he had only one—seemed to be attentively and distrustfully considering Eusèbe and his continued appeals.

"What the deuce!" he muttered. "Must I get rid of him?"

Certainly if these words had reached Eusèbe's ears, and he had comprehended them, he might have regretted his interview with the crocodiles. But seeing only that the man had stopped, and not discovering in him any hostile intentions, he noticed at some little distance a rock over which he could easily descend to the stranger, and to this point he resolutely began to advance.

The other waited, revolver in hand, shouting to him, but in English,

"Stop where you are, or I fire!"

He might have talked for an hour in the same strain without producing much effect. But Eusèbe was already very few paces off, and was propping himself up against a stone with the appearance of being much out of breath.

"Well, Monsieur," he said; "suppose you give me a reference."

At this voice, and at these words, spoken in the purest French, the unknown lowered his pistol and replied in the same language, though with an American accent,

"What do you want? Who are you?"

"He speaks French!" exclaimed Eusèbe, with a burst of joy. "Monsieur, I am a charming young man, who has found himself by chance a good way from home, and very much wants somebody to show him the way . . ."

" Advance."

" Here I am."

" Where do you come from ? "

" I don't know."

" Where are you going ? "

" I don't know." .

" Are you joking with me ? "

" Not in the least, honourable sir. I profess that I speak nothing but the truth. I come from Paris, but I have strayed rather out of my way; and as for knowing where I am going to, the deuce take me if I have the faintest idea."

The other darted a piercing glance at him from his one eye.

" You are a Frenchman ? " he asked, somewhat roughly.

" A Frenchman and a wit; yes, Monsieur."

" Then, what are you doing in Florida ? "

" Oh, that's a long story—which I will tell you if you like. Nevertheless, before beginning so long and so interesting a narration, can you not say whether you will consent to be my guide ? "

" Perhaps. What's your name ? "

" Oh! you are a policeman. Eusèbe Lodier."

" Lodier ! " murmured the man thoughtfully. " It seems to me that I have heard that name before—somewhere or other . . ."

He continued, aloud,

" Do you know any one here ? "

" Here ! In these wild deserts ! Heaven preserve me ! "

" But in America—no matter where : for you ask me to guide you—whither ? Can I possibly guess ? "

" There, my good fellow ; don't be angry. I am going to explain all that. Is it far from here to New Orleans ? "

" You are mad ! "

" I don't think so. I will give you my name and address. I must as soon as possible get to Battle Field, M. Valville's plantation. Do you know it ? "

" Battle Field ! Valville ! " exclaimed the man, starting forward in his surprise. " Yes, indeed. And your name—Lodier ? You have a sister ? "

" So I flatter myself."

" Who is called . . ."

" Alice ! Just so ; but you are not very polite."

" And you know M. Charles Valville ? "

" I dined with him not a month ago : also, with a good sort of Yankee, Doctor Freedy."

The man made one step towards him, placed his two hands on his shoulders, and looked at him with the attention of a police officer who wants to verify a description.

" This is possible," he said ; " but it is not certain. You have a Frenchman's head ; but other proofs are none the less necessary . . ."

" Eh, parbleu ! " cried Eusèbe, quite out of patience ; " there's my card."

And he presented a bit of pasteboard, which the other immediately perused.

" Under these circumstances, M. Eusèbe Lodier," he said with a slight bow, " I put myself at your disposal."

" And you will take me to New Orleans ? "

" At any rate I will take you to M. Valville."

" Soon ? "

" Before this evening."

" You are a charming man ! Would you kindly tell me, in your turn, whom I shall have the pleasure of thanking,—in other words, what is your name ? "

" As to that, sir," replied the other, " you would be no wiser if you did know it. Come, we have no time to lose : are you ready to follow me ? "

" I have left my luggage and my gun up there : I only want to fetch them."

" Do so : I will wait for you here ; but make haste."

Eusèbe was delighted. The conversation had ended better than it had begun.

The reader will have already recognised Ned Bark, the detective.

There was nothing astonishing in the fact that he should be found in Florida, on the banks of the St. John's River, if we remember the council of war held by Ned Bark, Freedy, Valville, and Woodman, at the latter's plantation.

But how did it happen that he had arrived at the very place where he met Eusèbe ?

Let us at first remark that the detective was absolutely unrecognisable. A fringe of beard and whiskers hid the lower part of his face, and his hat was drawn so far over his forehead as to render his infirmity of sight quite invisible at some little distance. Then the line in his hand gave him the appearance of a peaceful fisherman waging war with simple fishes, and not with the assassins of Battle Field. He was well versed in the art of costume, for in the rather fat, broad-shouldered man, one would not soon have recognised the peculiarly thin and agile detective.

As regards what he had been doing, we shall soon hear his own account.

Eusèbe did not lose a moment. He dipped his feet hurriedly into the foaming waters of the cascade: a summary way of making his toilet, with which he had to content himself. Then, in honour of his guide, he put on his socks and his one boot, for, as we well know, he had left the other as food for the crocodile family.

With the captain's bundle on his back, and the gun in his hand, he descended the rocky footpath, and stood again at Ned Bark's side.

During the short time that his absence had lasted, a complete transformation had taken place in the detective's appearance. He had removed the clothes which had given him a heavy look, and hidden them in the box beneath his arm; he had put away his fishing-rod, had fastened round his waist a belt containing two revolvers and a bowie-knife, and, in short, had metamorphosed the calm fisherman into a very warlike and active-looking individual.

"Don't be surprised," said Ned, seeing that Eusèbe was regarding him in utter amazement. "In order to reach this place without being recognised, I was obliged to take precautions which now are useless. I will be myself again."

And, to complete the change, Ned took off the beard which covered his chin, and put it in his pocket.

"Who can this fellow be?" thought Eusèbe, quite bewildered.

"Now," said Ned, "listen carefully to me. I have not the time at present to hear about your adventures, and I cannot take you away with me. You will be good enough to hide in a place which I will point out to you; and to remain there perfectly quiet for an hour or two. You will be so kind as to wait for me till I return for you; after which I will do what you have asked."

"Hum!" said Eusèbe with a grimace. "This is not very clear."

"Clear or not, don't trouble about that, unless you wish to resume your solitary walk across Florida."

"Not at all."

"Then you will obey?"

"I suppose I must."

"Come, then, and, above everything, bend down beneath the high grass. If your head rises above it, you run great risk of receiving a ball there."

"What an odd country!" said Eusèbe, beginning to feel quite accustomed to the singularity of his position.

They walked on through the tangled shrubs.

Eusèbe, with one boot off and one boot on, was not

very comfortable; but he kept up his spirits in spite of discomfort.

Ned said no more. They walked on in this manner for nearly an hour. They left the cascade behind them, and followed the course of the St. John's River.

At last Ned stopped short.

"You see that palm-tree?" he said. "You must climb it and hide yourself in the branches as quickly as possible."

"It is rather high."

"You are young, you ought to be agile. And you must do it. Let me see, you should be able to give me a signal. Have you, by chance, as a Parisian, any special cry, anything extraordinary by which I could recognise you anywhere?"

Eusèbe thought for a moment.

"I've got it."

And he uttered the strident cry of Parisian students and workmen:

"Pi—ouitt!"

"Bravo!" said Ned. "Well, listen. From up there you must watch the river. In an hour, or two hours at the most, you will see a flat boat loaded with wood, which will stop just opposite this place."

"Well?"

"Then you must give that cry as loudly as you can."

"Agreed."

"You will get down the tree and run to the bank."

"I will."

"There you must wait for me."

"And the boat?"

"Ask nothing more about it.   Come, climb! you have made me lose time."

"At your orders, my lord."

And he began to climb gaily enough.

"It will be quite comfortable up there," he said.

"Don't forget any of my directions.   I shall see you again presently."   And Ned Bark disappeared.

But this (presently) was long in coming.   The sun had begun to sink below the horizon before Eusèbe, whose patience had never failed him for a single moment, beheld from his perch the approach and arrival of a boat, easily to be recognised as the one of which he had been told.

"Pi—ouitt!" he shouted at the top of his voice.

Then he slipped down the tree, and made for the bank.

He had not long to wait, for he saw Ned Bark running towards him as swiftly as his limbs would carry him.

"Throw yourself into the water," he cried to Eusèbe, "or you are a lost man."

"But I cannot swim."

"Then trust to me."

Ned pushed him at once into the water and jumped in with him, holding him by the collar.   He struck out with all his might towards the boat.

But at the same moment several Redskins appeared upon the bank, armed with knives and hatchets.

And one of them threw himself into the river in pursuit of the fugitives.

CHAPTER IX.

THE PURSUIT.

NED BARK was strong; and in spite of his burden, he reached the boat with a few vigorous strokes.

Two black forms stood erect on the deck, and strong hands seized them both. In a couple of minutes the two men were safe.

"Fire! fire anywhere!" commanded Ned Bark.

Two reports were heard. Ned remained leaning over the side of the boat, trying to see through the shadows which darkened the face of the river. It seemed as if the man who had thrown himself into the water after them, had grown weary of his pursuit and retraced his path. No sound reached the ear; no movement troubled the calm waters.

"What has happened?" asked a young clear voice.

"Mr. Valville," replied Ned, "I found the track; though I fear we have only exposed ourselves to new dangers; but first of all, let us get away from here, for the Seminoles have got wind of us, and although they do not know who we are, it is evident that with their savage instinct they guess that we are their enemies. So to the oars, and let us reach St. Augustine as quickly as possible."

Valville and Freedy, for these were the two men to whom Ned Bark addressed himself, had become quite accustomed to render implicit obedience to the detective. They plunged into the water the long oars with which they were provided, and the boat—more lightly than one would have thought possible from its apparently heavy build, and the load that it seemed to carry—sped away into the night.

Meanwhile, Eusèbe, totally forgotten by everybody, remained at the bottom of the boat, drenched, dazed, and motionless. What had passed was so quickly over, that he had not had time to recover himself. Besides, he had a horror of cold water; and even at Paris preferred the lukewarmness of the Turkish baths to the swift current of the Seine.

But when he had sneezed some twenty times, Ned Bark, who was still attentively scanning the black depths before him, suddenly remembered the stranger whom he had hoisted on board like a parcel, and turned to him.

"A thousand pardons, sir," said he, "we will attend to you immediately."

"Ah! that's you," sighed Eusèbe. "Sapristi, how cold I am! Where am I?"

"With friends; at least if you told me the truth."

"I am true as steel, but I am frozen. I feel as if I had had a good beating with a stick."

"A little patience; keep still, you will be warm enough presently."

"To whom are you speaking?" asked Valville, addressing himself to Ned in English. Then he added quickly: "True, I had hardly noticed it: you were not alone just now."

"Silence, if you please," said Ned authoritatively; "we are in the enemy's country."

Eusèbe, who would certainly have recognised Valville's voice, if Valville had only spoken French, curled himself up in his corner, and said nothing; finally grew drowsy, and fell fast asleep.

The boat went on and on. Several times Ned Bark started and bent down to the water, almost near enough to touch it, as if he imagined that some adversary could rise up against them from its depths.

All at once, he cried: "Ship your oars! stop!"

At the same time a shot rang through the air.

Valville and Freedy sprang to the side of Ned Bark, who had fired.

"What is it?" they cried at the same moment.

"How should I know?" snarled Ned with an oath.

"Why did you fire?"

"Well, really," said the detective, "I do not know whether I am foolishly anxious in my old age, but ever since we set off it has seemed to me that we were followed."

"Followed! impossible! we have gone ten or twelve miles: a man could not perform such a feat of swimming as that!"

"A man? no! but a Seminole could! I will give you an example of the energy and obstinacy of these last remaining Indians. During their recent struggle with the troops of the Union, about thirty of them were hemmed in on the borders of the river Oclawaha. We thought we had got them: not at all! They threw themselves into the water, and for thirty hours—do you hear? for thirty hours!—they had to be chased. They dived, lay at the bottom of the water, reappeared, disappeared: the balls whistled round their heads without touching them, so supernaturally quick were their movements! At last, in order to terminate the contest, their lives were promised them, and they approached the banks. But as soon as they touched the earth, they sank down: some, never to rise again. They had had sufficient physical energy to resist up to the very last moment; and they died only when they were not obliged to defend themselves."

"Do you know," said Freedy, "that they are worthy of our admiration?"

"Hum!" returned Ned Bark, with a shrug of his shoulders; "say that they were very energetic, and I will agree with you. Nowadays they are merely brigands who find in assassination and treachery the satisfaction of a vengeance which is forbidden to them in loyal combat."

"So be it; but what makes you think that we are pursued?"

"Nothing, and everything. You must first know, that as I crept through the grass I found, down there on Long Island, as that barricade of the St. John is called, an encampment of Seminoles. I approached them on hands and knees, and watched them attentively. Bloody Foot was not with them. But they belonged to his tribe. You know to what a degree the senses of these men are sharpened, and how difficult it is to deceive their hearing or their sight. Happily I knew by what means to put them off the scent. I managed to approach them so closely, as to catch some of the words that they were interchanging."

" Then you know their language ?" said Valville, with some surprise.

" Oh, my education is complete," said Ned, laughing. " Cherokees, Creeks, and Seminoles have nothing more to teach me. But at first I heard nothing that was likely to be of any use to us, until suddenly a man appeared upon the stream, skilfully directing the course of his canoe until it reached the bank.

" The Seminoles rose, and then, with outstretched arms, fell on the ground before him. This time it was he—their chief, the Bloody Foot !"

" My father's murderer !" exclaimed the young man. " The wretch who dared to attack my dear sister ! Ah ! why was I not there ? How gladly I would have lodged a bullet in his head !"

" And you would have managed very badly, allow me to say," said Ned, with a coolness that nothing overthrew. " I covered Bloody Foot with my gun ; but, I thought, if he dies, we shall lose all trace of him, and it is by means of his movements that we may probably discover the whereabouts of Red Ralph and the other robbers."

" That is true !" murmured Valville.

" And by not killing him, I managed so well,"

pursued the detective, "that I should know now how to find my way again to these wretches."

"Ah! speak! tell me how! quickly."

"No, not yet: above all, not here. You think that on a river, at dead of night, we are in safety? No, for at the moment when a signal told me that you had reached the point of meeting which I had assigned to you, I was perceived by the Seminoles, who rushed in pursuit of me. You saw I had only time to throw myself into the water before one of those demons threw himself in behind me. Well! I tell you, that this man is following us, there, in the dark water; I tell you that while we are waiting, he is crouching there, somewhere, watching us with burning eyes that can see through the darkness . . ."

"He! help! help! the monster!" suddenly shrieked a voice.

And Eusèbe stood up in the middle of the boat.

"What? what's the matter?" asked Ned.

Eusèbe, his teeth chattering, spoke with extended hand.

"Here, under the bank, I saw a shadow, a head!"

"Ah! you saw right!" exclaimed Ned, springing forward.

"But who spoke?" said Valville, who could not believe his ears.

This time he was speaking French.

"Charles!" exclaimed Eusèbe. "Is it you?"

"Eusèbe! Eusèbe—here?"

"Yes, Eusèbe himself."

At this moment Ned Bark returned.

"Enough exclamations of that sort!" he said in his tone of command. "I knew quite well that I was not mistaken. Let us go no farther, but land at once. The man pursuing us will perhaps not risk his life on solid ground. Do this, and at once."

By the vigorous efforts of the two men, the boat was soon moored close to the river bank.

CHAPTER X.

INDIANS AND SNAKES.

SINCE the moment when Ned Bark gave the order to land, not a word had been interchanged between the different members of the party.

It was felt that they must endeavour to escape from this unknown but imminent danger as quickly as possible. Valville and Freedy, bending over their boat-hooks, directed the course of the boat along the coast, in search of a suitable landing-place.

In that place the eastern bank of the St. John's River was bordered by a sort of cliff, as if the water had worn for itself a channel through the fissure of some rocky mountain.

Its bed was also encumbered with water-plants, which wound themselves round the prow of the boat and rendered its progress very slow.

At last Ned Bark gave the word: "Stop."

The boat ran into a bed of mud and remained motionless.

With a vigorous bound Freedy gained the bank, where he unwound and knotted securely to a palm-tree the rope which Valville threw him.

For the last time Ned Bark walked round the boat

and carefully examined the neighbourhood with his piercing eye.

No noise. Had the Seminole really relinquished his pursuit? Had fatigue compelled him to land on the opposite bank?

Meanwhile Eusèbe, wet and exhausted, lay quietly at the bottom of the boat.

"Come! take courage!" said Ned Bark, giving him an energetic shake; "we have arrived."

But the lad seemed scarcely to hear him. His brain was in a whirl. The voice of Valville had certainly struck his ear; and yet it seemed to him as though he were living only in a dream.

"Johnson!" cried Ned; "lift up that fellow."

From the other end of the boat a tall form rose and advanced to Eusèbe, over whom it bent.

It seemed to be a form of colossal size. Eusèbe, whose eyes were dim, and who, in the early dawn of day, had a very vague perception of what was passing around him, believed that some enormous ghost was about to attack him.

"Here I am!" he murmured. "Come on!"

But the ghost opened its arms and seized him with remarkable vigour, and Eusèbe found himself perched upon vast shoulders in company with an immense bundle, which the ghost in question carried with extraordinary ease.

This form—gigantic, but not at all supernatural—was simply that of a Kentuckian named Johnson, whom the travellers had hired at Jacksonville to carry their luggage.

He had philosophically hoisted Eusèbe on his shoulders as one burden the more; a burden which he deposited on the bank with so little precaution that Eusèbe, recalled to a sense of the situation by the rude shock, exclaimed,

"Sapredié! this fellow's going to demolish me altogether!"

Valville had hastened to his side.

"Eusèbe! you here? This is perfectly miraculous!"

"Oh, miracles have gone out of fashion," said Eusèbe, shivering. "You simply see before you a charming young man who nearly died of ennui when he was left all alone in Paris, and who therefore thought of making a little tour with his walking-stick, but who is rapidly freezing on the way."

"My dear Eusèbe, you are really frozen!"

"Like iced coffee! Ah! a nice country, this is! crocodiles, and monkeys with feathers on their heads! Just give me Captain Queue-de-Rat's coat—it ought to be somewhere about. . . ."

The Kentuckian, always composed, had already returned to the boat, and now brought back Eusèbe's parcèl, as well as the gun and the fishing-rod. Eusèbe wrapped himself up in the coat.

"Don't let us lose a minute," said Ned Bark. "We must now get back to the St. Augustine road."

"Do you know the way?" asked Freedy.

"Certainly. We must mount this hill, and on the other side we shall reach the plain. We shall have to cross swamps and marshes, but we must go as fast as we can."

"Let us be off then."

To tell the truth, it was not a hill but a sort of rock that they had to ascend. There was no certain path; but it could be climbed by a sort of rough projection on the edge of a precipice.

It was a difficult ascent: so difficult, that at the end of a few minutes Eusèbe was warm enough—even too warm. They had to stop while he arranged his bundle on his shoulders again, and then, with somewhat feverish activity, and with the help of his famous fishing-rod, he marched on bravely, keeping to the front, and turning round from time to time to call to the others. In a few words he recounted his adventures to Valville; he had already recovered his Parisian gaiety and glibness of tongue; and with his usual admixture of street-slang, informed his friends that his journey had been a great success.

But Ned Bark kept apart, and advancing now and then to the extreme edge of the rock, he leaned over it, endeavouring to fathom with his eye the abyss beside which they walked.

He would not share his anxiety with his companions, but he had nevertheless very grave reasons for it.

The rock was covered with trees, which the wind, blowing from the sea, had bent and twisted into strange fantastic shapes.

This wood had formerly been turned to use by trappers. Down the ravine, which cut the rock in two as if it had been divided by the stroke of an axe, leaped a foaming torrent. Formerly, woodcutters wishing to convey the felled wood to the St. John's River, whence it would be floated down to its destination, had constructed in the ravine a way of descent, composed of the trunks of trees tied together and fastened to transverse bars, like those so much used in Alsace, which served to keep the rest in their place to the bottom of the cliff. These steps were now nearly destroyed; but in the dark shadow of the torrent, through which faintly gleamed the luminous whiteness of the falling water, Ned Bark could still distinguish the remains of this primitive ladder.

Several times it had appeared to him that he could also see a dark shadow crouching on the rungs of the ladder; but in vain he concentrated all his attention upon it. He was constrained to believe himself the victim of some delusion.

Moreover, what human being would be so bold as to follow that perilous course in almost complete darkness, where the slightest imprudence or the merest accident would infallibly lead to instant death?

"Here is the plain!" exclaimed Valville, as he arrived at the summit of the cliff.

At their feet there stretched away a vast extent of wood and swamp, beneath the clear light of rising day.

Once again Ned Bark examined with his eye the spot which had so long enchained his attention. Nothing. Evidently he had been mistaken.

They began the descent to the plain before them.

They entered the pathless cypress-groves. There is nothing more unpleasant than walking through a network of branches and creepers, amidst which can be heard strange noises and curious gliding sounds. With watchful ears, and fingers on the triggers of their guns, our friends hastened forward; but notwithstanding the desire to uphold his own dignity, Eusèbe was hardly able to walk any longer. Freedy had given him his arm, and encouraged him to proceed.

Pale, but laughing still, Eusèbe was murmuring,

"Ah, if a cab would only pass this way!"

But as one could hardly expect to get a cab, there was nothing for it but to walk and walk!

Ned Bark, continually haunted by one idea, darted aside into the deepest thickets several times. As they went on, it seemed to him that he heard behind him an occasional rustle of leaves, as if they were followed by some living being, not far off. He stopped; but all was still.

"I know," he said at last, "that at a short distance from the road we shall find the ruins of an old deserted fort. We can rest there for a few minutes, and decide upon our future plans."

These words restored a little strength to Eusèbe's failing limbs. What would he not have given at that moment to be able to lie down, no matter where or how!

Presently they came in sight of the much-needed resting-place. Amidst an inextricable thicket, a few heaps of crumbling stone marked the place where once had stood one of those forts built by the early occupants of the country, which nature was now reconquering by means of a luxuriant overgrowth of vegetation.

Within these mouldering walls there still remained

one room, the floor of which had long since been destroyed, but over which the trappers had made a sort of roof composed of interwoven branches.

"Oh, what a pretty dressing-room!" exclaimed Eusèbe.

Then with a sigh he sank down upon the ground, muttering,

"Oh, upon my word I can't keep it up any longer—I can't walk a step farther."

"You must sleep, comrade," said Ned Bark. "A few hours' rest will set you on your legs again."

"I hope so! but this seems a very hard sort of place to lie in."

"We will manage that. Johnson, undo those bundles."

"And then there's another thing!" said Eusèbe.

"Speak out."

"My feet are in such a state. Just look!"

"Ah! poor fellow!" cried Freedy, as he saw the bleeding feet, which, ever since the adventure with the crocodile, had possessed but one boot between them.

And such a boot, too! for the thin kid had not long been able to resist the roughness of the way. It was torn to pieces and hung in strips, which revealed the reddened sock between.

"Fortunately," said Freedy, "I have my little medicine-chest with me."

So saying, he helped Johnson to unfasten the straps that secured their luggage, and took out a box which he opened, and which proved to be full of phials of different sizes. In a few moments he had covered the young man's aching feet with bandages.

But Eusèbe's attention was suddenly fixed upon a certain object disinterred from the aforesaid luggage.

This object was a magnificent pair of boots.

"Oh, what nice boots!" said Eusèbe in the tone of a child who wants a piece of cake. "Do give them to me!"

"Most willingly," said Valville laughing. "You well deserve them!"

Eusèbe took possession of them with a delighted gesture. They were certainly splendid boots, and attracted him by a somewhat theatrical association. Dumaine, his favourite actor, had worn a pair precisely similar in the drama The Pirates of the Savannah. One may imagine their charm for him.

And while the others were spreading cloaks and rugs upon the ground in order to make him a softer bed, Eusèbe craftily slipped the boots into the place where his head would lie, against the wall : ostensibly for a bolster, but really that he might not be separated from his treasures.

Nature will not cede her claims ; and Eusèbe was not yet twenty. At the end of a few minutes he was sleeping—shall we say that he was also snoring?—the sleep of innocence !

The Kentuckian had also stretched himself in a corner, and was fast asleep.

The three friends were practically alone.

"Now," said Valville in a low voice, "it remains for

you, my dear Ned Bark, to tell us the story of what happened to you, and the information which you obtained."

"Unfortunately I cannot give you any important news," said the detective. "As I told you, when I crept on all fours to the Indian encampment, I found out that we had to do with Seminoles; that is, with the last remaining survivors of a wandering tribe of bandits, the mercenaries of crime, ready to sell themselves to any one who can· pay them. But when I saw Bloody Foot, I did hope that I should catch some words which would put me upon Red Ralph's track."

"Well?"

"The Indians are hard to deceive; and even when they suspect no spies, they take great precautions. They spoke in such low voices that none of their words reached my ears; but the pantomime of the chief—and in all these primitive races you know how eloquent gesture is—assured me that he was speaking of money to be received and booty to be divided. No doubt they were thinking of the reward which Red Ralph must have promised them; and perhaps also, according to the habit of these adventurers, he has made them wait an unreasonable length of time for it. Bloody Foot's attitude was a threatening one. The others approved, and received his statements with growls of anger. Finally, Bloody Foot—in this I am sure I was not mistaken— appointed a place of meeting. Pointing to the east, he gave them long and minute directions. But it was at this moment that, by that diabolical instinct which seems almost supernatural, one of these demons appeared suddenly to suspect the presence of an unseen auditor, and that they all rushed in pursuit of me. You know the rest. I escaped by a miracle; but I have to pay them out yet, and I shall not fail to do it."

"I count on you to keep your word," said Freedy. "But in the present state of things, it seems to me that we are just working at haphazard!"

"Not altogether. The presence of the Seminoles in this part of the country, where they seldom venture, must be connected with a set of facts which will not, I am sure, have escaped general attention. We will go on to St. Augustine, and there set minute inquiries on foot. Red Ralph is known everywhere. If he has been here lately, we shall soon hear—and . . ."

Ned Bark did not finish his sentence.

Suddenly he started from his seat, reached the door with one bound, and rushed out of the fortress.

Valville and Freedy rose also, full of anxiety, and, guessing that some new incident was about to occur, or that perhaps some new peril was near, they took their guns and followed in Ned Bark's footsteps.

But when they had passed through the door they perceived nothing.

We have said that the ruins of the old fort were literally hidden by the vegetation that covered them.

Where was the detective? Freedy listened, with head eagerly advanced.

Suddenly they saw that the branches at some little

distance were agitated by vigorous movements which might proceed from a struggle between men or animals.

And yet no noise, no cry had reached their ears.

" Forward !" said Freedy.

And the two friends ran in that direction.

In a few seconds they gained the spot, and there they beheld Ned Bark, standing calmly beneath the trees, with a smile upon his face, although his forehead was bleeding from a wound.

With his hand he pointed to a shapeless heap upon the ground.

" This time," he said, " I have made a trick."

They then discovered that it was an Indian who lay before them in the grass, with hands and feet tied.

" Is he dead ?" asked Valville.

" Surely not !" replied Ned. " I have too great an interest in keeping him alive."

" Do at least explain . . ."

" Nothing simpler. I told you that one of those devils was on our track from the moment I gained the boat. Eusèbe, too, saw the wretch ; so doubt was impossible. But, as I told you, I did not think that he would be so bold as to continue his man-hunt on land. I was mistaken. And while we were climbing the hill and crossing the cypress-grove, certain curious signs gave me much reason for anxiety. Now I know. This man, obeying his chief, climbed the rock by means of those wooden ledges, to which the most agile monkey might have hesitated to trust his weight. He followed us on all fours through the grass, so skilfully, that in spite of my suspicions, it was impossible for me to surprise him.   But here he was imprudent."

"Go on."

"While we were talking just now in the ruins, I kept my eyes fixed on the roof of branches.   I had noticed a sort of movement, and—in fact, by and by, the Indian, not being able to hear very distinctly what we were saying, ventured to separate the branches a little.   It was then that I saw him, and sprang up.   He thought he could again escape me.   But this time I wanted my revenge, and swore that I would not be beaten.   I dashed after him and reached his side.   He aimed a blow at me with his tomahawk, which fortunately glanced aside, and only grazed the skin.   But I threw myself upon him, brought him to the earth, and, you see," he added, pointing to the Seminole's bonds, "I have put it out of his power, I think, to go and give an account of his mission."

"But what do you mean to do with this man?"

"A very simple thing.   We are going to take this robber with us to St. Augustine, and there place him in the hands of the authorities.   And I promise you he will speak, and sell his accomplices."

"Do you think so?" said Freedy, shaking his head doubtfully.

"Don't be afraid.   They will not use torture.   It will be quite sufficient to shut the man up in Fort Marion. For these children of the forests the worst torture is that of the loss of liberty."

"But look!" exclaimed Valviile, "the man is dying!"

Ned uttered a cry, and bent over the Seminole.

What Valville said was only too true. The Indian's face was frightfully convulsed, and a greenish bloody foam was standing on his lips.

"He is dead!" exclaimed Freedy in his turn. "It is so really. Under our very eyes the wretched man has poisoned himself. Ah, Ned Bark, you thought that he would sell his accomplices! you see he chose rather to kill himself."

"But it is impossible!" cried Ned Bark. "He has made no movement; his hands have not even stirred."

"Look here," said Freedy, stooping down.

The Indian's head was resting on the trunk of a cypress-tree, half buried in the dank waters of the marsh.

The wood was almost entirely concealed by a parti-coloured growth of lichens, amidst which toad-stools of all shapes, heights, and colours, could be seen.

"He has poisoned himself, I tell you, with wonderful strength of will. It was quite sufficient for him to turn his head and bite this toad-stool, of which, you see, he has severed a portion with his teeth."

It was a white toad-stool of great beauty, supported upon a stalk of azure blue.

"A deadly poison," added Freedy. "He chose well."

There was a moment's silence. Although Valville had his own reasons for hating and despising this savage race, yet the calm fortitude of the Indian's death struck a thrill of admiration to his heart.

And this was the second corpse which had already marked the course of his avenging way.

"What men!" he murmured. "Why must their energy always be lost to civilisation?"

Then, turning to Ned Bark, he asked—

"Must we leave this wretched man without burial?"

"I'll take care of that," said the detective. "After all, he was a brave man, and I respect courage even in my enemies. But," he added, addressing himself to Freedy, "return to the ruins; it is not prudent to separate ourselves one from another. Go, and in a few moments I will rejoin you."

"Come," said Freedy, leading away Valville, whose emotion had communicated itself to his friend.

"Don't be long, Ned," said Valville to the detective.

"I will be with you in five minutes."

Without a word to each other, the two men returned to the little fort.

As they opened the door, Eusèbe, still half asleep, said suddenly,

"Ah! what is this horrible odour? Sapristi! one ought to have some eau-de-Cologne here."

And in fact a strange, penetrating, sickening smell filled the whole place.

"What can it be?" whispered Valville to Freedy.

The American started, but so slightly that no one noticed his emotion. With a slow gesture, he stooped and picked up Eusèbe's stick, then made one step towards him.

"Listen," he said, "and on your life do not say a word, or make a single movement, how small soever. Understand that the slightest movement is immediate, horrible death. You have courage : prove it now. I will tell you what is happening. Somewhere, amongst your wraps, or under your head, is a snake, the copper-headed snake, whose bite is deadly. If you do not move I will answer for your safety ; if you do, it will be your death."

There was a fearful silence.

Slowly, so slowly, that one could scarcely see him move, Freedy bent down. With his stick he gently rustled and scratched the cloak upon which Eusèbe's head was lying. The young man, with true courage, obeyed orders, and compelled himself not even to shudder.

At last something greenish, something that looked like a bit of bronzed metal, issued from one of the boots which Eusèbe had so carefully wrapped together for a bolster.

It was the head of the snake.

Freedy was close to it, and no sooner had the neck appeared, than, with a single blow, he nailed it down to the ground and crushed it.

The terrible creature was killed. From its crooked fangs oozed out a yellow liquid with an unbearably horrible smell.

"M. Eusèbe," said Freedy, offering him his hand, you may congratulate yourself on having, by your presence of mind, escaped the most terrible danger that a man can incur in this fortunate country."

"Thank you . . . thank you," stammered Eusèbe ; "but . . . it seems to me . . . that it was you . . . who killed . . . the snake. . . ."

" Just so ! but if you had moved in the slightest degree, it would have jumped out of its hiding-place, and one of us would certainly have been attacked."

Ned Bark entered at this moment, and seeing that every one looked pale, asked what had happened. For answer, Freedy pulled out of the boot the rest of the snake's body, which measured more than five feet in length.

" Heavens ! " cried Ned Bark, who was a brave man, nevertheless, jumping two steps back as he spoke, " what an ugly chance ! "

" Bah ! don't talk of it any longer," said Freedy. " Now tell us your plans."

" Oh, they are very simple. More than ever, we must go to St. Augustine."

" Have you anything new to tell us ? "

" Yes. First, I should say that I rendered the last honours of war to that rascal of a Seminole, whose courage touched me in spite of myself."

" Ah, that is right," said Valville. " You have committed his body to the earth ? "

" Whew ! " said Ned Bark, laughing. " It is easy to see that you don't know much of those gentlemen. If I had done that, he would have been ready to come to life again and scalp me."

" Which means. . . . ? "

" That an Indian would regard it as terribly shamefu to be buried like us white people. The corpse of an Indian is always placed in the branches of a tree, out of reach of wild beasts, but not of birds ; and it stays there until, as they say, it is restored to air."

"Then you have put your Indian up a tree?"

"Exactly so: but first I searched him."

"Ah! and what did you find?" asked Freedy. "I suppose he would not have a pocket-book with pencil notes about him?"

"No; but he had this," said Ned Bark, drawing from his pocket a thin layer of bark, on which certain marks seemed to have been irregularly traced by the point of an arrow.

Valville took the piece of bark in his hand, and examined it attentively.

"I cannot understand these hieroglyphics," he said.

"Then I will help you. You see this dotted line against which some horizontal marks are drawn—much like the lines by which the sea is indicated in maps?"

"Well?"

"Well, this is a map, too, and that is the sea. This other line parallel to the sea is the St. John's River. Now, here, this round place is St. Augustine. Then a pointed line follows the coast, and stops all at once. This stoppage is just opposite Pilatka. This is simply the map of a journey. And the Seminole in question was to go to this place, opposite Pilatka. What place it is, I do not know; but at St. Augustine it will not be difficult to obtain information. The man would not speak, but he could not but be aware that I knew the tricks of the Indian gentlemen as well as he did! It was this point—still unknown to us—that the Indian indicated by his gesture to the sea; and I swear to you, my good friends, that I will find it, and that there we will have good sport!"

"I hope so!" said Valville.

"On, then!" said Freedy. "Ned Bark has given us too many proofs of his clear-headedness, that we should lose confidence in him now."

"Oh, I do not doubt him!" cried Valville, giving his hand to the detective.

"Forward then! This is the time when the stage-coach passes. Let us be off to St. Augustine."

An hour later they were being drawn to that town by four fast-trotting horses.

About three-quarters of a mile from St. Augustine, the coach, or the omnibus, suddenly stopped before a wooden shed, from which several negroes hurriedly appeared. A moment later, the travellers, having left the coach, were seated in a tramway car—a real tramway car, exactly like those that in Paris pass between the Madeleine and Courbevoie; with a small platform before and behind, and a driver standing up, and flicking with his whip the two mules that he drove tandemwise. The rails were made of wood instead of iron. And the carriage rolled over them with a dull, almost an ominous sound.

If Valville had been less preoccupied, or Eusèbe less fatigued, each of them might have been struck with so curious a contrast; on the one side stood Nature in all her wildness, with her strange plants and savage animals; on the other, at only a few leagues' distance, a progressive civilisation which, little by little, was conquering the land.

As they approached the town, Eusèbe could not repress a cry of delight.

He had just perceived, on the banks of the Matanzas, which was crossed by a wooden bridge, one of those charming cities which have been built by northern tourists, almost surrounded by lovely woods. Civilisation and social life lay before him.

He was full of childish astonishment when, upon entering the suburbs, he saw an old negress seated beside a rickety table selling coffee; while a little negro-boy, who carried a basket of dates upon his head, regarded her with envious eyes.

"Hurrah for America!" Eusèbe exclaimed.

"Wait," said Ned Bark smiling. "You will have surprises still!"

Eusèbe thought of the crocodile and the snake, made a little grimace, and was silent.

CHAPTER XI.

NED BARK'S PREDICTION.

IT was about eight o'clock in the evening when our five friends made their entrance, behind two mules, in St. Augustine, the oldest town of the United States.

As they entered the city joyous bursts of military music filled the air. An artillery regiment was parading before the windows of the St. John's Hotel, and on the balconies stood a well-dressed crowd of sightseers.

As soon as they had reached the portico of the hotel, Freedy ordered a meal to be prepared for them in a private room. As for Eusèbe, he asked leave to go and lie down at once.

Valville himself was exhausted with fatigue, and Ned Bark, knowing that new exertions would soon be required of him, insisted that he also should go and rest.

Freedy and the detective remained by themselves. They had long been accustomed to similar expeditions, and they wanted to converse together for a time alone.

"Let us speak freely," said Freedy. "There is no one here now who needs encouragement, and whom we are afraid of depressing. So any beating about the bush would be absurd. Ned, what do you think of our situation?"

Ned was silent for a few moments, and then replied.

"You know better than anybody, doctor," he said, "that nothing can be done but by earthly means, and that sorcery and witchcraft are out of date. Well, we cannot hide from ourselves that our enemies have great advantages over us. They can watch us, and spy out all our movements; and nothing ought to surprise us less than an attack directed against us at the very moment when we least expect one."

"I have thought of that," said Freedy. "And I am astonished that we have reached this place without an obstacle."

"Oh, it is not in this part of the country, close to St. Augustine, that the robbers will dare to attack us. The civilising influence of the States is still felt here, and the Federal troops protect us. But we are not yet on the scene of action, and whichever direction we take south of Florida, we shall be left to ourselves, and shall be in the very midst of war, with its ambuscades and its treacheries. We may expect to be attacked by invisible enemies on every side."

"And yet we must do something!"

"Certainly. Don't suppose that I want to go back. But courage is not rashness, and if we can possibly bring about some equality of position between our own and the advantageous one occupied by our enemies, it will be by acting with the most extreme prudence."

"So be it; but do not forget that time is passing— that an unfortunate girl is in the hands of those wretches —and that every hour brings fresh peril to her!"

"I forget nothing : be sure of that. The death of that Indian who escaped us was a great misfortune ; but at any rate we have received a hint," and he pointed to the piece of bark, of which we have previously spoken, "which ought to serve us as a guide in the beginning of our search."

" It is very vague."

" Not so vague as you suppose."

At this point the waiter entered, and placed a small book before Ned Bark, who opened it at once.

It was a map of Florida. Ned spread it out upon the table, then, with his elbows on the paper, and his chin between his hands, he began most carefully to examine it.

Florida is a peninsula, long, but regular in shape, which measures from Tallahassee, the most northern point, to Cape Sable, about 300 miles.

Jacksonville and St. Augustine are the only places which have any right to the name of towns. Pilatka is only a large village, and New Smyrna, which is marked on the map as lying upon the eastern coast, consists merely of two houses.

The western coast is almost uninhabited.

It is only in the northern portion—about 'a fourth part of the whole territory—that civilisation has made any real progress.

Ned studied the map attentively. Freedy, standing behind him with his eyes also fixed upon the geographical symbols, tried in vain to divine the detective's thoughts. Suddenly the latter put his finger on the map, on a certain spot a little to the right of Volusia.

"It is there," he said, "it is evidently there that Red Ralph has arranged a meeting with his accomplices."

"There?" said Freedy bending over the map. "But I do not see why. From the island of Anastasia to New Smyrna the coast seems to be a mere desert."

"You are right. It seems to be so. But I know that on that part of the coast the Spaniards formerly built important forts, the ruins of which still exist, and which serve only too often as places of refuge for Indians and bandits. I remember that after the Seminole war, a band of Indians managed to escape from Ocala. We pursued them energetically, and as we drew near the sea, we never doubted but that they could not possibly escape from us. Their only resources were to throw themselves into the waves, where they would have perished, or to surrender. We surrounded them in a cypress-grove about a mile from the coast, and, as we were resolved to finish the business, we crossed the marshes, the bind weeds, the bogs. . . ."

"Well?"

"Well! Of these Indians, who numbered more than thirty, not one was ever found in the cypress-grove: it seemed as if they had sunk into the ground. And, in fact, so they had. After beating the wood in all senses, sounding the ground, risking our lives a hundred times amongst the poisonous creatures which crawl about the unhealthy pools and decayed roots, we ended by discovering a sort of hole lined with stone, of the same kind of which the walls of St. Augustine are built. It was the entrance to a subterranean cave. As we had no torches we could not search it. Besides, the officer in command dared not risk the lives of men in his charge in a place where they would have been entirely at the Indians' mercy. They escaped us."

"Why did you not explore the subterranean place afterwards?"

"It was done the week following. But the Indians had partly destroyed it, and it was with great difficulty that we penetrated even to five yards from the opening. We found out only that the cave extended as far as the ruins of an old Spanish fort, destroyed long ago by sea and tempest."

"And you think that we shall find Red Ralph there?"

"There, or in a similar place."

"But, by your own account, how are we to get to it?"

"We must decide how to-morrow. In the morning I will make inquiries. Either from the officers or the policemen I shall obtain—I am sure I shall—some information about the movements of the Indians and of Red Ralph, and I shall find a way of action."

"Just so," said Freedy. "You know, Ned, we have complete confidence in you. . . ."

"Even Mr. Valville?" asked the detective, smiling, for he had not forgotten the young man's early distrust of him.

"I assure you, Ned Bark," said the doctor gravely, "that he knows how to value your energy and your devotion. One word more before we separate. What do you think of that young man, Eusèbe, whom you found in so extraordinary a manner? He is a thoughtless fellow, not very strong, and I fear that he will be a burden to us rather than a help."

" Who knows ?" said Ned.

" Do you mean to attach him to our party ?"

" Why not?" said the detective. " The harebrained fellow has really shown some resolution in coming all the way from Europe, and the position in which I found him proved that he did not want for courage ; and then," said Ned, laughing, "is there not a proverb which says that 'Providence takes care of children and fools'? Chance will serve him better than it does us perhaps."

" I accept the omen," said Freedy.

And with these last words the two men parted.

But Ned Bark, in whom it appeared that Eusèbe had excited some interest, did not expect that his prediction was so soon to be fulfilled.

When Eusèbe awoke, after a heavy sleep of ten hours' length, he rubbed his eyes, tried to collect his thoughts, and naturally—according to the custom from time immemorial in all respectable dramas—asked himself the question : " Where am I ?"

The comfortable room made him smile to himself, and he stretched out his arms with a thrill of satisfaction. But suddenly he started. This slight movement had been immediately followed by a heavy thud, as if some hard body had fallen to the ground.

Eusèbe remained motionless. He had been dreaming of rattle-snakes, alligators, and other interesting but hungry creatures, and the first thought that now occurred to him was that a new specimen of the Floridan fauna was about to bid him welcome.

He would have liked to produce some small joke, but an overwhelming sensation of doubt and dread effectually closed his mouth. He had interviewed certain animals of Florida under auspices which did not render continued intercourse with them particularly desirable.

He held his breath and listened with starting eyes. Nothing. The wild beast—if wild beast it were—was so quiet that our hero began to regain courage, and at the end of a few minutes ventured to turn round and examine with his eyes the space enclosed by the four walls of his room.

The curtains were not quite closed. Eusèbe had been too anxious to get into bed the night before to take any precautions for his own safety; he had even forgotten to bolt his door.

Between the curtains, then, a ray of light glided in and rested on the floor. In this white faint gleam Eusèbe could see an object of an oblong shape and greenish-brown colour. A slight shiver ran down his spinal column. Certainly the thing was not very big, so perhaps the danger was not great. But Eusèbe loved not the unknown. He was soon disgusted. And whatever could that thing be?

Concentrating all his visual faculties upon the said object, Eusèbe remarked that it was clothed in a rough skin, something like shagreen : that it had no feet, and no head. He recurred to his profound acquaintance with natural history. If it should be a tortoise, were there any square tortoises? When he was at school he had kept one for six months in his desk, religiously feeding it on lettuces obtained from a greengrocer's shop. But this tortoise—which he had called Héloise—was oval, like all other tortoises.

It would have been much better if, instead of indulging in these somewhat lengthy reflections, he had jumped out of bed, and marched straight up to the enemy. Blame him if you like. At any rate he found out at last that a bell-rope was fastened to his bedstead, and he pulled it violently.

A negro entered the room.

Relinquishing all linguistic attempts, Eusèbe pointed to the object on the floor, and said in French:

"Take that away, negro." . . .

The negro did not need to be told twice. He picked up the thing, put it on Eusèbe's bed, and retired.

Ouf! Eusèbe turned pale. He shouted:

"Idiot! Fool! Take it off!"

But the negro was gone. The animal—*monstrum horrendum*—was there at his side. Oh, he would not look: he recoiled from it as far as the wall would permit.

Yet he must resolve on some mode of action. Eusèbe shut his eyes, and instinctively guessing the precise position in which the thing lay, pushed it off the bed with a violent kick.

There was a fall and a rustle, as of paper. Eusèbe came to the edge of the bed, and leaned forward anxiously.

The thing had opened, and a host of green and white papers were escaping from its side. Eusèbe burst into a roar of laughter.

"A pocket-book!" he cried.

And with one bound he was on the floor. Yes, it was nothing but that: a pocket-book of dark-green leather, with pockets full of greenbacks and bank-notes. Assuredly Eusèbe was well satisfied with this conclusion, but he was none the less surprised. He knew better than any one else that since his encounter with the excellent Captain Cotraw he had not possessed a shilling, and it was impossible to suppose that American hotel-keepers had the delicate consideration to supply their guests with pocket-money.

A note which he found in one of the folds of the pocket-book explained the puzzle.

"My dear Brother-in-law," Valville had written; "I do not want to awake you. But as I know that you have no money, I hope you will accept a small loan from me. I am going on a search with Ned Bark and Freedy, and we shall be back in about five hours. Be prudent. Yours,—Charles."

"Come! here's a good fellow," murmured Eusèbe to himself. "Little sissy has been lucky! such a brother-in-law ought to make a capital husband. Let me see. I have all the day to myself. I must go and explore the country in that nice get-up!"

For, with the boots that the snake had invaded, the captain's coat, and his own much-damaged trousers, Eusèbe would not have cut a very fine figure on the

Boulevard des Italiens, in Paris. But a man must be brave; so Eusèbe, although he grumbled, proceeded to dress himself, daring not, however, to look at his own reflection in the glass.

On his arrival downstairs he consumed with a significant grimace a breakfast chiefly composed of vegetables boiled in water, without salt or butter. When he had finished this deplorable repast he took his fishing-rod, which figured as a stick, or rather as a formidable club, and launched out into the streets of St. Augustine.

"Oh, what a wretched place!" he growled at every step. "And how dilapidated it is! The architect ought to be kicked out. What hovels! And there's a man who thinks no end of himself because he's a Spaniard! And there's another without either guitar or castanets. So much for the Spaniard of picture-books."

Thus arranging his notes of travel, Eusèbe went hither and thither by chance, when, as he was crossing the market-place, he experienced a sudden shock of surprise.

And this was why.

A few yards before him walked a negro of the deepest dye, who twisted and turned and gave himself the most extraordinary airs. Eusèbe could see his thick lips, the whites of his eyes, his fleece of crisped wool; but these were not the things that aroused his attention.

No: what astonished him beyond all expression—and indeed the most phlegmatic person might have been impressed by it—was the clothing of the said negro. Fancy a little coat, cut in a fashion that made your mouth water to look at! And the stylish trousers, falling straight to the ankle, and there expanding gracefully, so that only the tip of the boot was visible; and on the head a perfect love of a little hat, not bigger than the palm of one's hand!

The coat and trousers were of a bluish grey colour, as delicate as the tint on a dove's neck! He knew them by heart! he had chosen them himself, with his own hand, and in Paris!

Were there in St. Augustine, in Florida—fifteen hundred leagues from Paris, that paradise of dandies—were there drapers who sold these works of art, workmen to cut them out, and tailors to fit them on? Was such a miracle possible?

Eusèbe did not hesitate to reply in the negative. Was it a miracle? No! Was it a mystery? Yes! But what was the mystery? It was the work of a moment for Eusèbe to walk up to the negro, plant himself before him with his club in his hand, and execute a flourish with his right arm which did credit to his fencing-master, as he cried—

"You black thief! where did you steal those things?"

The ruling characteristic of a negro is not precisely courage. Moreover, this negro had been in the service of a planter at New Orleans, and understood a little French; so when he caught the words 'thief' and 'steal,' he trembled from head to foot and began to whine:—

"Massa, me no thief! me swear . . ."

Eusèbe, now quite beside himself, seized him by the lovely necktie, of the colour of stewed haricot beans with blue spots; an ideal necktie!

"Where did you find these things? Where? where? where?"

"Me not found! massa, pardon: not hurt poor nigger."

"You not stolen? you not found?" said Eusèbe, speaking the negro tongue in perfection—which proves once more how easy languages are to learn. "Then, who gave them to you?"

"Not gave—massa, me swear! Bought! me bought them!"

Eusèbe's fingers relaxed their hold.

"Bought!" he cried. "Where? Come, tell me, or I'll strangle you again!"

"But, massa! there—in the market! me paid!"

Eusebe took out a five-dollar note and spread it before the negro's eyes.

"You know that?" he asked.

"Oh yes, massa!" said the negro, turning purple with pleasure.

"And you know that too?" said Eusebe, showing him his club. "Well, you choose! you take me where you buy that, or me kill you! Eh! it's clear enough, isn't it, you fellow?"

The negro did not require to be told twice. Making a sign to Eusèbe to follow him, he led him through crooked narrow alleys, where the balconies of the houses nearly touched each other, and looked like drunkards leaning on one another's shoulders. But Eusèbe was not at all afraid. He would have gone anywhere with his guide. They reached at last a sort of shed, under which could be seen a crowd of negroes, while a man on the table shook out various garments, offered them for sale, and shouted their price with all the strength of his lungs.

"Here, you take!" said Eusèbe, who had turned exceedingly red, as he put the five dollars into the negro's hands.

And while the descendant of Ham expended his strength in thanks, Eusèbe, making play with his elbows like a woman who wants to see the fireworks at a show, pressed through the negro ranks, reached the table, jumped upon it at one bound, and seized the merchant by the collar.

"Ah, it is you! you dog of a Queue-de-Rat! You shall pay for this. No! Then you'll get a first-rate thrashing!"

Yes, it was Captain Cotraw himself, with his enormous breadth of shoulder and bony face! And he was selling to the negroes of Florida the contents of the thirty-three boxes, which were there pell-mell.

But more comical than anything was the way in which this formidable-looking gentleman received as sound a box on the ear as ever resounded on the cheek of a clown at fair time. Without any loss of time he received another of equal force from the same quarter. And yet he did not knock Eusèbe down with one blow of his gigantic fists! Perhaps he had not time to do so, for Eusèbe thumped and thumped so long and so well that the worthy Queue-de-

Rat, confounded, overwhelmed, half killed, went head over heels to the ground. The negroes laughed and squalled. Queue-de-Rat tried to escape. But Eusèbe was now quite a Hercules, and held his prize so securely that the other could not move a step.

" You'll confess that you are a robber !" cried Eusèbe; " and that all this belongs to me !"

" If you will only let me go," entreated Captain Cotraw.

" Not before you—you yourself, mind—have put all these things into a trunk and carried them on your own thieving shoulders to my hotel. Come now ! quick about it, or I will have you put into prison, you gallows' bird !"

Cotraw did what he was ordered to do. He did not seem to wish for any further public exposure, but obeyed implicitly; and enough of Eusèbe's things were found to fill three boxes. There were coats, shirts, trousers, hats : quite a collection of different articles of clothing.

Cotraw made evident haste. He hailed two negroes.

And Eusèbe, walking behind, with his stick in his hand, conducted the triumphal procession to the hotel, where everything was safely deposited.

" Go, and be hanged somewhere else !" he said to the thief.

Cotraw asked for nothing better, and departed amidst shouts of laughter and cries of derision. It is needless to say that throughout all this uproar the police were conspicuous by their absence.

.But if ever a conqueror was delighted, transported,

enchanted, that conqueror was our friend Eusèbe. He cared little for the thousand or fifteen hundred francs of which Cotraw had cozened him, as long as he possessed these delicious clothes! In five minutes, Eusèbe issued from the hotel in a short coat of red and green tartan, and sky-blue trousers, in which he perambulated the streets of St. Augustine, convinced that he was stealing every woman's heart.

He kept the club in his hand, by way of precaution, however.

But he was so delighted, so feverish with joy and excitement, that, wishful to display himself everywhere, he lost his way, turned to the right, to the left, backwards and forwards, until at last he found himself outside the town.

But what did that matter, when he was so well dressed?

Besides, he knew his way back again, did he not? He saw in the distance a wooden building, and persuaded himself that it belonged to the town. It was an old mill, worked by a little waterfall, which leaped down and expanded below the wheel into a clear pond. Eusèbe advanced to it, and stood upon the bank. There, beneath the clear waters, he saw some truly magnificent fish; and a thought occurred to him. What a success it would be, if that evening he could bring one of those splendid creatures to the hotel, where they ate cabbages boiled in water! Had he not with him a fishing-rod that had cost nearly fifteen hundred francs?

He screwed it together, and then, erect and in a fine attitude, with eager eye, he threw the line into the water.

But, alas! a very robust creature took the hook into its mouth. Eusèbe was not expecting a bite so soon; and the shock he received made him nearly lose his balance. In the effort not to fall, he relinquished his hold alike on line and fish. What a misfortune was this! After all, what did it matter, when he was so perfectly well dressed?

It was true that he had quite lost his way; that in regaining the bank near the mill he saw nothing on the right hand or on the left, that seemed likely to guide him to St. Augustine. But then he was so proud of his tartan coat; so satisfied with his trousers—particularly with the trousers!

So he went straight on, thinking that Providence would surely befriend a young man so exceedingly well dressed.

But there were cross roads and hills before him. Which of these roads would lead him to St. Augustine? He began to walk a little faster. He consulted his chronometer, which had never been contaminated by the touch of a Captain Cotraw, and saw that it was four o'clock; and dinner was to be at six. He began to feel hungry. Then, another and more worthy anxiety seized upon him. He feared lest Valville and Freedy should come to a sudden decision, and be hindered in their departure by his absence. He had some good in him, this little exquisite, so he set off running like a hare.

Suddenly, after climbing a steep rock from which he hoped to see something which should indicate to him the direction of St. Augustine, he found himself at the top of a narrow defile, which ran between two rocks rising straight and bare from either side.

"This is the Hölle Strasse, in little!" exclaimed Eusèbe, who had visited the Black Forest with a circular ticket.

So saying, he missed his footing, and would certainly have rolled into the abyss, but for a hand that seized his own, and dragged him back to safety.

It was a negro's hand. Nothing but negroes!

"Ah! where am I?" exclaimed Eusèbe, addressing himself to this individual.

The negro rolled his big eyes and replied:

"Me not know . . . you ask . . . there; people down there."

Eusèbe bent down, and perceived in the ravine a group of four or five persons who were walking in the shadow of the rocks by the light of a lantern.

Two ladies went first, and Eusèbe could just see that they were armed with guns.

"These are heroines of romance!" he exclaimed. "That's perfect, and will suit me exactly. Me get down," he added, turning to the negro.

"Sambo take you down," replied the black man.

Two minutes later, having managed to descend by a precipitous pathway, Eusèbe arrived at the bottom of the ravine, and exclaimed—

"Saperlipopette! Alice! and the Woman with the iron will!"

CHAPTER XII.

EUSÈBE AS CAPTAIN.

DECIDEDLY Eusèbe was the man for adventures !

But his surprise was nothing to that of his aunt and Alice Lodier: for it was indeed these two who had presented themselves so suddenly before him. His delight was, however, so great, that with a burst of thoroughly Parisian sentiment he threw himself upon his sister's neck, kissed her on both cheeks, and repeated again and again in a voice that was choked with something very like a sob :

"Oh, I am so glad to see you, dear little Alice ! "

Then, without leaving her time to answer, he proceeded :

"But this is most extraordinary ! how did you come here ? you, and the strong-minded woman, in the middle of Florida ! For we are in Florida, you know."

His geographical acquirements were of too recent date not to be made the most of.

"We are quite aware of it," said Alice, smiling. "But you—how did you get here ? "

"Oh, I ! " said Eusèbe, swallowing down his emotion. " It is quite an epic: Offenbach ought to set it to music!"

"Come, children," Madame Longpré interrupted them; "it seems to me that you will have plenty of time to talk, and that we ought to get to St. Augustine as soon as possible. . . ."

"Where my sister will meet some persons of her acquaintance—whom perhaps she will be glad to see."

" M. Valville?"

" Exactly! M. Valville, and Freedy, and the spy—no, the one-eyed detective."

"Mr. Ned Bark? You are right, aunt," said Alice; "we must make haste; and let us for once congratulate ourselves on having obeyed the inspiration that brought us here."

"Oh, I am never wrong!" said Madame Longpré. "When we heard—all that did hear, I said at once, 'Let us set off!'"

"And I obeyed, as usual," said Alice, exchanging a glance with Eusèbe.

She then turned to the guides, and requested them to lead them as quickly as possible to St. Augustine.

" Guides!" exclaimed Eusèbe, shrugging his shoulders. " How very pitiful! Did I ever need a guide? I? I! who came all the way from Havre by myself! And if I liked, could I not take you straight to St. Augustine? But I'll leave you to it! Come, Alice, I bet that your famous guide, who has a very hang-dog look, will go to the right!"

They had arrived at a sort of cross road, from which two paths lay in precisely opposite directions.

The guide, whom Eusèbe thought doubtless the worst of characters, hastened to turn to the left.

"That's the one I meant," murmured Eusèbe apologetically.

Then, thinking it better to change the subject, he turned to Alice, who had taken his arm and given him the gun she had been carrying.

"Come, sissy," he said, "tell me your little adventures. You must confess that for a brother who is not a block, and who prides himself upon his sensibility, there is something rather surprising in the sudden apparition of a sister armed from head to foot like a huntress, in an ugly ravine, too, which would be a disgrace to our worst decorators. Tell me everything."

"That is soon done," said Alice. "M. Valville left us in the care of an excellent man, a planter of Louisiana, a Mr. Woodman."

"What names they have in this country!" growled Eusèbe.

"And in spite of our anxiety, we intended to await his return, when an unforeseen occurrence changed all our plans."

"Ah! there was an unforeseen occurrence. I love that sort of thing. It is just like a novel when the word 'suddenly' occurs!"

"But your curiosity will have to remain unsatisfied," said Alice.

"Bah! why?"

"Because," said Alice, lowering her voice, "we must be prudent, and I do not trust the guides."

" But you are speaking French ? "

" I distrust them, nevertheless, and I should be very sorry to risk by any imprudence of mine the success of the enterprise upon which M. Valville and his friends are engaged.   But you shall hear everything by and by, when we reach St. Augustine."

" Well ! I am still very anxious to hear everything."

" This unforeseen occurrence—having happened, it was most important that M. Valville should immediately be informed of it."

" Well ! And the telegraph ? Or is that only for crocodiles in this country ? "

" A telegram might be intercepted."

" The deuce !—you seem to know all about it ! "

" Mr. Woodman was not well; and I should not in any case have liked him to leave dear Lucile. . . ."

" Lucile ! what's that ? "

" What's that ! Lucile, Monsieur Eusèbe, is a very charming girl—worth all your—what shall I say ?—all your Parisian young ladies ! "

" We'll allow her to be an angel ! there ! What else ? "

" She is M. Valville's sister ; and the sister, too, of poor Jeanne who has disappeared."

" All honour to unfortunate valour ! Good. Finally, Miss Alice Lodier, if I am not the greatest of asses, was not sorry to have a pretext for going in search of M. Charles Valville ! "

" Eusèbe ! "

" So she hastened—on account of unforeseen occur

rences—to set out upon her way. But why did Miss Alice Lodier bend her steps—as they say in a comic opera—towards the honourable Spanish city of St. Augustine?"

"Because we were told to address all letters and telegrams to M. Valville thither, in case of need."

"Really! he thought then that you might telegraph?"

"Missis—St. Augustine," said Sambo, approaching them, and pointing to the town, which could be faintly seen through the gathering twilight.

This interruption was not distasteful to Alice, who had blushed a little at her inability to answer Eusèbe's impertinent observation.

She told him that at Picolata they had not been able to procure carriages, and had therefore been obliged to provide themselves with guides to show them the way on foot.

In a short time they entered the town, and soon reached the St. John's Hotel. Eusèbe, who at last had found his way, was delighted to act as guide.

It was now nearly six o'clock. None of the three men had yet returned to the hotel.

"Oh, no need to be anxious," said Eusèbe; "with Ned Bark and Freedy, they are sure to fall on their feet."

Alice and Madame Longpré retired to their room in order to rearrange their somewhat disordered toilette, while Eusèbe installed himself at the door of the hotel, smoked a cigar, and waited for something new to happen.

In fact he began to be greatly amused with the events around him. He found everything great fun. It seemed to him as if he were witnessing a play, full of catastrophes and recognitions of the most sensational character. Only the music was wanting. He would have liked a few songs.

Freedy arrived first; and, on seeing Eusèbe, asked abruptly,

"Where is Valville?"

"I have not seen him."

"And Ned Bark?"

"I have not seen him either."

Freedy made use of a purely American expletive.

Just as Eusèbe opened his lips to tell him the news, Ned Bark appeared in his turn.

"Where's Valville?" he also asked.

"He has not returned."

A fresh ejaculation, more violent than ever.

"Well, what is the matter?" asked Eusèbe, utterly nonplussed. "Anything wrong? Sapristi! this is a bad time for it."

At that very instant Alice appeared on the steps. She had seen Freedy from her window, and never doubting but that Valville was with him, had run down to meet him.

"You! you here?" exclaimed Freedy, with a sort of anger. "And yet we begged you . . . . ."

"To stay at the plantation," Alice interrupted him. "When you know what brings us here, you will understand why we were obliged to come. But," she added, "I don't see Charles . . . M. Valville."

"And, by Jove, no more do I!" said Freedy, more moved than he wished to show. "I would give my right hand to see him here."

Alice turned as pale as if she had been struck to the heart.

"What!" she said. "Have you any reason for anxiety?"

Freedy and Ned Bark exchanged a quick glance, and were silent.

"Gentlemen," said Alice, in a firm tone, "I am the promised wife of M. Valville, and I beg you to tell me the truth, whatever it may be."

"Let us go in," said Freedy sharply, turning to the hotel.

They entered a private sitting-room, and then Freedy addressed himself to Alice.

"You ought never to have come, for here we have everything to fear from our enemies."

"But Charles? speak!"

"I fear he has been drawn into a snare."

"Charles?"

"Listen to the facts. Ever since the morning we have been searching St. Augustine and its suburbs, in the hope of discovering some information which should put us on the track of the ruffians whom we are pursuing. But our endeavours were fruitless. For one moment only were we separated. Ned Bark went to see the metropolitan police, I to visit an old filibuster who might have been able to help us, Charles to inquire at the post-office and telegraph-office whether anything was waiting there for him. Just as I left the house which I had visited, a negro approached me, and asked if I were Doctor Freedy.

"Upon my answering in the affirmative, he gave me a note, which consisted of these words written with a pencil in French :

"'I think I am on the track. Don't be anxious. Till this evening.'"

"Yes, that is indeed his writing," said Alice, who had glanced at the note. "But did you not question the negro?"

"Certainly, for my suspicions were at once excited. And what the negro told me only increased them. He had met Valville on the ramparts near Fort Marion. He was not alone, but accompanied by a person whom the negro described to me as one of the men whom we call 'carpet-baggers,' that is, adventurers capable of anything bad. Unfortunately, Charles has been absent from this country too long to be sufficiently on his guard against these rascals. They went in the direction of the open country. What can have happened? How can Charles, whom I have so often begged to be prudent, have allowed himself to be deceived by offers, promises, perhaps by mere lies! It is what I cannot understand. I met Ned Bark and he was of the same opinion as myself."

"M. Valville has fallen into some snare prepared for him by our enemies," said the detective.

"We must go to his help!" exclaimed Alice.

Freedy shook his head.

"Certainly, that is our intention! But the country round St. Augustine is broken up by cypress-swamps, woods, almost impenetrable thickets, and I fear that we may only arrive too late."

"What does that matter?" said Alice, carried away by her excitement. "Our duty is plain. Let us set off immediately."

"What! you, Mademoiselle?"

"Have I not told you that I love him, and that henceforward I consider that I bear his name?"

"Quite the right style, sissy!" said Eusèbe. "I agree with you: let us set off! see if I won't get him out of this mess."

Eusèbe was growing quite heroic.

In a few moments the four were ready to start.

Madame Longpré had, as usual, allowed herself to be persuaded, and authorised Alice to go without her. Eusèbe took with him a cane, which he had found in one of his recovered boxes: a little work of art, with a head representing a barking dog.

As he forgot to take arms, he had to be reminded to do so; but he flatly refused to be separated from his cane, which he brandished in one hand, while with the other he retained his hold upon the gun which rested on his shoulder. Ned Bark hastened to order the horses: for above everything it was necessary to gain ground. When they had left the beaten pathway, it would be time to abandon the animals.

Alice had fastened up her hair beneath a sort of fisherman's cap, which was not likely to be carried off by the wind.

The little troop consisted of five persons, including Sambo.

At this moment the moon was rising, and shone brilliantly down upon the city of St. Augustine.

" You seem to bring us good fortune," said Ned Bark to Eusèbe.

" Ah ! yes, I think I have a good chance of it," said Eusèbe with the air of a little conqueror.

They sprang to their saddles, and the horses set off at a gallop.

Ned Bark acted as their guide. He replied very evasively to the questions that were occasionally addressed to him. He trusted to his own detective-instinct. For half an hour not a word was uttered ; each ear was on the alert ; and Freedy kept close to Alice's side, fearing some ambuscade, but without daring to avow his fear.

The road that they had taken led to the river Matanzas.

The moon shone so brightly that one might have imagined its light to be that of noonday. The nights in Florida often retain this exquisite clearness. The smallest objects are visible, light colours and shadows are defined with perfect exactitude, and work is often not suspended until the night is far advanced.

At a distance of about two hours' journey from St. Augustine they perceived two men felling a tree in the midst of a clearing. Ned Bark gave orders that the travellers should halt, and slipped down from his horse.

A hut had been built against the trunk of a palm-tree, and a bright fire burned upon the ground.

Ned Bark advanced towards the two men and questioned them.

They made no difficulty about answering him, and he learned that three riders had passed down that road about an hour before.

"One of the three was a Frenchman," said one of the labourers.

" How could you tell that ? " asked Ned Bark. " Did you speak to him ? "

" Not I," said the man, laughing ; " but he spoke to his horse ; and, you know, we don't use the same words in speaking to animals."

" That's true," said the detective. " And where do you think they went ? "

" That would be hard to say. This road has no precise object ; in about three hours' time it loses itself in the cypress groves, which extend as far as the river Matanzas."

" And they went so fast," said the other, " that one might have thought they would take the distance over the sea to Anastasia at a single leap."

When Ned Bark returned to his companions his face wore a more sombre expression than ever. He could on longer doubt but that Valville had been carried off by some of Red Ralph's emissaries. There was nothing, however, to indicate that he was treated as a prisoner; so he must voluntarily have followed his worst enemies. What promises had he made to them? With what hopes had they lured him? How had Charles allowed himself to be deceived? These were questions which must all remain unanswered.

But he had obtained one piece of valuable information: the road was cut short by cypress swamps. Possibly, by quickening the trot of their own horses, they might yet catch up the others, whose progress could not be very rapid.

"Forward!" Ned Bark exclaimed.

And at a touch of the spur the horses dashed forward at their utmost speed.

In one hour they had crossed the space that separated them from the cypress groves. So far they had been threatened by no danger; on the other hand, they had also received no new information. Ned Bark asked himself if he were really on the right scent.

Before adventuring themselves in the labyrinth of cypresses, they were forced to dismount. They were consulting together as to whether they should content themselves with merely tying the horses to trees—a measure doubly dangerous on account alike of venomous reptiles and of horse-stealers — when Ned suddenly raised his head. He had just noticed a strange and regular sound, as of monotonously falling strokes.

They were then in the midst of a sort of ravine, one side of which was formed of white stone, like chalk, fully illuminated by the brilliant rays of the moon. Ned Bark turned the corner of the rock, and saw some blackish buildings propped up against it on the other side. It was an old sawmill, turned by means of a stream of water that issued from the rock. Negroes were still working in the moonlight, and a negro woman was kneading cakes of Indian corn.

Ned Bark did not hesitate. He addressed himself at once to the negroes, and easily obtained shelter for his horses.

These exiles from the rest of the world had noticed neither horses nor riders ; but Ned heard that by turning the flank of the chalky cliff he would find himself on the edge of the river Matanzas.

Was it in this direction, then, that Valville had been conducted ?

A sort of council of war was held. Ned, supported by Sambo's opinion, declared, after close examination, that nobody had entered the cypress grove for a long time, as there was not a single trace of footsteps.

But upon examining the soil more carefully, which the exceptional beauty of the night rendered it easy for them to do, they were soon convinced that the marks of footsteps were indeed visible in the direction of the river-bank.

There were no traces of horses' hoofs.

The riders had doubtless left their steeds in some nook where the little troop could not be noticed by passers-by.

The ground gradually sloped down to the edge of the river.

Suddenly Eusèbe uttered a cry.

"Sapristi ! down there ! Look !"

Their eyes followed the direction indicated by his hand, and they saw a boat gliding swiftly down the current, impelled by rapid rowers.

The river Matanzas, which divides the Island of Anastasia from the mainland, is nearly three-quarters of a mile broad, but it is dotted over with smaller islands which intercept the view.

The boat moved with great rapidity. It could not preserve a straight course, as its progress was constantly impeded by currents.

"And there is a boat doing nothing !" cried Eusèbe. "Let us get in."

He was right. A boat, furnished with oars, lay on the sand.

There was no need to hesitate. The four men pushed off the boat, which in a few seconds was afloat.

Alice, whose courage did not fail her for a single moment, placed herself at the stern. The men seized the oars.

"Shove off !" ejaculated Eusèbe. "This is like the regatta at Argenteuil. Let us show these fellows what it is to be a water-dog of the Seine ! Off ! Time, boys !"

Thus did Eusèbe constitute himself captain of the vessel. He feared nothing. If America had been there to conquer, he would have felt capable of conquering it single-handed.

The oars dipped, and the boat shot forward like an arrow from a bow.

"One, two! One, two!" said Eusèbe. "No nervousness now! Don't hurry the time! One, two!"

But the other boat had had a considerable start of them, and now appeared about to disappear in the maze of islands which dotted the watery plain.

In vain did the four companions redouble their efforts; they saw the boat hide itself completely behind a screen of earth and trees.

"Sapristi!" cried Eusèbe. "This is not child's play!"

Still they would not abandon their pursuit. The oarsmen were strong; but the current was rapid, and they were not sufficiently well acquainted with the dangers of the river. Twice their keel became entirely entangled in water-plants, and several minutes were lost in disengaging it.

And this was not all; for the moon was sinking rapidly, and darkness fast coming on. Alice, wringing her hands, felt with despair her impotence to defend or save the man for whom she would gladly have given her life.

They succeeded in coasting round the island behind which the boat had disappeared. But the night had become so dark that it was impossible to distinguish anything. It was useless to continue the pursuit.

"He is lost! he is lost!" murmured Alice.

"No, no, little one!" exclaimed Eusèbe. "Have I

not been through enough difficulty and danger? I, who have conversed with crocodiles in charge of a large family, and snakes which invaded. . . ."

"Alligators and snakes are less dangerous than men," said Ned Bark, shaking his head.

"Get along with you, wet blanket!" cried Eusèbe. "Do you, too, want to dishearten her? I tell you that we shall soon find her Charles for her, as fresh as a rose!"

He was rewarded for his encouraging speech by a gentle pressure of the hand.

"After all," said Ned Bark, "I am never discouraged, so I will not begin to be so to-day. Doctor Freedy, what do you think of the situation?"

"In my opinion," said the doctor, "this is what we ought to do: approach one of these islands, and moor the boat fast to the bank. Then wrap ourselves well up, and spend the night there. To-morrow, when the sun rises, we can carefully examine the place, and think what we must do."

"That would be the most prudent course," said Ned Bark. "And if Miss Alice has no objection. . . ."

"I am ready for anything," said the girl in a grave voice.

They took Freedy's advice, and in a few moments the boat was moored in a little creek in the bank of one of the islands.

There they spent the long and dreary night.

No one slept; yet not a word was interchanged.

What was happening? What fate was reserved for Charles Valville?

"Daylight!" exclaimed Eusèbe at last.

And in fact, a whitish tinge seemed to pervade the whole atmosphere.

But at the same instant, as if his cry had been a signal, the report of guns rang out upon the silence.

CHAPTER XIII.

"Do you hear?" exclaimed Alice. "They are murdering him!"

"Come, a Frenchman is not killed quite so easily!" said Eusèbe. "To arms, friends!"

The four men had already seized their oars.

In the deep silence of early morning the reports had been so distinct that it was easy to guess from what quarter they had proceeded.

Even had the listeners hesitated, a fresh succession of shots resounding in the distance might have served them as a guide.

The first explosion had been produced by several shots fired at once. But now single reports were heard at intervals, and it seemed as if the sounds drew nearer and nearer to the shore.

As they rapidly noted these facts, the rowers quickened their strokes, and the boat shot through the water with incredible swiftness.

Now that day had broken, they could see that beyond the islets that had served them as a shelter for the night, the course of the river was unimpeded as far as the coast of Anastasia, which was some two miles distant from them.

Above the clumps of trees upon the bank they saw a tiny cloud of smoke.

"Courage!" exclaimed Alice, who was standing upright in the stern of the boat. She had seized a gun, and laid her finger on the trigger.

Eusèbe jested no longer, for he felt, as indeed did also his companions, that a decisive moment was approaching. The boat cut its way through the current, under the impulse given to it by vigorous hands, straight to the shore. In a few moments they would reach it.

But at that very moment they beheld a terrible sight.

A man was running towards them, tearing his way through the tangled bind-weeds, while, at a short distance behind him, two forms could be seen standing upon a slight elevation with guns upon their shoulders, evidently waiting until he should reappear from beneath the trees in order to give him a mortal wound.

"Bloody Foot!" cried Freedy. "Oh, let us show no pity this time!"

And snatching the gun from Alice's hands, he rose up in his turn, saying:

"Ship your oars! Let her drift!"

And for a few seconds the boat, obeying the impulse already given, glided on steadily.

Charles—for it was indeed he whom the men were waylaying—had just issued from the wood. Before him lay an open space, which he began to cross.

A shot was heard.

One of the Redskins flung out his arms and fell forward.

But at the same instant the other fired at Valville. Did the ball strike him? They saw the young man stagger on for a few paces, then fall into the moving flood.

Had his friends arrived too late?

In the terrible silent waiting that followed, one might have heard their hearts beat with the agony of suspense.

But the voice of Sambo cried out—

" Here !—to the left !—in the water ! massa's son !"

In the direction indicated a dark form could now be seen. They rowed towards it, and Ned Bark, leaning half-way out of the boat, seized Charles Valville by his clothes.

It was Valville himself, but exhausted, bleeding, and so pale that Alice thought at first they had saved only a dead man after all.

She fell on her knees in the boat, and supported with both hands the head of the man whom she loved to call her husband.

" Alice !" he murmured in a feeble voice. " Alice !"

" He is living," said Alice.

And indeed it seemed as if love—true, deep, earnest love—had worked a new miracle. Yes, Charles was living, for the blood rushed to his face; he seized Alice's hands and pressed them to his lips as he returned her look of affection.

Meanwhile the boat, directed by the rowers, had

reached the shore of the island of Anastasia: a wild coast strewn with fragments, which told a tale of many a tempest-driven bark wrecked upon the inhospitable shore.

" Freedy," said Ned Bark, " give your best care to the wounded man. I and Sambo are going in chase."

" Prudence above everything !" exclaimed Freedy.

But the detective and the negro, gun in hand, were already crossing the cypress grove. Ned Bark had chosen his destination beforehand. It was the mound upon which Freedy's piercing eyes had recognised the Indian, Bloody Foot. He had fallen, struck by a ball, but did he still live ? Could not some last confession yet be wrested from his lips ?

This hope was disappointed. The Seminole was motionless : Freedy's ball had seemingly penetrated his heart. He had fallen face downwards, with a slight foam upon his mouth.

But he had not been alone. · What had become of his accomplice—the wretch who had fired at Charles Valville ?

From the height where he stood, Ned Bark could survey the whole extent of the long and narrow island of Anastasia. No vestige of a human being could there be traced.

They walked round the hill. Both uttered at the same time a cry of anger. For, a few yards only from the western coast, they saw a small sloop, rigged like a cutter, moving off from the shore with all sails set.

And, as if to prevent their doubting for a moment that the sloop was affording a means of escape to their

enemies, a man, the very Redskin whom they were seeking, had plunged into the water, grasped a rope thrown
to him from the vessel, and gained the deck.

With a furious exclamation, Ned Bark discharged his
gun after them; but the distance was already too great
for the shot to have any effect. The cutter sped rapidly
upon its way.

Ned Bark returned to Bloody Foot, seized, perhaps,
with a hope that his first examination had deceived him.
Sambo, understanding his intention, preceded him.
While Ned Bark was still examining the place, the negro
bent over the Indian. He found him stretched close to
the edge of a fissure in the rock, which divided it as
completely as if it had been severed by one stroke of
a giant's sword.

Suddenly the arms of the Seminole moved and seized
the negro by the neck, while the wretched man writhed
upon the ground and dragged his prisoner to the abyss.
Taken utterly by surprise, powerless to disengage himself, Sambo's chance of escape was as nothing. The
Seminole was dying, but in dying he attempted a last
revenge. His attack had been so sudden, that Ned
Bark, who at that moment was directing a parting
glance of anger at the cutter, did not even hear the
negro's stifled cry. When he turned round, he saw
Sambo suspended over the gulf, retaining his hold
merely upon a frail root which his hands had grasped
convulsively, while Bloody Foot was pressing him downwards with the whole force of his body. Ned ran
forward, and drawing a revolver from his belt, applied

it to the Indian's head. He fired. At the same moment Ned seized Sambo's arm, and with one vigorous
effort restored him to safety upon the surface of the rock.

A dull sound could be heard. The Seminole's body
rebounded as it fell from rock to rock. Then one last
thud: then—nothing. Their terrible enemy was no
longer to be feared.

Sambo bent down before the detective, took his hand
and kissed it. Ned was more moved than he liked to
show. He raised Sambo from the ground with a show
of brusqueness, and said :

" We have nothing more to do here. Let us go and
find our friends."

As he spoke, Eusèbe appeared.

" Well, what's the matter?" he cried. " You seem
to be having nice little games without us !"

" Where have you left Mr. Valville?"

" A few yards off; he is lying on a bed of leaves. Oh,
there's nothing to be afraid of. That scoundrel's ball only
grazed his shoulder. He's going on like a house on fire !"

And as Ned Bark and Sambo approached, they saw
Charles actually standing upright, still pale, but with
eyes sparkling.

" Ah, Mr. Bark," said Valville, holding out his hand ;
" I know what you have done for us !"

" Don't talk of that," said the detective. " Well?
speak out—are you wounded?"

" A mere nothing," answered Freedy. " One dressing
will suffice."

" In that case," said Ned, " we have no time to lose."

And he recounted to them what he had seen.

" You only can tell us, Valville, who the men are that are escaping in that cutter."

" Those men," said Charles, " consist of Red Ralph and his band of assassins."

" I was sure of it !" cried Ned. " Why have I not that robber at the mouth of my gun ! But you have yet to tell us why you were so imprudent—you will forgive the word, I hope—as to leave us and go off on a wild-goose search !"

" You shall hear everything," said Charles. " But pray believe that the man employed very powerful means in order to entrap me into this snare. And, above all, don't think it useless to search their hiding-place. Who knows but they may have left behind some sign which will put us on their track ? "

" Their hiding-place ? " said Ned, in surprise. " What do you mean ? "

" I was taken there myself: to an old deserted building . . ."

" Singular ! I saw no sign of it."

" Oh, the place is well hidden. But follow me, and I think we shall find it again."

The little band set out upon their way.

Alice, supremely happy, took Valville's arm. She had been easily pardoned for her disobedience to the order that she should remain at the Woodman plantation.

But as yet she refused to answer the questions, with which they plied her, as to the motives which had caused her to leave her dwelling-place so unexpectedly.

"I will tell you all," she repeated. "But I want to know what has happened already. The news that I bring will be really important only if it agrees with what you have heard yourselves."

The island of Anastasia was, in the last century, one of the strongest fortresses possessed by the Spaniards, its uneven ground adapting it admirably for purposes of defence. Traces of ditches and fortifications could still be seen. And after passing through the tangled wood which formed, as it were, a thick curtain upon the western coast, one reached a sort of high wall cut out of the solid rock, against which the sea, as yet invisible, dashed with terrible violence in waves that expended themselves in showers of foam and spray.

Upon the summit of this enormous natural embankment some wooden buildings—once probably used as a guard-house—seemed to hang over the abyss beneath.

"It was there that those men took me," said Charles, pointing to this erection.

"But I do not see any means of scaling the height," said Freedy.

"Wait. If we go round the base of the cliff we shall see a sort of lake, fed by small streams from the sea. There we shall find a wooden bridge, which leads to a stair cut in the face of the rock . . . ."

But he interrupted himself suddenly.

"The wretches!" he exclaimed. "They have cut down the bridge before leaving the island!"

There was a moment's hesitation.

But the fine gentleman, Eusèbe, who had hitherto

kept silence, now threw off the nicely-coloured coat which enwrapped his graceful form, valiantly pushed up his sleeves to the elbow, and hurrying to the edge of the lake, where he had noticed the trunks of some great trees, seized one in his arms, and cried—

" If there isn't a bridge, we'll make one, that's all ! "

He was right. Before them lay far more wood than was necessary to make a temporary footway. They set themselves to work at once. At a short distance from the waterfall they found a comparatively narrow portion of the lake. Sambo worked in the water; and in less than half-an-hour the six persons had crossed the foaming flood, and found themselves at the foot of the staircase of which Valville had spoken.

" Attention ! " said Ned Bark. " Have your guns ready."

They ascended the steps slowly, every sense on the alert. When they had attained the summit of the rocky wall, an involuntary cry of admiration escaped their lips. Below them the mighty ocean stretched away into the far distance. The waves burst furiously upon this vestige of Spanish power, still strong and massive enough to resist the continual incursions of the sea.

The wooden building was of more recent construction. No doubt it had been erected during the late civil war, and had served as a beacon to the ships which blockaded the north of Florida. Now it was nothing but a haunt for robbers or birds of prey.

" Here we are ! " said Valville, who was walking first.

Following the course of the embankment, he had reached a wooden staircase, and, having ascended it, he pushed open a mouldering door which gave entrance to a large room, where they found several traces of the recent bivouac of a band of men. A fire, still alight, shed a red gleam upon a wide, solidly-built hearth and fireplace.

The men began to search the premises, leaving no corner unexplored. But it was only too evident that the bandits had made a clearance.

" Listen to me," said Valville, when they found themselves once more collected in the room which they had entered first, and which contained several seats; "listen to me, and I will tell you the history of my strange and dangerous adventure.

"When, at St. Augustine, I left Freedy and Ned Bark, I went, as you will remember, to the post-office. I was wrong there, perhaps, in not taking any precautions when I asked for letters and gave my name. As I came out of the office, I was accosted by a tall personage, wrapped in a cloak, who asked me, in a most polite manner, if my name were not Charles Valville.

"Upon my replying in the affirmative, he continued—

"'Pardon me, sir, for taking this liberty; but I know that you are visiting Florida for grave reasons, and if you will consent to trust me, I can make important revelations.'

"I am young, my dear friends," said Charles, interrupting the course of his story for a moment. "I ought to have refused to listen to this man, but the mysterious tone in which his words were uttered provoked my curiosity. I followed him—the more readily because he spoke of the crime committed at Battle Field, and of Jeanne's disappearance. And when—with a last gleam of sense—I asked him what interest he had in giving me such information, and he answered, 'That is very easily explained: you are rich, and will pay me well,' I felt that nothing could be more logical. But still he refused to give me immediately the information that I expected. He explained to me that he, with others of his companions, formed part of the band of which Red Ralph was chief. He had not taken part in the crimes of Battle Field, but he had heard all about them. Since that time, he and his friends had had reason to complain of their chief, and had resolved to sell the secrets which they had discovered. But, as these men were naturally suspicious one of the other, they had resolved never to reveal these secrets except in presence of all the members of their confederation.

"All this seemed to me very plausible. Then my sister's name, uttered several times, threw me into a sort of fever. I consented to everything. We left the town, found horses outside it, and galloped off. What road did we follow? I do not know, and I am still surprised that you could recover any traces of me. We found a boat on the river-bank. Two men were already there, who seemed to be waiting for us. At last we arrived at this island and took the way that I have shown you, and I was led into the very room where we are sitting now.

" But scarcely had I entered it, when I understood that I had been tricked, and that my life was in danger.

"A dozen bandits, armed to the teeth, occupied the room, and amongst them I remarked two Indians.

"I was silent, waiting until one of the villains should inform me of what my fate was to be, when a door opened, and another individual appeared: a man of very high stature and stern features, with a face which bore an expression of savage energy.

"I do not know what instinct told me that my father's murderer stood before me, but, carried away by rage, I cried out—

"'You are Red Ralph! Curse you!'

"And although I was unarmed, I threw myself upon him. But at the same instant twenty hands were laid upon me, and reduced me to powerlessness.

"'Since you know my name,' said the man, with a sneer, 'there is no need for an introduction. You were looking for me, and you have found me sooner than you expected. Your first expression was one of anger. I hope, nevertheless, that we shall yet understand each other better; and to show you that I wish to make the first steps towards reconciliation'—here he turned to the men who were holding me—'set Mr. Valville at liberty.'

"The hands that had seized me were removed. I remained calm and motionless. I had had time for reflection. What would be the use of violence? And now that I found myself face to face with my enemy, ought I not, above everything, to learn his designs?

"'I will listen to you,' I said, looking him full in the face. 'Only remember that there stands here a murderer and a judge, and that I am the judge.'

"A strange contraction passed over the robber's brow, but he preserved his calmness.

"And now," continued Charles, "I beg of you, my friends, however improbable my story may appear to you, to give it your entire belief. I will not weary you with the interruptions which I made to the extraordinary ravings of the wretched man, and I will repeat to you the mere substance of his words.

"He spoke gently, and I must say that his manner was that of a man far superior to the atrocious trade which he had made his own.

"'Mr. Valville,' he said, 'I am a criminal, and I acknowledge it. But know, that not only did I never soil my hands with your father's blood, but I saved the life of Miss Lucile, Jeanne's sister, and yours. What I will not hide from you is that I directed the expedition against your father's plantation, but for what purpose? You shall know all. I love your sister; I love her madly, passionately. I went to her in all truth and honour, and said, "Be mine, and I will make you the happiest of wives."'

"Here a livid pallor overspread his face. With a gesture and a few words he ordered his companions to retire. Alone with me, he approached me, and spoke in a voice that came forth with a hissing sound from between his closed teeth.

"'To all my vows of love your sister replied by hate and disdain. Then I went mad. I said that in spite of her, in spite of all, she should be mine. That is why, Charles Valville, I burnt your father's plantation.　That is why your sister is now in my power.'

"You will understand, my friends, with what difficulty I contained myself.　When he had finished, I crossed my arms on my breast, and said—

"'Then you dare to tell me that you have used violence. . . .'

"'No! no!' he cried, 'I give you my word that I have treated your sister with every respect.　She repulses me, she hates me, she despises me, always!　Well—do you know why you are here?　Because Miss Valville said to me not long ago with that disdainful smile which cuts me to the heart :—"On the day when my brother consents to the marriage, I will be your wife!"　Do you understand that I might have made her obey me?　But no! I love her.　I, Red Ralph—the outlaw and the robber —I bend to her will—I submit to her!　It must seem almost impossible to you.　And yet it is the truth.　So far, my reverence for her has been unimpaired.　But take care!' he added with concentrated rage, 'all patience ends in time!—And, Mr Charles Valville, I come to ask for your consent—for the command which your sister waits for—and I will do everything to obtain it.'

"I was stupefied.　There appeared to be in this man an inexplicable mixture of greatness and baseness, of humility and ferocity, which overpowered me.

"'And if I refuse to obey you?'

"'Then,' he said, with a burst of rage, 'you are in my power, and I shall kill you!'

"'Kill me, then!'

"But the wretched man threw himself at my feet, begging and imploring me to grant his request. Time passed on; and a hope seized me—I know not why—that I should yet be saved. He said at last—

"'Listen, you do not know who I am. You think you see in me merely the robber Red Ralph. But I bear one of the names most honoured in America, for I am Ralph Staunton.'

"As you may well imagine, I remained immovable. Ralph was then attacked by a fit of rage, which seemed to be almost epileptic in character. At his orders I was seized and cast into a sort of dungeon attached to this room. Hours passed on; I asked myself whether the ruffian had not condemned me to that most horrible of deaths—the death of lonely starvation. Suddenly I perceived that there was an ill-closed opening in my cell, the side of which was level with the face of the rock. I called all my courage to my aid, and attempted an escape which only half succeeded, for I was seen at the very moment when I had reached the bottom of the wall, and pursued immediately. You know the rest.

"Oh, my sister!" Charles continued, "my poor sister is lost for ever! Who can tell me where I shall find her, or how I shall snatch her from that ruffian's hands?"

Then Alice Lodier rose and said—

"Take courage, Charles. I can tell you where your sister is."

CHAPTER XIV.

THE REVELATION.

"You asked me," said Alice, whose face had assumed an expression of gravity which contrasted strongly with the gentle and delicate character of its features; "you asked me why I came here; why, in opposition to your instructions, and more, in defiance of your wishes, I left Mr. Woodman's plantation, bringing with me my aunt, that kind-hearted woman whom I thus exposed to danger and fatigue. I will not believe that you, M. Valville, supposed that I was simply following a childish caprice. . . ."

Charles protested with a look. Was he not grateful to her for coming, and for illumining with her smile the darkness which surrounded all his steps?

"I only wished first to make you understand," said Alice, "that I would have respected your wishes, if there had not been grave reasons for my acting otherwise; and you shall judge of them yourself."

"I never doubted you, Alice."

"Thank you. And I feared to give you a momentary hope which might soon be found a mere illusion. It was for this reason that I so long kept silence."

"What do you mean?" cried Charles.

"I fear that if I tell you plainly what I know and what I think I know, you may conceive hopes which a single word will perhaps destroy."

"Go on, for heaven's sake!"

"Mr. Ned Bark," said Alice, turning to the detective, "you are acquainted with the southern coast of Florida?"

"Yes, Miss Lodier. I can affirm that there is not a single creek or opening which is not well known to me."

"Then tell me—speak freely. Have you ever heard of a place which is called . . ."

She hesitated, as if she feared a negative answer from the American.

"Go on," said Ned Bark. "I think I know every place on the coast. And yet, in the midst of so many out-of-the-way names, one may have escaped my memory."

Alice conquered her emotion, which proceeded simply from the feeling of fear that we have mentioned; made an effort and continued in a grave tone—

"Do you know a place on the coast called Devil's Rock?"

"Devil's Rock!" exclaimed Ned Bark. "Certainly; and all the coasters along Florida know it too: an enormous cliff, which in foggy weather is almost lost in clouds."

"Ah! Devil's Rock does exist, then?" said Alice, with a cry of joy.

"Does it exist! Go and ask the ships which have

been dashed against that rock by the high tides and destructive tempests of the Atlantic! Too often those who do not know it learn its existence in their latest hour!"

"It is a dangerous rock, then?"

"Devil's Rock," said Ned Bark, "derives its name not only from the imposing majesty of its gloomy form as it rises above the waves, but also from a special characteristic which makes it the terror of those who navigate the seas in its vicinity."

"Go on! go on!" murmured Alice, whose face expressed deep perplexity.

"Well! the Devil's Rock stands on the coast, about twenty miles from here, and is a great black mass. You, Doctor Freedy, who have travelled in America, you have seen the sombre ravines of our Black Forest, on each side of which rise enormous walls of rock? One of the rocks of which this Devil's Rock is composed looks like a gigantic monolith: the other, only like a detached portion of it. But what seems to us so strange is that in calm weather Devil's Rock appears to be more than a mile inland; but when the sea is high, the water gains on the earth more rapidly than in the highest tide, and rolls up, dashing and foaming to the very base of these rocks. More than one cutter has been seized by this inexplicable whirlpool and dashed to pieces against Devil's Rock! The rising sun has too often shone down upon broken spars and mangled human bodies at the foot of the cliff. I know this for a certainty. That is why I tell you that Devil's Rock is perhaps the most dangerous spot upon the coast of Florida."

"But why do you ask for this information, dear Alice?" cried Valville. "Do not play with my impatience! If you only knew the fever that consumes me!"

"Dear Charles," said Alice, "do not think that I act in this manner without good reason. I want to preserve you from sorrow, that is to say, from disappointed hopes. And that is why, if Mr. Bark will allow me, I will ask him another question."

"I am at your orders, miss," said the detective, bowing.

"Listen, and, before answering me, consider that upon your reply depends the whole campaign on which you have entered against the enemies of Mr. Valville's father—of him whom I also should have called my father!"

"Speak, miss."

"Could the rock of which you speak be used as a refuge for robbers?"

"Certainly," replied Ned Bark. "As I have explored almost all this part of the country, I know that the ocean has hollowed out caverns in the very heart of the cliff. I cannot call them subterranean places, as some of these retreats are a hundred feet above the level of the sea, but there are holes, vaults, grottoes—I can answer for that."

"Then I may speak," said Alice. "But forgive me, Charles," she added, turning to Valville; "I would not for the whole world have aroused in you hopes that were only to be dashed to the ground."

"Go on!"

"It is not I who will speak."

So saying, Alice took from her pocket-book a letter which she handed to Valville.

"I came," she said, "to bring you this letter from your sister. Read it, but, I beg you, weigh every word carefully, and, above all, be calm."

Valville was very pale. In his young and essentially sensitive nature all emotions assumed singular keenness. Alice knew him well when she refused to speak until she was sure that the story which she had brought him might at least possibly be true.

Charles took the letter with a trembling hand, and for some moments gazed at it as if he doubted whether his own name, there inscribed, had indeed been written by his sister's hand.

At last, upon an energetic sign from Ned Bark, he made an effort and broke the seal. His eyes were dim, and he was obliged to draw his hand across his forehead before he could decipher the characters, traced as they were in singularly large and clear handwriting.

"The best plan would be to read it aloud," said Ned Bark; "if, at least, Miss Lodier will allow us to do so," he interrupted himself, turning to Alice.

"You are right," she said. "In that manner you can all judge, and decide with more certainty as to the measures which ought to be taken."

"I will read it," said Valville.

He made a great effort to prevent his voice from trembling, and began the letter.

"Dear brother," Lucile's letter began, "another will bring you the news which I was the first to hear. But my wound has not yet healed, and gives me far too much pain at present to allow me to think of joining you."

"The ruffians!" murmured Freedy with compressed lips.

Valville imposed silence on him with a gesture, and then continued to read:—

"But I know that she whom you have chosen for your companion is brave, and that you love her with all your heart. It is to her then that I entrust these lines, certain that I cannot place them in better hands.

"I will tell you in detail all that happened. For before launching out on an adventurous expedition, where your life and the lives of our friends would be in danger, you should be able to weigh for yourselves every reason for and against it."

At the words 'our friends' Freedy smiled in spite of himself.

Doctor Freedy was a man of essentially phlegmatic temperament. But there is a time when almost every man, however impassible he may think himself to be, is conquered by an emotion which takes possession of his whole being.

Thus Freedy, sceptical and impassive as he pretended to be, had lately discovered that he loved with all his soul the young girl who had proved herself so pure and so simple in her heroism, whom he had first met at her father's house, and had not seen again until the moment when, after a miraculous escape from a horrible death, she had forgotten herself in thought for those she loved.

"This is what has happened," began Charles, as he continued to read his sister's letter. "Every day we expected some letter or telegram from you, to tell us that you were at last on the track of the wretches whom you were pursuing, and that above all—oh! above everything—you had some hope of finding our dearest Jeanne. Even when the postman's hour had long passed by, I could not make up my mind to despair, and waited on and on! Yesterday, almost ill with fever, which proceeded rather from over-excitement than from my own physical weakness, I could not sleep; and, wishing to cool my burning head, I opened the window which fronts the cascade at the end of the park.

"The moon shone brilliantly, and through the cactus and magnolia groves I could easily distinguish the smallest turnings in the paths, while my ears were filled with the monotonous sound made by the water as it dashed upon the rocks.

"Suddenly I started. It seemed to me that I heard a footstep upon the ground below. I do not think I am timid, but since the terrible events which terminated in my father's death and in Jeanne's disappearance, I have often found myself trembling, and unable to conquer a feeling of uncalled-for terror. My voice seemed to die away in my throat. I bent forward and gazed in silence. Suddenly I saw—though at first I thought it was a mere fancy on my part—a black form appear from behind one of the clumps of trees. I was nailed to my place with terror, and could neither move nor say a single word. The shadow approached—crawling—dragging itself, until it was almost close to the house. At that moment, though scarcely able to articulate, I managed to call out, 'Who goes there?' The form stopped suddenly, and, to my great surprise, I saw that it knelt down and extended its hands in the direction from which my voice proceeded. No mistake was possible; the unknown had assumed a suppliant attitude; and, moreover—I could hardly believe it, and yet I was sure that I could not be mistaken—the man staggered as though he were at the very point of death.

"It never occurred to me that I might fall into a trap. I do not know what instinct told me that I ought to go straight to the stranger; that he had come in order to speak to me in private; but as rapidly as possible I stole out of my room, descended the stairs, and gained the park. The man had made only a few steps forward. When he heard the sound of my steps, he raised his head, and I saw his face very plainly by the light of the moon.

"I could scarcely repress a cry of surprise and also terror, for I recognised a negro, once set free by my father, named Biji, who had disappeared with the assassins of Battle Field.

" He recognised me also, for he touched his forehead in token of respect.

" 'Missis,' he said, 'come to me, pray. I am dying, but I must speak first.'

"'What do you want with me?' I asked shortly. 'How is it you dare to appear at this place again? you, an accomplice of my father's murderers!'

"'Yes, I am a villain,' he said. 'And you cannot forgive me—yet I tell you I am dying—have pity on me, and I repeat it, listen to what I have come to say. I have come to tell you where Miss Jeanne is. . . .'

"At this name all my doubt and terror disappeared.

"'Jeanne!' I exclaimed. 'Oh, speak! and if you do not deceive me I will pity you.'

"'It is indeed the truth which you will soon know.'

"He had sunk to the earth, and I now saw that he was trying to raise himself in order to lean against the trunk of a tree.

"I helped him, and he thanked me.

"'You are good,' he said. 'I did well to come.'

"'You say that you are dying. What is the matter with you?'

"'Look here,' said the negro, and he lifted his hands to his head, and parted the thick tufts of his woolly hair.

"I leaned over him and shuddered. The poor man's head was laid open in a gaping red wound.

"'But who wounded you so terribly?'

"'Who? The ruffian, the robber, the coward—Red Ralph himself.'

"And over the negro's face passed a convulsive grin of fury and vengeance.

"'Speak!' I cried.

"'I will, missis. Yes, it is true that this man came

to the plantation; he promised if we would help him that we should have plenty of money, enough to let us live without working—the dream of us poor negroes, you know—help him to carry off Miss Jeanne. He did not speak of murder; he swore that no blood should be shed; I and several of my companions consented to listen to him. You know the rest; but I swear that I myself never touched a hair of your father's head!'

"'Go on,' I said, 'I believe you.'

"'The young lady was carried off, and we rode fast all night. We were guided by Indians, Seminoles, with Bloody Foot at their head. There was Sam Dorry, the New Orleans thief, and Phil Samster, who set fire to the Docks. Long, very long, we remained at a distance from any inhabited place—it matters little how we reached the borders of Florida at last.'

"'But Jeanne, my sister!' I exclaimed. 'Did she not sink under such frightful fatigue?'

"'No, no; do not be alarmed. Ah! she is a brave girl! really, it seemed sometimes as though Red Ralph were in her power. He trembled before her; she spoke plainly, she insulted him; he bent his head and did not answer. Still we had to watch every moment to prevent her escape; at night we built a hut for her, into which Ralph never dared penetrate, but round which we kept strict guard. At last we came to the St. John's River, and followed its course along the western bank as far as Pilatka, where we turned; and from that spot we entered upon ravines only known to the Indians, where it seemed as if no human being had ever trod before us. We thus arrived at the foot of a rock on the seashore. We were astonished, and could not understand the aim of our journey when our guides began to climb the rock by an almost perpendicular pathway. Between the clefts in the rock trunks of trees had been thrown to form bridges, on which one could scarcely stand upright; and finally, at more than a hundred feet above the sea, we entered a series of natural caverns, which had long served as hiding-places to the bandits. It was there that your sister was detained. We guarded her by relays, day after day. In vain did Red Ralph—we heard him distinctly—beg her to listen to him, to submit to him; always disdainful, always self-possessed, she repulsed him with contemptuous words. I have been very guilty! yet, little by little, repentance gained upon me; I admired and pitied the girl who had never done me harm, and for whom the danger grew greater day by day.'

" He stopped, and fell into a sort of swoon. I ran to the cascade, brought him some water in the hollow of my hand, and bathed his temples with it. He revived, and thanked me with a smile, which sat strangely on the pale lips of a dying man.

" ' One night,' he continued, ' I saw Red Ralph steal towards that part of the cave where your sister was sleeping. It was I who watched, gun in hand, with orders to kill her if she tried to escape. What happened I do not know, but suddenly I heard a cry for help! Obeying my better instincts I rushed forward; I seized Red Ralph by the throat, and threw him backwards on the ground.

How it was I did not kill him I do not know; but a few moments later I was dragged off by the others—by those who had been my accomplices. They pushed me to the verge of the cliff which overhung the abyss, and there they threw me down—a frightful fall! I felt the sharp corners of the rock cut my flesh—then came a last shock—then nothing more. How many hours I passed in that swoon I cannot tell. But when I came to myself I swore to repair the evil I had done. I swore to avenge myself upon Red Ralph; and, dizzy as I was, staggering like a drunken man, I set off—it is a miracle that I got here at all—but here I am! and I tell you, Miss Lucile, you must go to your sister's help; she must be saved.'

"'But the rock that you speak of, where is it? what is its name?'

"'It is called Devil's Rock,' he answered.

"In an hour Biji was dead. I told everything to Mr. Woodman and to our dear Alice; and as Mr. Woodman could not just then leave the plantation, and as I felt that I myself was too weak to brave the fatigues of the expedition, fearing that I should be a burden, and not a help, to you, I was in despair, until your Alice, Charles, accepted—nay, claimed the mission.

"What more shall I say, my dear brother? With all my heart I pray for you and for Jeanne. Have confidence and courage; and in the midst of danger, let you and yours not forget poor Lucile, who grieves so much at her absence from you all."

The reading of this letter was followed by a long

silence. All eyes were moist, all hearts touched by Lucile's simple words.

Eusèbe was the first to recover the use of his tongue.

"Well, she's been carried off, that is certain," he said. "Don't stop to think about it; let us find the said rock. It will be a nice affair! we shall have a hot time of it."

"What do you say, Ned Bark?" asked Freedy.

"What I say is, that the little one"—it was thus that he designated Eusèbe—"that the little one is right. Before forty-eight hours have passed we ought to be heading an attack on Devil's Rock."

"You know how to get there quickly?"

"I'll answer for that."

"Then let us go," said Charles. "And here I swear either to save my sister or to die for her!"

CHAPTER XV.

THE CRUSTACEAN.

IT was not easy to find at St. Augustine a vessel ready to start for the southern coast of Florida. The fishing-boats had already set out, and a week might elapse before their return.

Freedy and Valville were in despair, for well they knew that with each hour the danger increased. Half the day had already passed, when Ned Bark re-entered the hotel with a business-like air.

"Up with you!" he cried. "I can manage it."

"At last!" said Charles, springing up with a cry of joy.

"But one remark beforehand," said Ned. "I have had to play a part, and you must bear me out in it."

"What do you mean?" asked Freedy. "It is an understood thing that we do not wish to let strangers into our secret."

"Oh, if it were only that! But the schooner which I have discovered is not an ordinary one, particularly as regards the captain."

"Explain."

"This is the state of the case. As I explored the harbour, and questioned the sailors, one after the other,

I found at last a schooner, somewhat heavily built, but strong and fairly good for speed. Two or three men on the deck seemed to be making the last arrangements before setting sail. I asked what was their destination. They seemed amused at my question, but I repeated it. 'Where we are going?' said one of the sailors. 'If you want to know that, you must ask the master.' 'Who is he?' 'A fool.' Of course I did not content myself with that answer; and these are the facts which I gathered at last. The schooner, the 'Tortoise,' belongs to an Englishman, an eccentric naturalist, chemist, and physiologist, who, with three pupils, as little used to a seafaring life as himself, has been exploring the coasts of Florida for the last six months, in order to discover some animal or other which he wants for his collection. He has already spent thousands of dollars, and is ready to spend as many more; for he is, it appears, immensely rich, and is just setting off for the eighteenth time in the last twelvemonth to explore the coast as far as the Gulf of Mexico. After which, if he has not succeeded—if he has not found his monster, a sort of crab, I think—he will come back, quite ready to set off again in a fortnight."

"He may be a fool or not," said Charles; "at any rate he is a zealous servant of science. But will he consent to take us on board?"

"That is the question. But there is one way . . . "

"What?"

"You must pretend to share the good fellow's tastes.

I suppose you are both quite well able to play the part of scientific men ; you must go and see him and persuade him that you can help him in his efforts. When once we are off, we shall easily find means of making him stop at Devil's Rock."

"But if he should refuse ?"

"One must always be ready to take one's chance."

"Do you think that there is any likelihood of inducing him to take us on board ?"

"Yes, for I ventured upon the little fable that I have just mentioned to you, and he answered that if you had the same aim in view as himself he would have no objection to your company."

"Let us go and see him," said Charles resolutely. "Freedy, you may do the talking; Nature has no secrets for you."

"And I ?" said Eusèbe, "what am I to do ?"

"Come with us," said Valville.

"I shall have to pass for your pupil, the assistant head-cook and bottle-washer !"

This arrangement being made, the three men, directed by Ned Bark, proceeded to the street where the naturalist resided.

Of our three travellers, two—Charles and Freedy—at least, might have appeared to be well steeled against any emotion or surprise. But they were not prepared for the sight which awaited them when they were ushered into a so-called study in which the naturalist, whose name was Cartwright, very politely received them.

The room was flagged and sanded, and the floor was nearly covered by scores of living creatures of the most curious shapes, which crawled forward, sideways, backward, climbed one over the other, stretched out their claws, and entangled them with those of their neighbours; fought combats that Homer might have sung, and engaged in frightful battles that were worthy of an Iliad, with strange sounds of gliding and cracking of shells and scales. Round the room ran a shallow tank in which other guests were eating, sleeping, or fighting their lives away.

In the midst of this inferno of crabs—which Dante left undescribed—stood a crooked hunchbacked man, with a skin of parchment, and arms that were curiously like antennæ : a veritable crab in human shape, with great prominent eyes that seemed to be starting out of his head.

Eusèbe was livid with horror. This army of crustaceans seemed to him like a nightmare.

Cartwright had a crab in his left hand, a crab on his right leg, and a crab on his shoulder. In his right hand he held a magnifying-glass with which he had been examining the animal, that lay on its back, and held up its claws in the air as if in sign of protest.

"What is it you wish?" asked Cartwright of Freedy.

The doctor had already recovered his self-possession. Then, to Eusèbe's ever-growing surprise, he plunged into the midst of this chaos of crustaceans with a truly heroic courage ; and, taking the tone of a professor, he addressed the naturalist in a speech worthy of a scientific association.

"I see before me at last," he said, "a man who recognises how much there is of true beauty and grandeur in the study of brachyural decapods. I honour you; for here, sir, is the future of science, here the secret of nature. Yes," he added, uplifting one of the monstrous creatures, that flapped its claws wildly in the air, " here we may indeed behold the lobed crab of the Antilles, and there the rose-coloured crab of the Red Sea. And this one—what a splendid creature! Is it not an Australian crab? And surely, I do not deceive myself! What, sir, you have got an ocypodian, a gecarcinus, the robber, and the violet crabs! Would that I could give its weight in gold for this precious collection!"

The worthy Cartwright was in the seventh heaven of ecstasy. He regarded with a softened look his Pandemonium of crustacea. He smiled at the gelasimus, and made eyes at the gecarcinus.

Freedy was eloquent. Learnedly he set forth the reasons for his enthusiasm. The crab, rather than the retort of a chemist, contained within itself the true secret of creation! Even if one deprived it of its limbs, the amputated members would grow again! The crab was the king of animals; the crab was in fact divine!

He discoursed so long and so well that the man of crabs all but seized him in his arms—I nearly said his claws—and embraced him in delight. Freedy was then a fellow-student of crustacean lore? What did he want? Would he like a specimen of the rarer kinds?

"No, I have come to ask if you will allow us to share your labours and become your pupils."

"These gentlemen, then," said Cartwright, looking at Valville and Eusèbe, "have also been initiated into the mysteries. . . . "

At this very moment Eusèbe became conscious that two pointed claws were penetrating the skin of his ankle.   He had, nevertheless, the strength of mind to smile like a Spartan and reply :

"I? Oh, I have always been fond of crab !"

Cartwright's resistance to Freedy's proposition was not of long duration, more particularly as Freedy's next piece of information overbore all his objections.

"They tell me," he whispered, "that you are looking for a little-known species—may I hear what it is?"

The naturalist shuddered slightly, and laid his hand over his eyes.

"You recall the memory of one of my sorrows, gentlemen," he murmured in a mournful tone.   "For three years I have sought the spinomanus."

"The spinomanus!" exclaimed Freedy, "that is the crab with prickly claws, connected with the acanthus!"

"What! you know it?"

"We were at school together!" said Eusèbe in a low voice aside, with a furtive kick at the imprudent crustacean which had attacked his heel.

"Do I know it?" said Freedy.   "Ah, Mr. Cartwright, how mysterious are the ways of Providence!"

"Tell me," said the naturalist, with a gasp.

"Sir, the spinomanus may be found a few miles from

St. Augustine, upon the coast, at the foot of a high cliff, popularly known as Devil's Rock."

"Great heavens! Let us start at once."

Freedy had gained the victory.

An hour later they all embarked on board the 'Tortoise.' Cartwright was so preoccupied that even when the six friends appeared—for Alice, Ned Bark, and Sambo had been added to the party—he never dreamt of feeling surprised that so many crab-lovers existed in the world! Sambo and Ned Bark hastened to bestow themselves in the hold of the schooner, in order to escape notice. Alice wore a dark dress, and was enveloped in a long cloak, which covered her whole figure.

At last the word of departure was given. The schooner was not built for speed, but it was of very solid construction. Freedy was already on intimate terms with Cartwright, who reposed every confidence in him, and, as his acquaintance with nautical matters was not large, soon committed the management of the schooner to his new friend.

The boat, under skilful handling, made rapid way through the deep waters of the Gulf of Mexico.

Our friends were too anxious and in too great haste to attain their end to pay much attention to the fine scenery which they passed along the coast of Florida. Eusèbe was inexpressibly disgusted when once, in the middle of a meal, Cartwright calmly placed a jelly-fish upon his plate and examined it through a magnifying-glass.

In twenty hours from their departure the travellers found themselves near Devil's Rock. Night had fallen, and in spite of their impatience they were forced to wait till daybreak before disembarking.

They were also obliged to use great precaution, as there was a heavy sea, and the ship might easily have been wrecked upon the enormous rocks that frowned upon the coast.

At last the little band landed upon a narrow strip of earth, above which frowned the gigantic masses of the Devil's Rock.

But when they gazed at the colossal wall of stone, cleft in twain by a great fissure, through which the waves dashed with a sound like thunder, it seemed to them a veritable madness to dream of attacking the bandits in their stronghold.

Where, moreover, could they find the robbers? In what direction should they go? Even to climb that rugged cliff appeared impossible!

And what was worse than anything to bear was Cartwright's despair when our friends were obliged to confess that they had tricked him, and that they had not the shadow of a wish to hunt the spinomanus.

Fortunately, the naturalist was a good-natured man, and a brave one too.

"Good heavens!" he said, when he heard their story, "then you cheated me? You shan't have the laugh against me, however!"

"What do you mean?"

"I mean that I'll join your party; the crabs can wait. I put myself and my companions at your disposal; and if it comes to a bit of fighting, well, I'll prove to you that one may be rather mad, and not want for courage or resolution either."

"I will find you the crab you seek!" exclaimed Freedy, with a burst of feeling. "I give you my word I will."

"First let us find the young lady," sighed the naturalist, who was now somewhat doubtful of his friend's good faith.

Meanwhile, Valville and Ned Bark had set out on a reconnoitering expedition. In order to escape notice from their enemies, they explored the base of the rock as stealthily as possible, clinging to the trunks of scattered trees, or to projecting pieces of granite ; for they felt sure that a footpath must somewhere exist that would lead them to the robbers' cave.

The rest of the party hid themselves in a sort of grotto, which seemed to have been hollowed out by the action of the sea, and waited.

We have already said that day had scarcely dawned. The place seemed deserted ; no sound could be heard but that produced by the breaking of the waves upon the rocks ; a dull and dreary resonance re-echoed from the barren shore.

Suddenly Ned Bark stopped and turned to Valville.

"Up there, look !" he said.

At the same time, with the stick which had served to support his steps upon the slippery pathway, he pointed out to the young man a fissure in the rock, now gilded by the rays of early morning.

"Do you not see there," he said, "something like men's forms which seem to be ascending the cliff?"

"Indeed I do; and now they look as if they were hanging in mid-air, which shows that a ladder or staircase must exist there, and that they are mounting it."

Soon they could doubt no longer; there could be no mistake. The robbers were evidently returning to their hiding-place, and the travellers were at any rate on their track.

The two men returned hurriedly to their friends.

But as they approached they heard a cry. It was Eusèbe's voice.

"Ah, poor boy!" exclaimed Valville, "what misfortune can have happened to him now?"

In a few seconds they reached the cave, where they saw Sambo on the point of throwing himself into the sea, Eusèbe, always rash, had strayed beyond the border of stones which guarded the entrance to the grotto, and had then slipped and almost disappeared in a hole full of water. But Sambo at once jumped after him, and succeeded in bringing the young man to the surface.

"Sapristi!" cried Eusèbe, as he clambered up the bank, "that was a jump! Aie! whatever is that?"

"That" was something that had attached itself to his trousers, a something which was driving its claws into the fleshy portion of his leg.

But a second cry responded to his own.

"It's he! it's he! Oh, what luck! The spino-manus!"

And a strong hand detached an enormous crab from

Eusèbe's trousers, together with a piece of the material of which they were composed.

In an ecstasy of enthusiastic delight Cartwright continued to exclaim—

"Yes, the spinomanus indeed! Oh, eternal bounty of Providence!"

Freedy had not deceived him after all, and the valiant naturalist, energetically brandishing his gun, declared that he could now die in peace!

For he had got the spinomanus! In two minutes the very ugly creature was enclosed in a tin case, and confided to the care of one of Cartwright's pupils, who received it with the veneration usually accorded by a neophyte to a relic.

Ned Bark and Valville gave an account of what they had seen. Their plan of action was soon decided upon. The little troop was separated into two parties. Ned Bark, Freedy, Valville, and Cartwright were to scale the ladder; while Eusèbe, Sambo, Alice, and the naturalist's pupils were to keep guard lest the robbers should escape them.

"Alice," said Valville, taking the girl's hand, "we are near the decisive moment. If I die, I confide to you the care of those whom I love."

"You will live, Charles; I know, I feel you will. Our cause is just, and your sister will be restored to us."

"Forward!" said Freedy.

At first the two groups marched side by side, seeking for some suitable spot for the disposition of their reserve corps.

"Look," said Alice suddenly, "is that not a path-way ?"

And certainly upon the side of the rock they could distinguish a winding outline.

"Well, you had better wait here," said Ned Bark. "Although that path seems to be almost impracticable, the ruffians will perhaps try to escape by it. Hide your-selves behind that point of rock, and there, gun in hand, wait for us. And now—Heaven help us all !"

The four friends regained the spot which they had searched a short time before. They began immediately to climb the rock, directing their course towards the ladders, which they could now distinguish much more clearly.

CHAPTER XVI.

As we have said, the four persons who had entered upon this perilous road were Ned Bark, Freedy, Valville, and the crab-lover Cartwright.

The two first-mentioned preceded the others.

"Ned," said Freedy, "this is no doubt the decisive moment.   Do you augur well of our enterprise?"

The detective shook his head.

"To tell the truth," he said, "I have lost my bearings. My much-bepraised acuteness is all at fault.   We have to do with so extraordinary a criminal!"

"What do you mean?"

"Did you not hear Miss Lucile's story as well as myself?"

"Well?"

"Well! did you not notice that just where we thought we had to do simply with political foes, avenging imaginary grievances on Mr. Valville, we were encountered by a strange wild passion, complicated by incredible weakness on the part of a man who has never hitherto recoiled from any sort of crime?"

"You mean Red Ralph?"

" Exactly so.   You know this man belongs to a very good family, and although his insatiable ambition has dragged him far down the road of crime, I think that there is still a spark of noble feeling in him."

" But what has that to do with it ? "

" It shows that we have no common adversary to deal with, and I doubt whether we shall succeed as quickly as we had hoped."

By this time the little party had reached the foot of the cliff, and its members were attentively gazing at the ladders of which we have spoken.

It seemed almost impossible to set foot upon them, placed as they were upon a dizzy height, from which they seemed to lose themselves in the distance.

By what means could they be attained?

Some time elapsed in fruitless search for the means of ascent.   At last Cartwright, who for some time had been making the neighbouring rocks resound beneath repeated taps of his geological hammer, exclaimed suddenly—

" It sounds hollow.   There is a cavern here."

"So be it!" said Ned.   "But where is the entrance ? "

" We can look for it."

And Cartwright persisted in affirming that upon the level of the first stratum of the rocks they would find the opening of a sort of natural tunnel.   And he supported his opinion by pointing out the fact that a stream of water issued at that point from the very heart of the rock.

" Understand me," he said.   "I am quite sure that

there is an opening up there, and that through that opening our enemies reach the ladders which we can see."

"Then what do you think we ought to do?"

" Climb up to the point from which the stream gushes out; once there, we can consult about our next movements."

"Come along then."

The method proposed by the crab-lover was certainly not easy to put into practice. As no beaten track existed, they were obliged to scale the rugged cliffs by means of jutting rocks or trunks of trees to which they clung, hanging at times above the abyss into which the slightest false step would have precipitated them.

Happily the four men were strong and agile, and the naturalist was not the least vigorous of the four. The strength of his arms was extraordinary. He clambered over the slippery stones in exactly the fashion of those decapods whom he had made his lifelong study—so true is it that men identify themselves at last with the creatures in whose habits they take continual interest.

As they were obliged to choose in their dangerous ascent only the points which offered some support for their hands and feet, they deviated little by little from the course which they had meant to take.

They lost sight of the opening whence the torrent issued, and which they thought might be the entrance of the cavern. Still they did not lose heart, but climbed on and on.

At last they emerged upon a sort of open plateau.

Valville, in his impatience, had scaled a rock which seemed almost inaccessible. Ned Bark was just behind him.

Charles advanced to the overhanging edge of the precipice and called out:

"Ned, don't let the others come up!"

"What can you see?" asked the detective.

"I can see the stream which we noticed before; its source is obstructed by a great heap of wood."

"Let me see too," said Ned Bark.

And with marvellous courage, the detective—who, when the bargain was made at the plantation, had taken the risk of death into account—by the help of a bare pine-tree which lay upon the cliff and extended far beyond it into space, lay down, crept out as far as he could, and bent over the abyss.

"You are right," he said to Charles, as he drew himself back.

He made a speaking-trumpet of his two hands, and shouted loudly to Freedy and Cartwright. Their voices answered him, saying that they could hear.

"Go no farther," he said. "Turn to your right, and you will find a sort of natural staircase cut in the face of the rock. There: you have got it; now climb!"

The two men obeyed his instructions. They thus reached a ridge of rock exactly opposite a large dark hole, to which, however, as Valville had said, entrance was forbidden by the mass of trunks and branches piled before it.

The ridge of rock was so narrow and so slippery that it was almost impossible to stand erect upon it.

" Wait ! " cried Ned. And he called to Valville, who hastened to rejoin him.

Ned, always prudent, had compelled each of the travellers to provide himself with a long stout cord, which he wore coiled round the waist.

" This is what we had better do," said the detective· " We will throw these ropes down to them, so that they can fasten them to their own. And while we hold them fast, they can throw down those trunks of trees into the stream below, and thus force an entrance for us all."

Cartwright, accustomed to dangerous expeditions, had already thought of a similar plan. Once more climbing to the summit of the rock from which they had descended when they turned towards the ridge, he fastened two ropes to some trees which grew there. He then tied himself and Freedy together at their belts.

And when Ned and Valville had lowered the ropes with which they also were provided, Cartwright and Freedy were so securely fastened and supported that a fall was hardly possible.

" Now to work ! " said Freedy.

He had thrown off his coat, and his sinewy form displayed itself in all its vigour beneath his well-fitting woollen shirt.

" You content yourself with directing the course of the wood," he said to Cartwright, " while I move it."

Then, seizing an enormous branch, he plunged it into the midst of the heap of wood, and, leaning forward, gave it a tremendous shake. The weight to be removed was immense. But beneath a graceful exterior, Freedy concealed perfectly Herculean strength.

Beneath repeated thrusts the mass began to give way.

" Have a care, Cartwright ! " he cried.

And the great branches, sliding and twisting, lost their balance and fell into the torrent. A frightful overthrow, a gigantic ruin then was seen. The pieces of wood dashed against the rocks and again rebounded, awakening in their fall a thousand echoes which seemed to resound throughout the whole extent of the mountain heights.

A dozen times was Freedy almost caught in the falling mass. A dozen times, at the risk of his own life, did Cartwright turn aside the course of the falling branch that might have crushed him; and in half an hour the ridge was clear from all obstruction, and before it yawned the fissure in the rock.

" Hurrah ! " cried Freedy. " Now, come down, Ned and Valville, and let us boldly penetrate the depths of this inferno."

In an instant Ned and Charles were at his side.

Before they entered the cavern, Freedy said to the detective in a low voice :

" We are going to the unknown ; for, to all appearance, this is not the way ordinarily used by the bandits."

" So much the better ; we shall surprise them the more easily."

" Heaven grant it ! " said Freedy, shaking his head.

They secured the ropes once more around their waists, and took up their guns, as well as the torches with which Ned had furnished them.

"Forward !" said Valville.

The torches were lighted, and the four friends plunged into the darkness of the cavern.

Cartwright had rightly inferred the existence of a cavern. The course of the torrent soon diverged and left the way free. But had this opening any other way of issue ?

The slippery ground beneath their feet rose gently. By the smoky light of their torches they could see that the roof of the cavern was of considerable height. They could walk upright with ease; but as they advanced, and the ground still continued to rise, they were obliged to stoop, and finally to creep forward upon their hands and knees. Ned went first, backwards, with his torch held close to the ground, in order to give light to his companions. The air grew thick and foul, yet none of them dreamed of turning back.

But suddenly Ned's course was stayed. The cavern seemed to be completely closed by a wall of rock. After so many efforts they had traversed only a blind alley. At this point the roof was higher, and they recovered some freedom of movement.

But in vain they lighted their torches and gazed about them : the granite wall presented no way of issue.

"We have gone too far," said Ned. "Some cross-passage must have escaped us."

"Let us go back," said Freedy philosophically.

After several moments' consultation the friends agreed that this was their only resource. They would not be discouraged. They had resolved beforehand to sacrifice their lives rather than leave the mysteries of Devil's Rock still unexplained.

But just as they were about to retrace their steps Ned cried suddenly—

"Silence ! Listen !"

And, curiously enough, they heard, at apparently an immense distance, the sound of voices. It seemed at first as if they issued from the very bowels of the earth; yet, by degrees, the sounds became more and more distinct.

The four men listened with feverish anxiety. Whence did these sounds proceed?

Cartwright, who never lost an opportunity of displaying his scientific knowledge, was already whispering an explanation of a phenomenon not unfrequently encountered in mountain-sides.

The rocks themselves transmitted sounds, often to a very great distance. The friends listened accordingly, and suddenly distinguished amidst the echoes the sound of a woman's voice.

"It is Jeanne's voice !" cried Valville, dashing himself like a madman against the wall.

The voice was high and vibrating. Although it was impossible to distinguish the words that were spoken, it was certain that they did not consist of cries for help or exclamations of terror. Their accent was imperious, almost solemn ; but another voice—a man's voice— responded in threatening tones.

"I would risk my life to save my sister!" cried Charles. "Oh, let us not lose a minute! It may be our last chance!"

Possessed by the same idea, they hastened along the passage. Before very long Ned cried—

"There is the opening! Down there!"

And upon their left hand they saw a long passage, the entrance to which had been so well concealed by a projecting piece of rock that they had passed by without noticing it.

This passage was so narrow that they were obliged to go in single file.

This time Cartwright went first. He walked on hurriedly, expecting every moment to be brought up by some unassailable wall of rock.

The passage seemed to be a winding one. How long the minutes were to the four men! They heard nothing more, and yet they could not doubt but that Jeanne was in danger. She was there—at only a few steps' distance, perhaps—and they might arrive too late.

Valville's blood seemed to turn to ice in his veins at the very thought.

At last Cartwright exclaimed—

"Daylight! I can see daylight!"

And in fact a band of light could be seen at some distance from them beyond the shadows of the rocks. Pushing aside the naturalist, Charles sprang towards the opening. His friends saw him raise his gun to his shoulder, and almost immediately the sound of a shot rang through the cavern.

Ned joined him.

"What is it?" he asked.

"Look there! the ladders!"

They were now above the great fissure in the rocks where the curious rope ladders were suspended which they had noticed that morning; and through a sort of fog they could dimly distinguish upon them certain human forms which seemed to be trying to escape.

"Don't fire!" cried Freedy. "You forget that your ball might strike your sister!"

He had forgotten that! Fully sure that the bandits were before him, he had fired, and seen one dark figure lose its hold and fall into the abyss.

Freedy's words awoke a frightful fear within him.

But without more delay the four friends began to descend the mountain-slope. They wished to reach the ladders at all risks, although it seemed as if everything had fallen back into its primitive condition of solitude and silence. Rapidly they made their way onwards till they arrived at a sort of amphitheatre hollowed out of the bare rock; before them stood a grotto, like the entrance to some magician's palace—a majestic-looking place of great size, supported on pillars that looked like bronze.

The four men entered it unhesitatingly.

They reached first a great hall, of prodigious height, in the middle of which a fire was still burning, as if to attest the recent presence of the robbers.

Beyond the hall the grotto was divided into a number of apartments, separated one from another by doors adorned with hanging mats. In any other circumstances this retreat might have excited admiration, so beautifully had it been shaped by nature's hand.

Furious and desperate, Valville searched the rooms, calling loudly upon his sister's name. But no voice replied.

Followed by Ned, he entered at last a room which had evidently been furnished with some attempt at elegance. Silk hangings hid the walls; plaited mats, prettily arranged, formed a bed and seats; in the middle of the room a bamboo table supported a lamp, still alight.

"Look!" cried Charles, sadly.

Upon this table an unfinished piece of needlework lay in a work-basket. Doubt was now impossible. It was there indeed that Jeanne, his beloved sister, had been held prisoner. It was there indeed that her wretched lover had tormented her. It was thence that he had dragged her but a few moments earlier!

And she had escaped her brother's pursuit!

"But I will follow them!" cried Charles, almost beside himself with grief.

"Wait," said Ned Bark.

Guided by his keen instinct, the detective had at once set to work carefully to inspect every corner of the room, and he had just discovered on the ground a crumpled piece of paper, as if the girl, suddenly surprised, had thrown it away from her to let it fall where it would. Half of it had been torn away, but these lines still remained visible—

" I await
have been able so far
keeps me in his power
are seeking me ; he knows
rescue his victim.   He will take me
overheard a few words interchanged between
he spoke of a
Louisiana
to understand
to Wood   help !"

And that was all !

In another moment the four friends had quitted the cavern, where all research was now useless.

An easy road led them to the rope ladder.

' But there a new disappointment awaited them.   The fugitives had severed the ropes with blows from their hatchets.   Their last hope was wrested from them.   And Jeanne remained in the bandit's power !

It was with great difficulty that Valville and his companions regained the friends who were waiting for them. And even there they found only new sources of anxiety.

Nothing had been seen.   Not one of the robbers had shown himself.   But this was not all.   Imprudent as ever, Eusèbe had quitted the little band more than an hour ago, and had not since returned.

In vain they searched the mountain-side ; in vain they called his name !   Eusèbe had disappeared.

CHAPTER XVII.

THE RETURN.

THE fragment of a letter found by Ned Bark and Valville in the grotto which had served as poor Jeanne's prison, though to a great extent incomprehensible, seemed yet to convey some information which had to be taken into account.

The letter was written in French.

Doubtless the bandits who were Red Ralph's accomplices did not understand this language, which was probably the reason why the captive had chosen it, in order to hide from them the object of so important a message.

The question which first presented itself was this: Why had Jeanne written these lines at all? It was an imprudent action, which could not be explained except on the supposition that she thought herself able to count upon the help of a messenger.

Perhaps pity had entered the heart even of some of these wretches? Perhaps there were some who, like the negro Biji, were ready to avenge themselves by treachery upon the chief who had treated them badly?

But what could scarcely be doubtful was, that Red

Ralph had surprised the girl in the act of writing, and that she had only had time to tear in two the letter and partly to destroy the fragments.

It was a pity that the greater portion of it was wanting.

Ned Bark and Freedy—the latter, thanks to the logical nature of his mind, the former, by reason of his detective habits—were both apt at deciphering the most abstruse problems of cryptography.

But here the difficulties were numerous.

First of all, the manner in which the paper was torn rendered it impossible for them to know the size of the sheet on which she had written, or, consequently, the length of the lines upon it and the number of words missing. A few points, nevertheless, were beyond dispute.

Thanks to the exactness of the expressions, it was easy to discover the sense of certain phrases.

"I have been able so far . . ." to defend myself? " He will take me . . ." " I overheard a few words interchanged . . ." between him and some one else? "He spoke of a . . ." town? "in Louisiana. . . ."

But the three last lines were untranslatable.

Had the words " to understand " been preceded by " I have been able," or " I have not been able"? They evidently applied to the name of the town chosen by Red Ralph as a fresh prison for his captive.

Then "to Wood . . ." What did that mean?

The thought that occurred most naturally to the mind was that she was mentioning Mr. Woodman the planter, whom she knew to be one of her father's truest friends.

Then the word " help !"   It was her final prayer.

In view of this problem, of which the solution seemed yet so far to seek, Valville and his friends experienced a feeling of great discouragement.

What should they do ?   Whither should they direct their steps?

In vain they repeated half a dozen times the perilous ascent of Devil's Rock, explored its recesses, and examined its steepest cliffs.   They found traces of the supports on which the rope ladders had formerly been hung.   But notwithstanding all their perseverance, they could not understand in what manner the bandits had escaped and carried away with them the unfortuuate daughter of the planter of Battle Field.

They had not gone by sea ; for the men on board Cartwright's schooner had seen no other vessel leave the shore, and their position allowed them to survey the coast for a very considerable distance.   When they made their way over the enormous blocks of stone which constituted the granite promontory of Devil's Rock, they found nothing but masses of rocks which were lost by degrees in impenetrable cypress thickets.

Although nothing there indicated the recent passage of a body of men, it was still possible that the ruffians had disappeared by this route.

To all these causes for depression, another was now added.   Alice regarded her merry young brother with a deep affection.   Valville also was much attached to him.

Certainly they had often laughed at the harebrained lad who himself made a jest of everything; but amidst the strange circumstances in which they had been placed, he had shown so much courage, so much joyous carelessness in the face of danger, that he had revealed himself in quite a new light.

And he had disappeared! Had he lost his life in one of the torrents that rushed down the mountain-side? Had he been surprised, entrapped, killed by the bandits? The field of conjecture was vast, but, unfortunately, every hypothesis was equally unbearable.

Were they all to be vanquished in the combat in which they had engaged? Would they fall one by one, without rescuing Jeanne from her persecutors, or avenging the unfortunate planter who had fallen a victim to a frightful crime?

These were the thoughts that tortured Charles Valville's heart.

Had he a right to bind to his side those whom he loved, and lead them into these ever-recurring dangers, —Alice, above all, who had devoted her life to him so faithfully? And if, perchance, some misfortune happened to her, how should he dare to present himself before the excellent, generous Madame Longpré, to whom she was more than life—the last hope of her old age?

No, it was Valville's duty no longer to accept these sacrifices. It was too much already that Eusèbe should have paid his devotion with his life; other victims must not fall. To him alone belonged the duty of continuing his task.

And, resolved upon carrying out his determination, Valville drew Alice aside.

They sat down upon the rocks. Before them a water-fall, white with foam, fell over the stones into a sort of gulf below.

"Alice, my own love," said Valville, "listen to me: we ought to separate . . ."

But his words were cut short. With a cry of despair, Alice guessed and comprehended all.

"Not a word more!" she exclaimed. "I am your companion, your friend, your wife. Whither you go, I will go. Whatever your arguments may be, however powerful you may think them, they will never change my resolution."

And as the young man entreated her to listen, she added—

"Your task is mine also. If it is true that my poor brother has fallen, we must discover his murderers; and if there is time we may save him yet."

Valville yielded. And the two young people, obeying their feelings of generous enthusiasm, vowed, in face of a scene which nature had rendered at once terrible and magnificent, to live and die together: a new betrothal which bound them yet more closely one to the other.

Hesitancy had lasted long enough. It was time to look the situation in the face and take a decisive re-solution.

A council was held. The brave Cartwright, who had forgotten his passion for crabs in real emotion, was asked for his opinion.

Ned Bark was, however, the first to speak.

The worthy detective had had his share of humiliation, although he had neglected nothing; and, according to the terms of his contract, had bravely risked his life.

But there was no use in dissimulating the fact that all his efforts had ended in failure, which was serious, if not irreparable.

In his opinion it would be best to follow out the vague intimations given in the letter, which he thus explained.

"So far," he said, "the ruffian, Red Ralph, has not dared to abuse his strength by forcibly imposing his wishes upon your sister. He sees that neither menaces nor fears have any effect upon that courageous heart; and perhaps he wants now, by taking her again to Louisiana, to attempt other methods of intimidation: possibly to threaten the life of her sister Lucile."

The danger was thus shifted, but not diminished. Still if it were true, according to Ned, that Red Ralph had chosen this new field-of action, it would be easier to call him to account there than here.

In any case there was not a minute to lose. They must regain the Woodman Plantation, and place Lucile in safety at New Orleans.

Afterwards they could act according to circumstances.

"But," added Ned Bark, "I have a scheme in my head which I will tell you later, a scheme which may help us to win the day."

In fact, although their new hopes were so precarious, it was evident that the safer plan was to leave the unexplored regions where Red Ralph possessed unknown resources. And a study of Jeanne's letter led them all to believe that the detective's suppositions were not inadmissible.

It was therefore decided that they should return immediately to St. Augustine and Jacksonville, and make their way thence by train, as quickly as possible, to New Orleans.

As it was certain that Red Ralph and his accomplices would not risk a journey by frequented ways—a fact which would necessarily retard their progress—it would be prudent to precede him in Louisiana, and prepare their batteries before his arrival.

Cartwright's schooner was quite ready to resume its course. And on the evening of the very day when our friends landed, full of hope, on that accursed coast, the ' Tortoise' sped rapidly northwards. They waited a few hours only at St. Augustine in order to take up Madame Longpré, and also in the hope of gaining in the town some information as to the movements of the bandits. But Ned Bark could hear nothing of them.

At last they reached Jacksonville.

Here Cartwright took leave of his new companions.

He was about to quit North America and pursue his scientific researches on the coasts of Brazil.

He was most assuredly a very eccentric individual. But he had shown once more, that any man who loves science with his whole heart must needs possess some of the finer qualities which do honour to the human race.

His allies for the last few days took leave of him with

many a hearty clasp of the hand. Would they ever meet again ?

Tears were in Cartwright's eyes as he parted from them, and when the Florida Atlantic Railway was carrying Valville off to Tallahassee, the naturalist was seen in the small boat belonging to his schooner, at the mouth of the St. John's River, waving them a last adieu.

It was not without deep sadness that Valville again performed the journey which he had taken with Freedy upon their first arrival from Europe. Long days had rolled away since then, and nothing had yet been done.

The distance of six hundred miles between Jacksonville and Mobile was traversed with the rapidity of lightning. The American trains, at full steam, leave our prudent European railways far behind. But are not Americans travellers exposed to greater danger of accidents? Perhaps not, if we take into account the distances they travel and the number of travellers. And Americans commonly think very little about danger so long as they go fast enough. We have heard of the achievements of their steamers, which run races on the Mississippi. The same thing happens sometimes on railway lines. They have actually devised races by railroad.

They are conducted in this manner. Upon two parallel lines, two trains start at the same time at full speed. Which of the two will outdistance the other? The stokers and engine-drivers use the wildest means of accelerating the pace of their trains. They madden themselves with excitement, and gladly risk their very lives in the struggle.

But the most curious, and not the least interesting, part of the matter is, that, after the interchange of bets to a considerable amount on the swiftness of their respective engines, the men who bet and the judges of the result should all be seated in the trains.

When the speed is equal, menaces and insults are hurled from one train to the other. The passengers shout to the stokers to quicken the pace, and promise them immense rewards in case of victory.

And if the engine-drivers obey these demands so far as to put on steam until the boilers burst, why, then, they all blow up together—engine-drivers, betting-men, judges, and all! Thus no jealousy is left behind.

Indeed the Americans treat their locomotives rather like toys. They exert their ingenuity to make the engines look like diabolical faces, thanks to the two lanterns fastened on each side, and an open grating which allows the glowing furnace to be seen. At night the aspect presented is actually startling, all the more so as the chimney is very large and emits an enormous jet of smoke and flame, which, just above the fiendish-looking face, much resembles a fiery plume on the head of a demon.

Our travellers arrived at Mobile, however, without any accident.

We may remind ourselves that the first time this journey was made, Valville and Freedy performed it with Alice and Madame Longpré, on horseback, by way of precaution.

But now it was useless to seek to deceive the enemies, against whom war had been openly declared.

A steamer was already getting up steam in the Mobile harbour, on the point of starting for New Orleans. Freedy had just time to go to the hotel and see whether any letters had arrived there for him, but upon receiving an answer in the negative, he rejoined his friends, and they went immediately on board.

Nothing occurred to disturb their journey, and they landed at last on the wharf at New Orleans.

It had been decided that Valville should proceed to Pontchartrain, with Freedy and Sambo; and that Alice and her aunt should seek hospitality at the house of some friends of the Valville family, who lived in the French quarter of the town. As for Ned Bark, he was bound on further expeditions, as he still held himself to be in the service of those whose cause he had espoused.

The three men set off in the direction of the Woodman Plantation on horseback.

Alice and Madame Longpré were received with open arms by a family of French origin, living in the Rue Bourbon, and consisting of the father, M. Blanchemont, his wife, and their four daughters.

The two visitors felt as if they were once more on French soil. Did we wish to flatter the national vanity of a Frenchman, we might say that only in a French family can one find that real hospitality without constraint which sets a guest as much at ease with his hosts as if he were in his own house.

M. Blanchemont, whose ancestors had helped to found the town of New Orleans, belonged to those Protestants whom an iniquitous and impious measure banished from France, after the revocation of the Edict of Nantes.

Although the family had prospered far beyond its dreams, it had never forgotten its mother country, whom it did not hold responsible for the sufferings it had undergone. Bound by interest to America, it was attached by the far stronger ties of affection to France. And it had taken pride—perhaps not an unworthy pride —in the fact that in the veins of each member of the family the blood of old Gaul yet flowed in all its purity.

The Blanchemonts had never married into any race but their own. And it was easy to see, by a glance at Madame Blanchemont and her daughters, that the type of race remained unchanged.

It was the same with their speech. The father of the family had constituted himself his children's tutor, in order that they might not be led away by the charm of that Creole dialect, which is really the admixture of two tongues. The French language had been preserved in this family with really extraordinary accuracy; and even in listening to the most casual conversation in that house, a purist would have rejoiced to hear, with scarcely any alteration, the correct idiom and accent of the eighteenth century. So with the manners and habits of all the members of the family. Although M. Blanchemont had no claim to high rank, and was as proud of his position as a commoner as others are of the possession of pompous titles, yet the exquisite refinement visible at every moment in his address recalled to mind the best days of old-world French courtesy.

He had known Mr. Valville very well, and sincerely deplored his sad end. Accordingly he was delighted to receive the young lady, whom his old friend's son confided to his care as his future wife and most valued treasure.

"You come direct from France," he said to Madame Longpré. "I shall be delighted if, in our midst, you feel as though you were no longer in a strange land. It seems to us as if you formed a part of the old home which you bring back to us unchanged, whilst ours is never long at rest! . . . "—and a sigh concluded the sentence.

Notwithstanding their energy the two fair travellers were almost sinking with fatigue. The woman with the iron will herself was bowed down with sorrow. The disappearance of Eusèbe had inflicted a sad wound upon her heart. She had long considered the two young people as her children, and could hardly separate them one from the other in her maternal affection; but it must be confessed that in one corner of her heart she cherished a tiny preference for the fastidious lad whom she knew to be really so good and kind.

Rooms were quickly prepared for them.

Although Madame Blanchemont and her daughters

refrained with true tact from asking any questions, they could easily see that some great grief was weighing down the spirits of their new friends. When Madame Longpré was about to retire, she drew towards her Madame Blanchemont's two younger daughters—lovely girls of twelve and fourteen years old—and pressed them to her breast.

"Happy mother!" she said with tears in her eyes. "May you be made happier still by these dear children, whom I bless from the bottom of my heart."

The two elder girls, Pauline and Marthe, already seemed to look upon Alice as a sister.

In spite of herself, Alice felt a sort of peace descend upon her heart and calm her troubled spirit at the very sight of this happy and united family. Here was the happiness for which she herself had prayed; and she asked herself whether she was indeed called upon to renounce such hopes for ever.

It seemed as if Madame Blanchemont—a fair woman of some forty years, with a sweet, good face—had guessed her secret thoughts, for when she bade her good-night she said, smiling—

"I wish you pleasant dreams. And remember there is no trial too great to bear, if only one's conscience is pure."

Alice felt comforted by the gentle words, and the peaceful shadow of a quiet home enveloped her once again.

No sooner had she reached her room, and sent her best thoughts and wishes after those she loved, than she fell asleep, and slept with all the soundness of her twenty years.

Meanwhile Valville, Freedy, and the negro were galloping with loose rein towards the Woodman Plantation.

To them calm did not come. On the contrary, new anxieties assailed them. When once a man has felt himself borne down by what seems the force of fate, he must possess rare strength of mind if he can avoid belief in dark presentiments.

Had Lucile also been threatened?

When they saw from afar the magnolia groves which formed an almost impenetrable hedge round the plantation, the hearts of the two friends beat so violently that they suddenly drew rein, as though by mutual consent.

They looked at each other, and Valville clasped Freedy's hand.

"Come!" said Freedy, "courage! The future belongs to the brave!"

And they spurred forward to the magnolia grove.

CHAPTER XVIII.

RED RALPH'S FOREFATHERS.

FORTUNATELY the fears of our friends were not justified by fact. If the efforts of their enemies were to tend in this direction, their time had not yet come, for the plantation had not, so far, been the object of any hostile attack.

Thus they were informed by Mr. Woodman, whose anxiety of mind had been very great, and who listened with deep interest to the narrative rapidly given by the travellers.

"I quite approve," he said, "of your prudence in leaving Miss Lodier and her aunt at New Orleans, at my friend Blanchemont's house."

"You are then of opinion," said Valville, "that I ought to take my sister there too?"

"Certainly, without any loss of time."

At this point Lucile, who had been informed of the arrival of the two young men, appeared upon the scene, and threw her arms round her brother's neck.

"It is you at last!" she cried. Then, looking round her with an expression of terror, she added, "But where is Jeanne, my sister?"

The two men hung their heads. Freedy especially grew

very pale; for, although he had done his duty and risked his life without considering danger, he could not forget that he had vowed never to return to Lucile, the woman whom he loved, until he could restore her sister to her side.

And had not Lucile guessed that silent vow which Freedy had registered in his secret thoughts? Could not Freedy read her faith in him in the sad glance which she gave him, the glance in which he read so bitter a reproach?

Woodman understood the situation and hastened to interpose.

"Lucile," he said quickly, "a defeat does not mean that we must needs despair of ultimate victory."

"No, indeed!" exclaimed Freedy. "If you only knew, Mademoiselle, how earnestly, how fervently we have striven!"

Lucile's face grew inexpressibly sweet. She felt that she had been unjust, and wished to repair the wrong that she had done them. She held out her hand to her brother.

"Forgive me," she said; "but you know that I grieve and that I suffer; I love my dear Jeanne so much."

"At least," said Valville, with an angry gesture, "one of my father's ruffianly murderers has expiated his crime already."

"Our father must be avenged," answered Lucile quickly; "but would he not himself, if he were here, tell you to think first of his beloved daughter?"

"Dearest Lucile," said the young man, "pray do not think that I have renounced the work which should be first of all with us; we are just starting again, but this time either we shall die or Jeanne shall be restored to you."

"Die? Oh, how terrible! What would become of me if you were all to leave me?"

"In my turn, Lucile, I must tell you not to despair. But, you see, we must first be relieved from the anxiety which, in spite of ourselves, limits our liberty of action."

"What do you mean?"

"I mean that we have returned so quickly only because we have serious reason to believe that unknown dangers await you too."

"Await me?"

"And we wish to have nothing to fear on your account, at least; so we are going to take you immediately with us to New Orleans."

Mr. Woodman explained in as few words as possible the reason for this sudden decision. The girl had no objection to make. She even added, with a shake of the head—

"You are right, perhaps; I may not be safe here."

"What do you mean?" asked Freedy. "Have you noticed any sign of danger?"

"Nothing positive," said the girl; "and yet . . ."

"Pray continue."

"It is perhaps only a fancy of my overwrought brain, but sometimes it seems to me as if an invisible watch were kept over me. If now and then, wishing to escape from the cares which pursue me, I wander as far as the end of the park, I seem to hear steps behind me among the bushes, steps which follow me . . ."

"You never mentioned this before," interrupted Woodman.

"Because I did not wish to make you anxious, and because it may be folly on my part; and yet it seems to me as if enemies were watching and spying out my movements."

"All the more reason for not delaying your departure an hour longer," said Freedy.

"I am ready to go with you."

As Lucile was not yet strong enough to ride, Mr. Woodman ordered a carriage to be in readiness, and while she went to her room in order to prepare for the journey, the two friends remained with the planter, and Valville completed the story of his past adventures.

There was one detail which he had not yet made known. The reader will remember that when Valville had been surprised into a visit to the island in the Matanzas, he had met Red Ralph face to face, and the robber, in a fit of rage, had told him his real name.

"Ralph Staunton!" exclaimed Mr. Woodman when Valville mentioned this fact. "What! does that ruffian belong to so respectable a family?"

"He told me so himself."

The planter became thoughtful.

"I knew his father very well," he said. "He was, and I believe is still, a brave man, but imbued with a fierce prejudice against the negro race. And I remember to have heard that one of his family—his eldest son, in fact—was banished from his house on account of some dishonourable action. It was great severity on the father's part, and see what has been the result: he has made a robber of the son whom perhaps he might have saved."

Then, striking his forehead with one hand, Mr. Woodman added—

"Who can tell? He may yet have some influence with his son. Suppose I were to appeal to our old acquaintanceship; no doubt he does not know what has become of Ralph . . ."

" Your idea may be a good one," Valville interrupted him quickly. " I tell you that I do not think humanity is quite extinct in that wretched man's heart. For proof, look at the ascendancy which my sister has established over him! She is in his power, but she has made him treat her with respect."

" Well, as soon as you have started for New Orleans I will make my way to Mr. Staunton. I think he lives at Galveston; I shall be there in two days, and you may be sure I will plead your cause with him. If the father has still any power over his son, we may perhaps gain more than we imagine."

" Heaven grant we may !"

"It is a strange thing that in that very family there have already been several examples of the singular case that we have before us to-day. It never occurred to me before to recall the memories which cling to the house of Staunton; but now that I know Red Ralph's true name, these old stories thrust themselves forward in my mind, and I cannot refrain from asking myself whether we dare doubt the existence of terrible fatalities, such as immortalised the house of Atreus in the days of antiquity."

" Explain yourself," said Freedy.   " Such stories have reached my own ears, but I never attached any credit to them."

" Nevertheless they are true, and while Lucile is getting ready I can tell you the most terrible story of all."

" We shall be glad to hear it," said Valville.

" Oh, my story will not be a long one.   During the War of Independence the Stauntons lived in Savannah, in Georgia, and boldly espoused the cause of the country against the English.   Edward Staunton, the head of the family and father of five sons, had raised a body of soldiers; and it was marvellous to see the energy and courage of these patriotic men, as they struggled, with neither truce nor intermission, against the enemies of American liberty.

" But a dark day rose at last, which left a terrible memory in the history of the Staunton family.

" One morning, out of the five sons of Staunton, one was missing at the roll-call.   Where was he?   Had he been surprised and taken prisoner by the enemy?   In vain they exhausted their ingenuity in conjecture.   But, strange to say, the more closely they pursued their inquiries, the less possible it seemed that the absentee should have fallen into a snare.

" The sentinels, the outposts, had not been attacked. No one had noticed any of the enemy's troops in the vicinity.

" The son who had so mysteriously disappeared was named Ralph Staunton, as is also the one who lives now. He was the youngest of the five sons, and his father's favourite.

" The little camp of the patriots was situated at the foot of a hill, on the bank of a stream swollen by the winter rains, over which they had been obliged to throw a temporary bridge made of trunks of trees tied to·gether.

" One of Staunton's companions affirmed that at day-break he had seen a man cross the bridge and leave the camp. But that it was Ralph Staunton he could not positively declare.

" The father's head was bowed as though he felt that disgrace was near. If his beloved son had been sur-prised and put to death his heart would have bled ; but then, fixing his eyes upon the banner which floated above the camp, he could have told himself that his son had suffered and died for the independence of his country. But Ralph seemed to have gone of his own free will ! He had abandoned his father, his brothers, his companions in arms, on the eve of com-bat ! This was desertion and cowardice !

" Edward Staunton was destined to receive, all too soon, a confirmation of his worst suspicions.

" On the following night the camp was attacked by a superior force. The little troop of Americans performed prodigies of valour. Hand to hand they fought their enemies, and two of Staunton's sons were killed. Of the fifty brave men who defended the post, only twenty at most escaped and sought refuge in the mountains.

" But the worst blow of all fell when, in the midst of the combat, a jesting voice—the voice of the chief on the enemy's side—cried to the father—

" 'It was your son who showed us the way to the camp.'

" His son ! was it possible ?   Yes, true indeed it was. Staunton lost no time in filling up the blanks which death had left in his little band. Nobody took pay at that time.   Everybody was ready to be a soldier and to fight for the liberation of his country.

" A few days afterwards Staunton gained a first advantage. He surprised some English troops and made several prisoners.

" He longed above everything to hear his son spoken of—to disabuse his mind of the terrible doubt that tortured it.

" Well, he heard that Ralph Staunton had fallen in love with an Englishwoman, and had left the camp in order to join her ; and that this woman had known how to transform the madman into a traitor, and obtain accurate information from him as to the plans of the Americans.

" When this frightful révelation was made to old Staunton he turned as pale as death. But not a single word escaped his lips, and nobody could guess what resolution he was about to form.

" Meanwhile the war was carried on more vigorously than ever. The English began to feel that the soil of a free America was no longer theirs. By his splendid manœuvres Washington fatigued and exhausted the enemy.

"Staunton had offered his services to the General, and often accompanied the advanced guard of the Federal army.

"He seemed to have forgotten the past, and the name of his youngest son was never heard.

"One day Staunton, after a forced march of unusual rapidity, surprised several English officers in a lonely house. Amongst them was Lord Clifton, one of the leaders of the English army. It was a most important capture. Staunton returned to Washington's camp with his prisoners, and the General congratulated him warmly.

"'Name your own reward,' he said.

"'Allow me to dispose of my prisoner.'

"Washington looked at him in surprise.

"'Staunton,' he said, 'remember that prisoners of war are protected by their rights as men. Republicans, above all others, ought to show an example of humanity.'

"'Reassure yourself, General; Lord Clifton's life shall be respected. More than that, in a few days I hope I shall set him at liberty, imposing on him only a promise not to serve against us any more.'

"'Then do as you like.'

"Lord Clifton was placed in a tent next to Staunton's, and was treated with the greatest respect. What was old Staunton's project? Nobody knew, not even his two remaining sons.　All that was known was that he had despatched a messenger to some unknown destination.

"Several days passed away without result before the messenger returned.

"Staunton questioned him.　He had succeeded in his mission.　And what do you think that mission was?

"The Englishwoman for whose sake Ralph Staunton had become a coward and a traitor was Lord Clifton's daughter.　The messenger had been to seek her and to say—

"'Your father has fallen into Edward Staunton's power.　Restore to him his son, and your father shall be free.'

"And she, expert in treason, and impelled, not by filial love, but by family pride, had consented to deliver up Ralph Staunton in order to purchase the liberty of the English peer.

"An interview was arranged between Staunton and the officers of the English army.

"The father came to it, accompanied by a small escort.

"The two parties met on the borders of a forest of giant trees, whose trunks when felled are found to be of such dimensions that men on horseback can ride through one of them as through a gateway.

"Staunton restated the terms of the agreement.　He would exchange Lord Clifton for his son Ralph.　The conditions were accepted, and Staunton returned to the camp in company with his son.

" The young man had not addressed a single word to his father. Although no threats had been uttered, he understood well enough that retribution was very nigh.

" Staunton presented himself to Washington and demanded a court-martial, which was immediately held. Ralph was placed before his judges, and Edward Staunton denounced and accused him.

" The old man displayed no anger. He spoke as coldly as if the accused had not been of his own blood. He demanded that Ralph should be condemned to death.

" The crime was patent. The prisoner confessed his guilt. The judges could not hesitate in sentencing the accused. And yet they pitied the father whose inflexibility ill concealed his suffering.

" They never doubted but that Staunton would ask and obtain his son's pardon. Ralph was condemned to death.

" The father bowed and left the court.

" Two hours afterwards Ralph Staunton was paraded before the whole army and publicly degraded from his rank.

" This alone was a terrible punishment. Would this not satisfy the offended father's wrath? But Washington waited for Staunton in vain. What! dared not the father claim pardon for his son? The General sent his aide-de-camp to him.

" ' Do you wish for Ralph's pardon ? ' he asked.

" ' I asked for justice,' responded Staunton. ' Let justice be done.'

"And Ralph Staunton was shot.

"When his son had fallen before the balls, Staunton lifted up his body and buried it with his own hands. Then, and then only, he wept. But he had accomplished his task, even to the bitter end!

"Such are the terrible memories which the name of Staunton recalls," Mr. Woodman added. "And let me tell you that I know the old Staunton, who is living now, and I believe that, like his forefather, he would be an inflexible judge."

As the planter concluded his story, Lucile reappeared in travelling costume.

The carriage was ready. Woodman kissed the young girl tenderly.

"Courage!" he said to her. "And do not despair of seeing your sister again."

Sambo drove, and the horses set off rapidly in the direction of New Orleans.

The road from Lake Chamberlain to New Orleans lies between cypress swamps, and the winter rains had ploughed great furrows of mud across it. All the negro's skill and the horses' strength were necessary to surmount the difficulties of the way.

Valville went inside the carriage with his sister, while Freedy occupied the seat beside Sambo.

Suddenly the negro started.

"Look, master," he said to Freedy, "the storm is coming!"

It was true. Enormous masses of black cloud covered the sky; for the tempests of Louisiana, veritable hurricanes, which sometimes lay waste a large extent of territory, burst forth with a suddenness which defies all preparation.

Scarcely had Sambo uttered these words of warning when torrents of rain began to fall, the forerunners of the tempest.

The terrified horses reared and refused to advance any farther.

They were already too far on their way to think of returning to the Woodman Plantation. Yet they must at all hazards obtain shelter.

"Hold the reins," said Sambo, springing to the ground. "I will try and find some sort of cabin in which we can at least place Miss Lucile in safety."

The danger increased every moment. The maddened horses could hardly be reined in.

But at last Sambo returned.

"Come quickly!" he said. "I have found a place of refuge."

The rain had already drenched the garments of the shivering girl. Valville took his sister in his arms and followed the negro, while Freedy, seizing the horses' reins, dragged them in the same direction.

Thus they arrived at some wooden huts which formerly had been erected by woodcutters.

They stood upon the edge of a pond. A negro, seemingly indifferent to the tempest, sat upon the very brink.

Lucile and Valville entered one of the huts, the disjointed rafters of which would serve at least as a temporary shelter.

Freedy unharnessed the horses and led them into a shed.

" It seems to me," said Lucile, " that this storm is of evil omen for us all ! "

CHAPTER XIX.

THUS an hour passed by. The wind drove against their frail shelter with such violence that several times the travellers had reason to fear that it would fall about their heads.

Fortunately these tempests, so frequent in Louisiana, are not of long duration. The fury of the storm soon subsided, and Freedy was able to go out and explore the neighbourhood.

On one side, the house in which they had taken refuge fronted a small waterfall, now considerably swollen by the rain. Several trees had been uprooted, and the road was almost impracticable, especially for Mr. Woodman's carriage, which was solidly built and rather heavy.

The travellers consulted together. It was evident that even if the carriage were driven into the midst of the ruts and hollows made by the storm, its course would soon be arrested by insuperable obstacles.

On the other hand, waiting was an impossibility. These wooden huts were inhabited already.

"We must come to some resolution," said Charles. " We cannot stay here and risk the approach of night.

A few hours of daylight remain to us : let us take advantage of them at once. How far, Freedy, do you think Frenier, the nearest railway station, is from here?"

For, by reason of the situation of Mr. Woodman's plantation, the travellers had intended to follow the coast-line of Lake Pontchartrain, by which route, if they had met with no accident, they might have reached New Orleans almost as quickly as by rail.

But as matters now stood Charles's idea was practicable.

"The station must be about eight miles off."

"What kind of roads?"

"Hum! very little frequented, and they must have suffered under this torrent of rain."

"Never mind, the horses are strong and active. If Lucile will consent, I will ride one, and she can ride behind me; you, Freedy, can take the other. Sambo will stay here and manage to send the carriage back to the plantation. What do you think of the plan?"

"It is possible," said Freedy. "I think it is perhaps the only way practicable. What do you think of it, Mademoiselle Lucile?"

"As for me," said the girl, "I am ready to go with you wherever you go."

And these words were accompanied with a slight but significant glance, which proved that Lucile was becoming very submissive to Doctor Freedy's wishes.

"Then let us set off," said Valville.

. Sambo approved of the decision at which they had arrived, although he regretted the separation from his master. But he felt sure that he could obtain means for sending home the carriage, and then he would immediately follow the others to New Orleans.

They made haste to unharness the horses. Freedy and Valville were first-rate horsemen, and troubled themselves little about the absence of bit and saddle.

They arranged a more comfortable sort of seat for Lucile by means of cloaks. She was not nervous, and feared nothing so long as her brother was before her.

They cut long switches from the trees for riding-whips, and then started at a good pace for Frenier. They were often obliged to slacken their pace, but their horses were surefooted, and the distance could be accomplished in less than two hours.

At last the travellers caught sight of the suspension bridge which crosses an arm of Lake Pontchartrain; the station was in sight, and a distant column of steam announced the approach of a train.

They quitted the side of the lake and reached the station. This time chance served them well, for the train was expected in a few minutes. They had only to find some one to take charge of their horses, a task speedily accomplished.

And at last Lucile and her two companions had the pleasure of finding themselves whirled away in the train to New Orleans.

Our readers, doubtless, accustomed to European modes of travel, might find it difficult to realise the comfort presented by American railway trains, especially in the Southern States, where they have been more recently introduced, and are therefore even better constructed than in the North.

The American cars, large, lofty, well ventilated, are capable of holding some fifty passengers. The seats are arranged in two rows, with a passage down the middle. One may sit face forward or face backward, for the seat revolves upon a pivot.

What a difference there is between these comfortable cars, and some of our Procrustean stalls, in which the traveller is packed like an unfortunate herring !

Each compartment contains a lavatory with a wash-hand stand, water-bottle, and glass; also a stove which can be lighted in winter. A cord which runs the whole length of the train puts every traveller into communication with the guard at will.

And let us remember that with us, on some lines, a traveller in any danger may break the pane of glass which divides him from the signal-ring, pull the ring violently, and obtain no result at all, because the said ring communicates with nothing and nobody.

One may walk through all the compartments of an American train while it is still in motion, and even stand outside them, leaning against a railing for the better contemplation of the landscape.

A man sells newspapers, books, and eatables as he walks up and down the cars. From time to time the guard examines the tickets, without inconveniencing the travellers, however, as they generally fasten them into the band of their hats.

In certain compartments smoking is now allowed,

but, every picture has its darker side, and Americans chew everywhere. Chewing is a peculiarly American weakness.

Still, addressing ourselves to smokers, we may ask whether even those who are most accustomed to the fumes of tobacco are not sometimes nearly suffocated in our narrow smoking compartments? Twelve cigars, or twelve pipes, in a space of a few cubic feet!

There are reserved carriages for ladies, whom Americans profess to treat with great respect, but their husbands or escorts have the right of entering these reserved compartments with them. They are simply carriages where smoking is strictly forbidden. No gentleman, however, can enter them without the consent of the lady who is with him. We must say that in America a bachelor is at a decided disadvantage, and it has even been said that a foreign nobleman, who was unmarried, used always to take his female cook about with him, so that under the protection of this lady, at least, he might pass in and out, and, not being a smoker himself, fly from the fumes of American lovers of the weed.

The seats can also be transformed into beds at night by a very ingenious process; and one can sleep in them quite as well as in the berth of a steamer, especially as there is no sea-sickness to be feared. The beds are one above the other; and the only danger is that of receiving on one's head the fellow-traveller who sleeps in the upper story, and who has proved too great a weight for the support afforded.

The palace-cars, or state-rooms, which may be occupied by one passenger, are still more comfortable, and can be made quite home-like.

Every facility is certainly given for travelling in the United States, and we cannot but regret that in Europe a traveller is regarded with little more consideration than if he were a bale of goods!

But during our digression the train has left Frenier, stopped at Kenner, and finally entered New Orleans.

Our three travellers took a carriage and at once repaired to M. Blanchemont's house.

This time at least anxiety was uncalled for; it seemed as if fortune was weary for a moment of persecuting our friends.

They were once more united, and could talk together over the terrible events that had happened; above all, unfortunately, of the dark fears awakened by the absence of Eusèbe and the fresh disappearance of Jeanne.

About ten o'clock in the evening a servant approached Freedy and whispered a few words into his ear. Freedy made a gesture of surprise, and quickly dismissed the man.

This incident passed unnoticed. Pauline and Marthe, the two elder daughters of M. Blanchemont, were endeavouring to dispel the sad memories which clouded the faces of Madame Longpré and her niece.

Freedy drew close to Charles and bent over him.

"We must go out," he said.

Valville looked up at him in amaze, but upon a sign from Freedy he understood that any remark would be imprudent. He felt instinctively that they might be on the point of solving a problem which hitherto had sadly taxed their ingenuity.

He found a pretext, therefore, for taking leave of Alice and his sister at once. In another moment the two men found themselves in Canal Street, the great thoroughfare which divides into two nearly equal portions the city of New Orleans, with the French part of the town on the right hand, and the American on the left.

There Valville asked—

" What is the matter ? "

" Ned Bark has sent for me."

" Does he know anything ? "

" I don't know.   But he is not the man to act without a motive."

" Where are you to meet him ? "

" At the foot of Henry Clay's statue."

" Come, then."

In a few minutes the two friends arrived at the appointed spot.

A man stood leaning against the pedestal of the statue, but Freedy and Valville really hesitated to believe that this was the man whom they had come to meet. Ned was small and wiry-looking, this man was tall and stout. And yet it was the same man, only the detective knew how to alter his stature and appearance in a manner which might have deceived the most experienced eye.

As soon as they had gained his side, Ned Bark made them a sign and began to walk towards the American quarter, first through the commercial streets, where the shops were now closed, then into a maze of narrow alleys, lighted here and there by a yellow jet of gas, while Freedy and Valville followed the detective without receiving a single word of recognition.

They arrived at last at some cross roads, something like the Seven Dials in London, the Five Points of New York, or the old Place Maubert of Paris. This place was called Muddy Cross, a curious name, which fitly characterised the muddy space from which branched out several dark and narrow roads of peculiarly uninviting appearance.

Here Ned Bark stopped, and the two friends rejoined him.

" Are we at the place ? " asked Freedy.

" Nearly."

" What have we to do in this vile neighbourhood ? "

" Follow up our search ; and this time I am certain of obtaining some important result. You see," added Ned Bark, " I do not insult you by asking if you are ready to confront danger, however serious it may be."

" Of course ! You know that you may count upon us."

" Are you armed ? "

Each of the two men carried a revolver.

" That is well," replied the detective. " But you must remove the cartridges. In what we have to do it is important that we should not attract the notice of the thieves who frequent this neighbourhood. A shot would compromise the success of our expedition, by exposing us to attacks which we could not possibly resist."

"Our revolvers are uncocked," said Freedy. "I think that will be sufficient, and you need not fear any imprudence from us."

"Very well. But unless our lives are really in danger, don't fire."

"Agreed. Now what have we to do?"

"You must go with me into one of those wretched holes called gaming-houses, the haunts of theft and drunkenness. The most important point is that nobody must guess who we are. You, Mr. Valville and Doctor Freedy, are not known, and you need only disarrange your clothes a little to appear like any other gambler or 'scalawag,' like those with whom you are about to mix. You can easily tell from this what sort of manner you had better adopt."

"Good," said Valville; "we will do our best."

"As for me, I intend to use some old methods which always succeed, and I am sure of passing unrecognised. As soon as we go in I shall take my place at one of the tables, and you must draw near and feign to be deeply interested in the game. Upon a sign from me you must take part in it. Only, don't forget one small detail. When you risk a few notes place your revolver beside you with some ostentation; that is always done in this land of mutual confidence."

"And then?"

"Do not trouble yourself about anything else. I shall

be there, and will let you know what we must do, according to circumstances."

"Let us go then," said the two friends.

"One last word," said Ned Bark. "As you know, I distrust the metropolitan police too deeply to drag them into this affair. That is why I have had recourse to you. And if any of these wretches guess what is my profession, you may be sure that neither you nor I will leave their haunt alive."

They entered one of the streets which diverged from Muddy Cross. It was composed of old buildings, which seemed as if they could hardly stand upright, and were staggering like a drunkard on his legs. On the ground-floor, through windows the dirt of which seemed redoubled by the reddish reflection of the filthy curtains, one could see, by the gaslight, the shadows of gesticulating figures, and the sound of hoarse, rough voices could be heard.

Sometimes one of the doors would open, and into the street men rolled out, quarrelling, swearing, and falling, as they staggered away into the night; sometimes the group engaged in a fierce fight, enlivened with oaths and savage grindings of teeth.

Before such a house Ned stopped at last. It was dark, but seemed to be inhabited. A wooden door, secured with iron bars, guarded the entrance.

The detective raised a knocker, and knocked several times in a peculiar manner. There was a long silence. Then a voice from the interior uttered a few slang words, to which Ned replied. A sound as of the unfastening of chains was heard, and the door was half opened. Ned and his companions found themselves in an ill-smelling passage, dimly lighted by a wick floating in a vessel of oil.

The man who had opened the door exchanged a few more words with Ned Bark. Thieves are not chary of precautions, and it is always more difficult to enter their abodes than those of honest men.

It seemed, however, as if the explanations given by the detective were satisfactory; the man went forward, and, having opened a second door, retired behind it in order to afford our three friends entrance.

Imagination could hardly picture a more alarmingly disreputable hole than that into which the three men were introduced. At first the smoke of pipes and cigars was so thick that nothing could be distinguished. For a moment Valville felt as if he should choke.

At one end of the room was a large leaden counter, loaded with bottles and mugs of every size, against which leaned a number of men, all talking at once. Whisky, gin, and brandy flowed copiously. There was a continual coming and going between hand and lips at the table. Behind the counter a red-haired man, of immense size and colossal stature, phlegmatically performed the functions of barman, serving in turn all those who wished to drink.

The rest of the room was filled with long tables and benches, the latter so crowded that they were completely hidden by the throng of human beings.

One could hear the sound of dice rolling and rebounding, then the exclamations of the gamesters, imprecations from the losers, joyful shouts from the winners. As Ned Bark had said, each place was marked by a revolver. It could be easily seen that in cases of dispute powder and shot would soon be called into requisition.

Ned Bark had some difficulty in forcing his way through the crowded room. Valville and Freedy did not quit him, but paid heedful attention to his slightest movements, and made ready to obey the least sign from him.

The detective advanced slowly, seeking to pierce the fog with his one eye. A slight tremor agitated the muscles of his face at last. He marched deliberately to one of the tables, elbowed aside two players, and sat down, throwing a handful of greenbacks upon the table. The game was one played with dice, called 'crabs,' now little known. It is somewhat complicated, and, on account of its complication, requires great watchfulness on the part of the croupier.

The croupier who dealt at the table which Ned had chosen, was a tall man, frightfully thin, with a face terribly scarred, either by smallpox or from the effects of a fire.

At the detective's movement he had fixed his eyes upon him, and regarded him for some moments, evidently trying to discover who this new arrival could be.

His examination did not seem to afford him any reason for disquietude, however, for he threw the dice again and repeated the cry peculiar to the game of 'crabs.'

" Chance !"

Freedy and Valville had felt a moment's anxiety. Although Ned Bark was so well disguised, the robbers might recognise him ! But they were soon reassured. The game began.

Three throws were made. Ned lost.

Then he leaned forward to the croupier and said a few words to him in a low tone, at the same time glancing at Freedy and Valville. The croupier seemed surprised, but smiled and said something in his turn to his companions, who immediately made room for the new-comers, while Ned invited them with a look to install themselves at the table.

The two friends obeyed without understanding why. Their confidence in Ned Bark was absolute.

They seated themselves.

" You have money ? " said the croupier.

" A little," answered Freedy.

" Well, then, we'll make a night of it."

" And to put some life into it," added Ned, winking to the croupier, " I'll stand the drink all round."

" Bravo ! Old Tom, best quality, then !"

The big tavern-keeper brought out an immense bottle, and the glasses were filled. Ned poured out bumper after bumper, drinking the croupier's health each time, and the croupier halted in the game only to drink also. Ned kept pace with him so courageously that Freedy and Valville were able to dispense with the potent spirit.

The game became very animated.

Freedy and Valville had not forgotten to place beside

them their revolvers, which served as paper-weights to their rolls of bank-notes.

With burning eyes the croupier threw the dice.

It is unnecessary to say that Valville and Freedy lost largely. More than a hundred dollars speedily went to swell the treasure of the successful croupier, who laughed and drank meanwhile, intoxicating himself alike with gin and with avaricious joy.

Time passed on.

Several changes of fortune prolonged the game. But luck always returned to the croupier. Fresh bottles of gin went round. The croupier was frightfully drunk.

As for Ned, although he had swallowed a large quantity of spirit, he was as calm as if his glass had held nothing but water.

Four o'clock struck. This was the signal for departure, according to the rule of the house, which was generally submitted to with tolerable alacrity, although with many a seeming grumble.

Ned rose, and passed his arm through that of the croupier.

"They have gold still!" he said to him in an undertone, but distinctly enough for the two friends to hear.

Following this indirect counsel, Valville plunged his hand into his pocket, and allowed the croupier to see between his fingers the gleam of gold.

"Well, Old Mother Sammy's house is open still," said the croupier. "If these gentlemen would like . . ."

"I should think so!" said Freedy. "We want to have our revenge yet!"

And they left the tavern together.

They were soon in the narrow street, Ned·arm in arm with the croupier. They were alone, having left the house as slowly as possible, in order to let the others disperse.

They were just beneath a gas-lamp when Ned Bark suddenly drew a revolver from his pocket, and placed it immediately under his prisoner's nose.

" Phil Samster ! " he said in a stern voice, " resistance is impossible. You must come with us."

This Phil Samster, once a beggar in the docks at New Orleans, was one of Red Ralph's accomplices. On hearing this name Freedy and Valville understood all. And as Phil endeavoured by a violent effort to free himself from the detective's grasp, the revolvers of the two friends quickly made him understand that he could do nothing but submit.

" I'll come with you," he said in a hoarse voice. " Where are you going to take me ? "

" Not far," answered Ned. " You need not be afraid ; we do not want your life."

The robber shrugged his shoulders and walked on, with Ned's grasp still firmly fixed upon his wrist.

CHAPTER XX.

THE END APPROACHES.

THE grey dawn was breaking. Phil Samster, seeing into what hands he had fallen, made no further resistance, but followed his three companions quietly. They proceeded towards the quay by means of the long Tchapitoulas Street, which still preserves its Indian appellation, in the direction of that part of the city which bears the name of Lafayette.

They stood at last on the bank of the Mississippi.

The river seemed all alive. Tall steamers were passing up and down. Travellers were making their way to the railway which winds along the bank, protected by no barrier.

They arrived at last at the foot of a hill where several wooden cabins had been built by pilots, in view of the frequent inundations of the river. Ned Bark directed his steps towards one of these buildings. Standing before it, he drew a key from his pocket and opened the cabin door: a door of somewhat mouldering appearance, but which was really of solid oak and covered with ironwork inside.

When the four men had entered, the door was shut.

They stood in a tolerably large, furnished room.

"Sit down," said Ned Bark to Samster.

The croupier seemed to have made up his mind how to behave. Having recognised Ned Bark, he knew that he was at the mercy of a man who did not easily relax his hold on those who had fallen into his hands. So he obeyed.

Ned Bark advanced to a cupboard which he opened, thus displaying to the astonished eyes of Phil Samster and the others a considerable quantity of provisions. What did it all mean?

"My dear Phil," said Ned Bark, "I wish to show you first of all that I have no evil intentions towards you. If I have brought you here it is because I want to make a bargain with you."

Phil Samster was ready for anything.

"A bargain? just so!" he said. "What's the stake?"

"Your liberty and your life," answered the detective plainly.

"Well, speak; I'm listening."

"You know, Phil, you were sentenced to death for firing the Docks?"

"I know."

"You know too, that, thanks to your comrades and to the complicity of certain traitors in the metropolitan police, you have hitherto escaped from justice?"

"Exactly so."

"And you know also that I, Ned Bark, concern my-self very little with party-questions, and although you may have committed this crime by order of your political chief, I consider you none the less a bandit of whom the country would be well rid ? "

" What then ? "

" It is well to put the situation clearly before you, so I will go on. I have arrested you without any regular authority, without any legal right at all, I may say; for I ought to have obtained a warrant, which I did not do. So you are not now exactly in the hands of the law, and it depends entirely upon myself whether I do what is necessary or refrain from doing it."

" All quite true. Proceed."

" I will not take you unawares, and I will leave you time for reflection. I am going to ask you some questions; if you answer them I will set you at liberty, reserving to myself the power of nailing you again some other time. . . ."

Phil Samster smiled.

" If I once get out of here you won't catch me again," he began.

" That is our affair. You are the game and I am the hunter. We have each of us our own devices. Now come to the second point; if you do not answer. . ."

" Well ? "

" Well ! I have shut you up here; just look round this hut, Samster. You may imagine, from its dilapidated appearance, that you have only to knock over the wooden walls and get out. But I will show you your mistake. You are quite wrong. You may use your fists, your teeth, and your nails for weeks against these walls without being an inch nearer free-dom.   Still, as you see, I give you every assistance towards the preservation of your strength.   You may stay here, like a fattened ox, with everything at your disposal ; but out you will not come, or, rather, you will come out to tell me everything I want to know, or go and meditate in prison over the foolishness of obstinacy."

"Why, it is a case of sequestration !"

"Exactly so: but a very mild one, for you will want for nothing.   Now that you understand me, think it over, and ask yourself whether or not you are inclined to obey me."

Phil Samster looked round him.   The room was com-pletely closed, being lighted only from the top, at a height which it would be impossible to reach.   He knew Ned Bark, and knew that he never threatened in vain.

"At least," he said, "I ought to know what you want."

"Quite right.   I will tell you.   You have not forgotten the Battle Field tragedy, the burning of the plantation and the murder of Mr. Valville ?"

Phil bit his lips.

"I don't know what you are talking about."

"As you please.   You refuse to answer my first question.   Well, good evening ! come, gentlemen," said Ned, rising.

Valville and Freedy followed his example.

"The devil !   One moment," said Samster, who saw that he was fairly trapped, and wanted to retain a chance of escape. "Of course I have a slight remembrance of the affair, like everybody else."

"Excuse me, not like everybody else, for you must have some personal reminiscence of it. You were there, I think?"

"I?"

"You, yourself, with Red Ralph, with Bloody Foot, with. . . ."

"The rascals have denounced me, have they?" cried Phil Samster furiously.

"They or others; at any rate I have been told the truth, have I not?"

"Well, yes . . . I was there . . . but I neither killed nor burned. . . ."

"I am glad to hear it. But you were in the pay of the assassin and the incendiary, and you helped him to carry off a young lady. . . ."

"She went with him of her own free will," muttered the bandit.

"You lie!" cried Valville, unable to restrain his anger.

"You! I've not got to answer you," said Phil, shrugging his shoulders.

"Nevertheless," said Ned softly, imposing silence on Valville by a gesture, "I warn you that this gentleman is the son of the murdered man, and brother of the young lady who has been carried off."

Samster started, and, in spite of himself, turned pale. The situation was a more serious one than he had at first imagined.

"You understand then," said the detective, with his

usual calmness, "that I do not question you in a spirit of idle curiosity. We know that you are not the chief culprit in the affair. You are quite sufficiently embroiled with justice without any superfluous addition to your offences. But in order to sum up your account exactly, we must know its different items. The real criminal is Red Ralph. Tell us where he is and you are free."

Samster rose in his turn and exclaimed roughly—

"I! turn traitor? never!"

"Ah, bah! how scrupulous we are! You are a thief, an incendiary, an assassin, and yet you have scruples! As you please, but what you will not tell us you will have to tell the judge, who will be less indulgent to you than we are, for he will remember the fire at the Docks, and by virtue of the sentence there delivered will very soon send you to the gallows."

"But I don't know where Red Ralph is."

"You lie."

"What?"

"I say, and I repeat to you, that you lie, for Red Ralph caused you to be informed of his approaching return to Louisiana."

"That is not true."

"Why should I lie, my good friend?" said Ned, smiling. "Here is a note under his own hand which condemns you."

So saying, Ned drew from his pocket a greasy note-book.

"My note-book!" exclaimed Phil, hurriedly feeling his clothes.

"Yes, indeed your note-book, which I quietly abstracted from your pocket while I was bringing you here, and where I found this, that is to say, a short note written in thieves' dialect, which I will translate as I read."

And Ned Bark read aloud—

"We have escaped pursuit. Prepare the house you know of. Prudence."

"It is true," he added, "that neither date nor any indication of place is given. But you must know from what spot this note has been addressed to you."

Phil Samster was silent.

"At any rate," continued Ned, "mention is made of a house that you know. Tell me where it is and you are free."

"And if not . . . ?"

"If not, you will never leave this place except to go to prison; I have already said so, and I never fail to keep my word."

Phil Samster's perplexity was evidently very great. Compacts are often made between bandits which they feel bound to respect. Yet the peril was imminent. Phil had escaped all pursuit for two years; for, as Ned had guessed, the police-officers, in league with the 'carpet-baggers,' had secured his immunity. But if he once fell into the hands of justice he was lost.

Freedy could trace the alternations of internal combat in the bandit's face, at the same time he noticed that Valville's agitation each moment grew greater. The young man's hand was in his pocket, where, no doubt, he grasped his revolver, in readiness to take swift and sudden vengeance on the robber.

"I have not yet spoken," said Freedy suddenly. "I think that conciliatory methods are best. Let Phil Samster speak, and I will give him on the spot a thousand dollars."

Ned could not repress a shrug of the shoulders. It seemed to him that this was useless prodigality, as he was certain, by means of threats, to lead the bandit to confess.

But the face of Phil Samster suddenly brightened.

"A thousand dollars?" said he, looking curiously at Freedy.

"Here they are, which proves to you that I make no idle promises."

And Phil saw the notes rustling between Freedy's fingers.

The affair became more serious than ever.

"And if I speak," he said, "it is really true—you will pay me?"

"I will pay you at once."

"And I will add another thousand dollars," said Charles, coming to Freedy's aid.

There was no further question as to compact, delicacy of feeling, scruple of any kind that could chain Phil's tongue! Two thousand dollars and liberty! This time he would take care not to be caught again; he would go to the north—to Canada, perhaps—and there lead a joyous life, without any need to fear Red Ralph's resentment.

"Well," said Freedy, "have you decided?"

"Faith, yes; you shall know all."

"One moment," said Ned Bark, whose matter-of-fact brain was always on the alert. "I have delicate feelings too, and I do not wish Phil to accuse me of having taken him prisoner. . . ."

"I am not treating with you, however," began the robber insolently.

"Excuse me; it is I who arranged this conference, therefore I have the honour of warning this gentleman that even when he has given up the secret information which we require, even when he has received the two thousand dollars which have been mentioned, still he will not leave this place."

"What?"

"He will not leave this place," Ned Bark repeated, "for four days at the least."

"Why not?"

"Because, dear sir, your first care would be to inform Red Ralph that we are on his track, so the dollars would be lost, and we should be green enough to let ourselves be tricked like babies."

"I will hold my tongue then," said Phil.

"Ned," said Valville, "you must let us act."

"Not in the very least Friend Phil will very soon hear reason. He will remain here four days, well lodged and fed; for in that cupboard there is plenty of food and plenty of brandy."

"Of brandy?" exclaimed Samster.

"Yes, indeed, old boy!" said Ned, laughing. "You

see I have forgotten nothing which could render your life agreeable. Yes, brandy and whisky, tobacco, fuel, and everything. Come, Phil, accept our conditions once for all. Two thousand dollars, four days' captivity; after that you may go and get hanged wherever you like and however you like."

Ned was right. It was impossible not to yield on these terms. Only, as Phil was still suspicious, it was necessary—first, that Freedy and Valville should give their word that the arrangement proposed by Ned should be carried out to the letter, and that on the morning of the fifth day Samster should be set free; secondly, that the two thousand dollars should be paid down to him at once.

The treaty being thus ratified, Phil spoke.

While our friends were climbing one side of Devil's Rock, Red Ralph and his accomplices were making way, by underground passages known only to themselves, to a certain spot on the coast, at some miles' distance, where they were secure from any surprise. Phil supposed that Red Ralph had despatched the message from this place. He affirmed that he had not seen any messenger. The letter had been slipped into his hand in a crowd, probably by some ' scalawag,' who was one of Red Ralph's accomplices.

He did not know in the least by what road Ralph would return to Louisiana. But the mission with which he had been entrusted was this. Red Ralph possessed a house, situated in a wood, near the village of Woodville, between Bayou Sara and Natchez, a building

which had several times served as a refuge for the bandits after their adventurous expeditions.   It was there
that Phil Samster was to await his chief.   He had not
set off on the previous night, because he lacked funds
for the journey, and it was in order to procure some that
he had repaired to the gambling-den in which Ned Bark
had surprised him.   The detective had been on his track
for several hours, and had found little difficulty in following up the trail.

He could tell nothing more.

" And now," said he, " give me the dollars and let me
alone.   Ah ! one word more, and it is to Ned Bark that
I address it.   I think he is enough of a man of honour"
—how oddly the words came from the lips of such a
ruffian — " not to denounce me to Red Ralph.   For,'
he added, with a sort of shudder, " if he knew that I had
betrayed him I should be a dead man."

" Set your mind at rest," said Valville.   " You have
our promise."

The result, thus gained, of their expedition was very
valuable.   Thanks to Phil Samster's information, they
were certain of surprising Red Ralph at last, and, perhaps, of rescuing his victim.

" Sir," said Valville to the incendiary, " you have
committed many crimes, but the service which to-day
you are rendering to honest men may in some degree
atone for your past life."

Phil shrugged his shoulders.   He did not care for
that : he had his brandy and his dollars ; the rest mattered
very little to him.

Ned made himself sure once more that the doors were fastened, and that all chance of escape was impossible; then he placed within Phil's reach every possible means of relieving the tedium and the solitude of his captivity.

" Good-bye for four days then," were his last words.

The three men left the cabin, and the heavy bar of the outer door fell into its place.

"Now to New Orleans," said Ned. " I don't think we have managed badly. Really, Red Ralph must be the devil himself if he escapes us now. Let us go and reassure the friends who are waiting for you, whom your long absence must have disquieted, and then let us be off to Woodville."

" Do you notice," said Freedy, " that we have obtained an explanation of that letter, the fragments of which were found in poor Jeanne's retreat? Had she not heard a name uttered which began with the syllable ' Wood '?"

" True," said Valville, " I have some hope at last. My poor sister, how much she must have suffered! How much care and tenderness we owe her to make her forget her miseries!"

The three men made their way very rapidly to New Orleans.

There a carriage conducted them to M. Blanchemont's house.

Lucile was gazing out of the window. When she saw her brother and Doctor Freedy appear, she pressed her hand to her heart and turned deathly pale.

But no one dies of joy. She had passed a night of agony, thinking of her brother, and also of her brother's friend, whom she feared that she might never see again. Madame Longpré had not quitted her side, and had received her whole confidence. She smiled therefore with a slightly mischievous air when the young girl held out her hand to Charles, with scarcely a glance at Freedy, and said—

"How unkind it was of you, Charles, to make us all so anxious!"

Ned Bark was invited to join the family repast. At first he refused decidedly to do so, for this is a peculiarly French custom. Any one who renders a service to a Frenchman becomes his friend. But Ned Bark found this difficult to understand. He was a paid servant. If he rendered any service he was only earning his wages. And yet—American though he was—if he had seriously and carefully questioned himself he might have discovered that he, the detective, had begun to feel positive affection for those whom he was resolute in considering only as his employers, and that he was now expending in their business far more interest and emotion than was at all necessary for the completion of a mere bargain.

It was decided that they should start for Woodville that very evening. It was an expedition which might prove dangerous, for they were about to stand face to face with the bandits, and would probably have to lay siege in good earnest to the house before they took possession of it.

Ned promised his friends the help of two men for whom he could vouch. Valville, Freedy, and Sambo were ready to start. Thus their force consisted of six determined well-armed men, all the stronger—as M. Blanchemont said—because they were upholding a good cause.

M. Blanchemont, however, hazarded one objection.

"Why not apply to the regular police? Why not call in the aid of the military?"

Ned grew somewhat impatient.

"Because, as I have said a hundred times, the regular police, as you call them, have lately been irregular enough to ally themselves with all these brigands, and we should have treachery to fear."

They adhered, therefore, to their first plan.

How should they reach Bayou Sara? There is no railway line extending the whole length of the Mississippi. The trains from New Orleans go to the west of Vermilion and Opelousas, and it is only at the latter station that a branch line to Bâton-Rouge can be found. From Bâton-Rouge one must go by water to Bayou Sara, whence there is a short railway line to Woodville. A journey thus made would be long and complicated. On the other hand, the steamers which navigate the Mississippi stop at a great number of stations in order to take travellers or goods on board.

"Our best way," said Freedy, "would be to engage the services of the captain of some little steamer, which would then be entirely at our own disposal, and would accomplish the distance in a very short time."

Money will indeed do everything, and fortunately our friends were rich.

At sunset, therefore, they stepped on board a lightly-built steamer with a flat keel, and at the sound of a bell the engines began to work, while Alice and Lucile stood on the bank with full hearts, and waved their handkerchiefs in token of farewell to the men who were once more about to risk their lives.

Even the woman with the iron will had tears in her eyes!

Ned Bark had kept his word. Two Georgians of colossal size had been introduced by the detective, and were ready for vigorous action.

The little band was full of confidence.

"At last we approach the end," said Valville. "The time seems long. I want to stand face to face with Red Ralph, and punish him as he deserves for the misery he has caused."

Meanwhile the vessel, flinging high into the air its jet of steam, glided swiftly down the waters of the Father of Rivers.

When a traveller finds himself for the first time in sight of the Mississippi, he is apt to experience a feeling of disappointment.

But a contrary feeling arises little by little within him, and his admiration increases by degrees. The more one sees and knows of the country around this mighty river the greater becomes one's appreciation of its grandeur and beauty.

It was first discovered in 1672, but its true source was not known before the explorations of Schoolcraft, who, in 1832, announced that it rose in a small lake, called by the French Lake La Biche, but generally known as Lake

Itasca. This lake is a fine sheet of water, irregular in form, and eight miles in length, situated amidst wood-covered hills and fed by fresh-water springs. Its waters form a cascade at one end, and here the Mississippi is born. The lake is about fifteen hundred feet above the level of the sea, and more than two thousand miles from the Gulf of Mexico.

The river drains an extent of country which is un-equalled for beauty and fertility. The territory, called the valley of the Mississippi, extends as far south as the Gulf of Mexico; east, to the Alleghany Mountains, and west, to the Rocky Mountains. The length of its course is two thousand four hundred miles.

The Mississippi is navigable by steam-vessels, with but slight interruption, as far as the falls of St. Anthony, at a distance of about four hundred miles from its source. Its course is extremely tortuous, and détours of twenty or thirty miles are frequently necessary in order to accomplish a distance which could easily be traversed, as the crow flies, in two hours. In other places, the dis-tance is, on the contrary, shortened by means of narrow canals called 'cut-offs,' through which the water rushes with so violent a current that the earth on each side is torn away, and a stream quite sufficiently large for the passage of steamboats is speedily formed. What renders navigation difficult is the existence of enormous mounds of earth, surmounted by trees, which are detached from the banks by the force of the water, and which, like floating islands, form obstacles well-nigh insurmount-able.

Sometimes, also, great banks of mud rise to the surface of the water, and occasion many a shipwreck. These mud-banks are called in the special dialect of the place, ' snags ' or ' sawyers.' They are generally as round in form as if their shape had been traced by the point of a compass.

On leaving New Orleans, the first station of any importance is Plaquemine, in the parish of Iberville. It is situated near the mouth of the Plaquemine Bayou, twenty-three miles south of Bâton-Rouge. Before the war, enormous quantities of cotton used to be transported from this point to New Orleans.

After Plaquemine comes Bâton-Rouge, the ancient capital of Louisiana. It is one of the wealthiest towns in that part of the country. It contains a college, an arsenal, and barracks.

It is said that the name of Bâton-Rouge was first given to this place because at the very spot where its earliest inhabitants built their huts there stood a red-barked cypress-tree of immense bulk and height, but entirely bare of branches. One of the settlers observed to a companion that this tree would make a splendid cane. And from this simple joke the name of Bâton-Rouge was given to the town. The story may perhaps be true.

The next landing-place is at Port Hudson, which was attacked in 1863 by General Banks, and surrendered to the Northern troops in July, after the news of the fall of Vicksburg.

Our friends disembarked at Bayou Sara.

Thence they went by train to Woodville.

And on the morning of the following day they entered the woods, in the midst of which, according to Phil Samster's instructions, they hoped to find the house belonging to Red Ralph.

CHAPTER XXI.

PUNISHMENT.

WOODVILLE, a small industrial town, has, it seems, gained for itself the right of inserting its name on the map of the United States. Yet it is neither a hamlet nor a village, but a manufacturing place, where hundreds of workmen in iron show how much needed was the short railway line which runs to Bayou Sara and connects the interior of the country with the Mississippi.

Woodville means a town in the woods. Therefore some resolution is necessary on the part of a tourist who knows that such a town exists and wishes to reach it, for it is completely hidden by the surrounding forests. Yet Woodville may congratulate itself on standing in a very pleasant situation.

The Blue River, descending from the hills and spreading itself abroad upon the plain until it loses itself in numerous streams which are almost rivers in themselves, expands near the town of Woodville into a sort of lake, bordered by manufactories and ironworks. A canal has been constructed from the Mississippi to the Blue River, in order to facilitate the arrival of vessels at Woodville. The river presents the appearance of a large basin, and recalls, in miniature, the view of the Thames from London Bridge. From the enormous chimneys a dark fog hovers over the town, which is noisy with incessant activity. A bridge crosses the water ; and, to continue the comparison, the dome of St. Bartholomew, surmounted by a cross, rises in the distance, and brings to mind the great dome of St. Paul's.

If it were not for the railway, for an almost impracticable road, and for the Blue River quays, it would seem as if the inhabitants of Woodville disdained to open communications with any other part of the world.

The town is surrounded with a broad belt of verdure, as on all sides of it arise great forests of trees of every kind. This part of Louisiana seems to retain all the peculiarities of the Mexican flora. From the bay-cinnamon tree, the bark of which produces an aromatic oil, from the pyramid-shaped clove-tree and the shaddock, whose branches form a refuge for a magnificently beautiful butterfly, to the magnolia, developed in vigorous splendour unknown in France, the baobab tree, with deeply-cleft leaves extending over an area of more than forty or fifty feet, and the white hazel, whose rugged bark resembles an alligator's skin, everything grows in wild luxuriance, and forms a strong firmly-planted fence which no human labour has yet pierced through.

There are no paths. The royal palm-tree, the sturdy oak, the banyan, and the date-tree interlace their branches, until they look like reptiles doing battle in the air.

It was into this labyrinth that our friends had plunged.

Perhaps it would have been wise to secure a guide. For what did they know? Only that Red Ralph possessed, somewhere in these solitudes, a place of refuge carefully concealed from every one. Certainly Phil Samster had given them directions, which, from afar, seemed most precise. But in the midst of this maze of trees, would it be possible to pursue the track that he had indicated?

But Freedy and Valville had not hesitated. To take a guide was only a way of exposing themselves to fresh treachery. Ned Bark finally agreed with them.

They went forward, therefore, rather by chance, attentively listening to the slightest sounds, each man carrying a loaded gun in his hand.

For this time they knew that the combat was for life or death.

Several hours passed in fruitless search. None of them felt fatigue. But a slight feeling of discouragement arose in every heart. Had Samster deceived them?

Certainly it seemed as if he had had every motive for speaking the truth, since his liberty and his life depended upon the success of his enemies' enterprise. But who could boast of having clearly read the robber's heart?

It was quite possible that, at the moment when they least expected it, there might arise any one of those complications which set all warnings at defiance and put to confusion the best-considered schemes.

The sun was touching the horizon. In an hour it would be dark.

By the aid of the compass, however, our friends were certain of being able to regain Woodville.

But none of them uttered a word about turning back.

There was a sort of general presentiment felt amongst them that the crisis was approaching. In spite of the failure of their search amongst the thicknesses of the dark forest, they felt a sensation of confidence which no discouragement could overcome.

"If necessary," Valville had said, "we will spend the night in the wood."

"As you please," Freedy had replied.

Ned Bark was equally determined not to abandon the contest.

"At the point where we stand now," he said, "the least delay, the least hesitation, may ruin everything. Who knows whether Red Ralph will not merely touch at his house near Woodville, and then drag his victim to more remote districts? We must wait for him at all risks, seize him, force him even by violence to obey us."

The night closed in. Nothing is stranger than the impression produced by the gathering of the evening shadows in a wood. And what a wood was this! There was no opening through which a ray of light could penetrate. A dome of darkness seemed gradually to settle down upon the traveller. First the leaves began to lose their distinctness, until they looked like crayon-drawings.

Then the darker lines of the branches alone stood out in black outline. Then it seemed as if leaves and branches alike became confused, intermingled, lost. A black platform was built up by degrees above the heads of the wayfarers.

In the gleam of the fading twilight, Ned Bark had again consulted the notes which he had made of Phil Samster's confessions. It was impossible, if the ruffian had told the truth, that they could be far from the spot indicated. But where was this accursed house? Hidden in a ravine? Concealed by a grove of trees on the summit of a hill? No answer could be given to this question.

"Let us trust to chance," said Freedy. "Let us remain here, but no one must sleep. We will place sentinels at the different points which give access to the spot where we are, and then we will wait for Providence to direct us."

"It is the wisest way," said Ned Bark. "Either Red Ralph has already gained his retreat in these solitudes, and will have to come out of it, or he has not yet arrived; and how prudent soever his attendants may be, it will be impossible for them not to betray themselves, if only by some rustling of the branches. The first supposition is highly improbable. We have made such haste that Red Ralph could scarcely have been before us. The second case is much the more likely one. Let us wait."

Not one of them felt any desire for sleep.

The men whom Ned Bark had hired, stimulated by the prospect of a high reward, were only too anxious to prove their zeal.

As for the others, they were seized with that fever which sometimes precedes the taking of decisive steps. Ned Bark had the honour of his profession at heart. He wished to succeed. Valville thought of his dead father and his lost sister. Freedy could not forget that at New Orleans there were two lovely eyes which would thank him for his efforts by their gentle glances.

And it was not Freedy the impassible who was the least moved of the party.

Ned Bark's two acolytes were placed on guard. They were used to forest solitudes, and their ears were quick to catch the faintest passing sounds. Ten years before they had been engaged in the last contest with the Indians.

Sambo, apparently indifferent, was stretched upon the ground. But his ear touched the earth. He was ready to give the alarm.

Ned, Freedy, and Valville, leaning against tree-trunks, waited with the immobility of statues. As each hour passed, Ned Bark uttered a few words concerning the time, and the others replied, thus showing that they were not yet overcome by sleep.

That was all.

It was already eleven o'clock. Nothing unusual had been heard or seen.

Suddenly Ned started. No one noticed his movement. His forehead contracted, his one eye gleamed with a singular lustre. Suddenly he turned round, and, with the rapidity of a machine worked by a spring, bounded into the midst of the thicket.

A stifled groan was heard.

Nothing more.   A few seconds passed in silence.

Then Ned Bark reappeared.

" Up !" he said in a low tone.   " I have caught one !"

Scarcely had he said these words when a shot was heard.

One of the sentinels had just discharged his gun at a black form which he had seen creeping through the shadows.

Then came a sort of general rush forward.   Each of our six acquaintances found himself confronted by an adversary.   It was easy to tell, on such a night, that these newcomers were adversaries indeed.

For men who would adventure themselves in this manner in almost impracticable woods were almost sure to be bandits.   Therefore Valville and his companions did not hesitate to throw themselves upon the persons whom they saw.

Blows were interchanged, and balls sped hither and thither.   But the men thus suddenly attacked did not seem disposed to sustain a long conflict.   Disengaging themselves from their assailants, those who were un-wounded took to flight with surprising swiftness, considering how nearly impossible it was to thread the labyrinth.

Out of the troop which had attacked Valville's men, three remained prostrate on the ground.

One of them had had his chest pierced by the ball of a revolver.   He gave no sign of life.

The second, who had fought with Freedy, had had his forehead laid open by a knife, and was insensible.

The third, upon whom Ned Bark had thrown himself, was safe and sound in life and limb. The detective had, in a second, tied his hands and feet so securely that during the combat he had been utterly unable to move.

"Here is the man who will guide us to the place," said the detective. "Come! it is useless to hide ourselves. War has been declared. Let us light the torches."

In a few moments Ned Bark's order had been executed. The glossy leaves reflected the lights a thousandfold. Not one of Valville's six men had been wounded.

Ned Bark forced his prisoner to stand upright, and pushed him into the circle.

"Listen to me," he said. "You see this"—and he showed him a revolver—"and this." 'This' was a purse, through the meshes of which the gold pieces glittered brightly. "You may choose . . . money, or a ball through the head. You see, the situation lies before you."

The prisoner was a short, fat man, with starting eyes; one of those wretches who, in their poverty, hire themselves at any price to any man for any cause.

"What do you want of me?" he asked in a hoarse voice.

"Tell us where you were going with your companions."

"To rejoin our chief."

"That is Red Ralph, I suppose?"

" Yes."

" What were you going to do when you had joined him ? "

" Get our money; he has made us wait for it a long time."

" That is clear enough, and we will put your frankness down to your account. Now we come to the decisive question—What had Red Ralph promised you ? "

" Twenty dollars."

" This purse contains fifty. If you like, it shall be yours."

" What am I do ? "

" Lead us to your chief's retreat."

The man started, and a livid pallor covered his face. It could be seen that the very idea of treachery caused him profound terror.

" What do you fear ? " Ned Bark asked.

" The chief will kill me."

" Yes, if you fall into his hands. But you may be sure that if you tell us the secret which we wish to know, you will have nothing more to fear from him."

For an instant the man gazed at the faces around him.

He understood two things at once.

First, that these were honest men, and that if they sought Red Ralph, it was in order to punish him for his crimes.

Secondly, that they were courageous and well armed, and that their success was possible.

" I accept your terms," he said.

" At last ! " exclaimed Valville. " Let us lose no time."

" I make one condition," said the man.

" What?" asked Ned Bark sternly. "·Make haste to speak, for we may yet remember that you are only a brigand, and Red Ralph's accomplice."

" I will guide you to the place where you will find him. It is a house in the depths of the forest, called Green House. But, after I have shown it to you, you must let me go."

" That is to say that you are afraid we shall not capture Red Ralph, and that then he may think of vengeance?"

" Supposing that it is so, have I your promise?"

Now, that Ned Bark and his companions were on Red Ralph's track, they cared very little for the capture of this inferior accomplice of the bandit.

" You may go then; we promise it."

" Then follow me."

" But don't forget that I have my eye on you," added Ned Bark, " and that at the slightest sign of treachery I shall blow your brains out."

As they were about to set out, the man who had been wounded and whom the midnight coolness had revived drew himself into a sitting posture, and cried out to his old companion—

" Judas! Coward! You are selling us!"

The other shrugged his shoulders.

" He is sorry that you did not apply to him," he murmured in Ned Bark's ear.

While the little troop made its way through the thickets, Freedy turned to Valville.

"Do you remember," he said, "the Indian who preferred death to the possibility of treason?"

"I have never forgotten him. That man was truly brave."

"Well! compare the two. See what civilisation does for those to whom it gives no morality. The guilty savage guards his point of honour; the civilised bandit has not even the elements of moral sense."

"Is it a long way?" Ned asked of the guide.

"In less than half an hour you will reach Green House."

"But what is to prove that you are not leading us into some ambuscade?"

"My own interest," replied the robber cynically. "If you were attacked, the assailants' balls would strike friend and foe alike. My life would be imperilled; whilst now I risk nothing, unless you are cheating me and do not give me the promised sum."

"You know that you have nothing to fear."

They were now mounting a height. The brushwood around them grew thicker and thicker, and walking became extremely difficult.

The man—forestalling a question from Ned Bark—said to him—

"This is not the way that the others took. If they are awaiting you, it will be on the other side of the hill."

Suddenly a voice cried—

"Who goes there?"

"Put out the torches," said Ned.

Utter darkness reigned in the woods.

" Before you, over that hedge, lies Green House."

" Well, wait a moment," said Ned.

He threw himself on the ground, and began to crawl towards the place indicated by the bandit.

There, through the darkness, he could see the blackish mass of a building surrounded with trees.

He returned and unloosed the robber's bonds.

" You are free," he said. " There is the money. Go."

The man thrust the purse into his belt.

" One piece of advice," he said. " We were twenty; you are six. Take care."

At the enumeration of their men, Ned could not repress a slight start. But at the same instant the report of a gun was heard, and balls began to whistle round the little troop, cutting and tearing the boughs and trunks beside them.

" Forward!" cried Ned Bark, " and God protect us!"

They rushed forward. Quickly they crossed the thick hedge which separated them from the open space in which Green House was standing. It was a sort of hut, two storeys high, built of the trunks of trees, and having one large window, now brilliantly lighted.

Shoulder to shoulder, the six men dashed upon the dark shadows grouped in front of the house, without waiting to fire. Surprised by this unforeseen attack, the bandits faltered at first, and some of them lost their footing. The others, however, soon regained their self-possession, and bullets again whistled through the air.

One of the attacking party fell. It was one of Ned Bark's men.

The combat grew fiercer and more terrible; it was a hand-to-hand contest in which each blow told.

Freedy had seized his gun by the barrel, and was using its butt-end as a club.

Suddenly Valville, carried away by fury, cried out—

"Where are you hiding, Red Ralph?"

The window was thrown violently open.

"Is it Charles Valville who speaks?"

"Myself! Ah! you are there, ruffian! Well, then! . . ."

He discharged his gun at the form which had appeared at the window.

But the passion that moved him caused his arm to swerve aside.

Red Ralph's voice resounded once more through the night. He called to his companions—

"Stop fighting, and let these men come in to me."

The ascendency exercised by the bandit over his accomplices was strange indeed. At his order they ceased the combat, and turned towards the door of the hut.

Charles advanced to it resolutely.

Ned Bark laid his hand on the young man's arm.

"Take care," said he, "Once inside that house, and you are in his power."

It might have been thought that Red Ralph had heard these words, although uttered in so low a voice, for suddenly the door opened, and he appeared upon the threshold alone. And, so great is the effect of courage when displayed even by the most hardened criminal, that Valville, who had his revolver in his hand, involuntarily lowered his arm.

"Enter," said Red Ralph. "And you, men, retire. Remember that you will answer with your heads for the lives of these men."

Then, re-entering the house, he signed to Valville and his companions to follow him.

We may perhaps recall the slight sketch of the bandit's appearance traced by Valville after his first encounter with Red Ralph in the Island of Anastasia.

"A man of high stature," he had said, "with stern features, and a countenance full of savage energy."

Was this the same man who now appeared before him?

The tall form was bent, as if the weight of misfortune, perhaps of remorse, had lain heavy upon him; on his features, worn, weary, sunken, there was a shadow of dejection and sinister resignation.

He turned to Valville.

"Now," he said, "you may kill me."

"Not before you have spoken, wretched man; I have no false generosity. Yes, I would have your life," cried Valville with redoubled fury, "for you are my father's murderer! But before anything else, you must give me back the beloved sister whom you have so basely carried away from us!"

There was a silence.

Red Ralph passed his hand over his forehead, and then said in a trembling voice—

"My life belongs to you, but I am no longer able to restore to you her whom you seek."

"What do you mean?   Take care; my patience is at an end."

"I tell you that your sister is not in my power . . ."

"What!   You are deceiving me!"

He fixed his burning glance on Red Ralph's face.   A sudden desolating thought crossed his mind.

"Dead!" he cried.   "She is dead! and you have killed her!"

"No, no!" said Red Ralph with vehemence, "I swear that I never touched her!"

"Where is she, then?"

"Your sister has disappeared."

"You lie!"

"She disappeared on the day after I escaped from your pursuit, at the foot of Devil's Rock!"

Ned, Freedy, and Valville were terrified.   They would have been glad to believe that this story was a lie.   But the bandit's accent of despair, the agony of his expression, showed that he spoke the truth.

"Look at me," said Red Ralph sadly, "and you will understand why I renounce the contest.   Yes—I committed a crime—but I have told you already, it was because a mad unconquerable passion had taken possession of me, and to vanquish the resistance that maddened me, I bent before her, I knelt at her very knees. At other times, beside myself, I threatened her with death; but her implacable contempt pursued me always —always; yet all the tortures I suffered are nothing to those that rend my heart now."

"She has disappeared!" exclaimed Ned Bark. "But how? under what circumstances?"

"Do I know myself? We left Devil's Rock—can you tell why? Because I did not wish to fight—not from cowardice, you will not imagine that!—but because I feared that the brother of the woman whom I loved would fall, and that his corpse would prove another barrier between herself and me. By almost impassable roads, known only to myself, I regained the seashore,—we passed one last night in Florida; there, in a spacious cavern, I had arranged a shelter for her. But that night I slept not: dark presentiments disturbed my rest. I had already sent by one of my men an order that this house should be prepared, for here I wished to make one crowning effort. In the morning, when I gave the word for departure, your sister did not appear. I had never penetrated to her chamber, but that day I resolved on doing so. Woe is me! in the night she had escaped. How? I have never been able to understand. Ah! what I felt was both rage and despair! In vain I sent my men in all directions; in vain I searched the whole neighbourhood, even to the most inaccessible heights! That is why I tell you I cannot give you back your sister. Kill me if you like."

There was no room for doubt. This story must be true!

New agonies of suspense and anxiety thrilled the hearts of Valville and his friends.

"You offer me your life," said Valville. "I will not murder you. You have arms, you may defend yourself."

"So be it," said Red Ralph.

A moment later the two men found themselves face to face, at a distance of twenty feet from each other, in the wide space in front of Green House.

"Listen," said Red Ralph to his men. "I have paid you. If I die, you will find in the house a considerable sum of money. Divide it among yourselves. Now, whatever happens, remember that the man against whom I am about to risk my life is to be sacred for you—the man himself, and all who accompany him."

A murmur of assent was heard.

The torches were relighted. The scene was striking, and at the same time intensely sad.

"Are you ready?" asked Freedy.

"Ready," answered the two men.

The American clapped his hands three times.

At the third blow a shot was heard.

Red Ralph threw out his arms, and fell, face forward to the ground. Valville's bullet had pierced his heart.

The bandits pressed round him.

"Dead!" said one of them. "Go, gentlemen, you are free."

With shoulders bowed, and faces pale, Valville and his companions turned away from Green House.

The Battle Field planter was avenged.

But Jeanne? his daughter! Alas, she had doubtless met with a frightful death in the solitudes of Florida.

CHAPTER XXII.

NEXT morning the little band embarked at Bayou Sara.

Few words were interchanged during the sad journey.

Notwithstanding his energy, Ned Bark now found himself destitute of the confidence which he had hitherto exhibited.

An accident to their steamer forced them to stop at some leagues' distance from New Orleans. Fortunately, America is covered with a network of telegraphic wires, and it was possible for them to announce their return to the Blanchemonts' house.

They hired horses, and were sure of reaching the town in two or three hours by a cross road.

Ned went first, probably in order that he might reflect at his ease upon the chances which still remained to them. As his one eye was endowed with the faculty of piercing sight, he perceived at some distance from their party a person who was riding towards them from an opposite direction. The horse and rider seemed to strike him peculiarly.

He allowed a host of contradictory exclamations to escape him.

4 Y

"Yes? no! it is impossible! and yet! . . ."

And then Ned Bark, who was of an essentially inquisitive nature, determined to solve the problem which so deeply perplexed him.

He spurred forward his horse and galloped up to the person in question, without much regarding the chance of a fall over a precipice near the road, where a torrent dashed wildly down the rocks.

But when he was but a few yards from the man he uttered an exclamation.

"Good heavens!" he cried.

"Good morning, Mr. detective!" said a laughing voice.

"The deuce! it is he himself! it is you! impossible!"

And the worthy detective, who was not easily moved, found himself stirred by singular emotion, for the man whom he had just recognised was no other than the fop Parisian, Eusèbe, in flesh and blood, and not dead at all.

The detective had taken a great fancy to the brave, reckless lad, who had really given signs of true courage and self-devotion.

"But this is not to be believed," exclaimed Ned. "Where do you come from? Where have you been?"

"You shall hear all the details, my old Vidocq," replied Eusèbe. "I am like a cat, I always fall on my feet. But wait awhile; where are the others?"

"Behind; see, here they are."

And, in fact, anxious to know what had become of the

detective, the friends had urged their horses to their utmost speed.

In another moment Eusèbe was beside them.

What exclamations followed! His reappearance caused great delight to Freedy and Valville. Indeed, Freedy, the phlegmatic, leaned over to Eusèbe and fairly embraced him with both arms, while Charles nearly crushed his hands with squeezing them.

Then all manner of questions had to be asked.

" What had happened to him? Why had he left the band at Devil's Rock?"

" My little lambs," said Eusèbe, with his most malicious air of fun, " you must allow me to tell you, that at the receipt of your telegram . . ."

" What! you are at the Blanchemonts' house?"

" As safe as a barndoor fowl."

" How long have you been there?"

" Since last night."

" This is really wonderful; but tell us . . ."

" Please let me finish my sentence. I was telling you that at the receipt of your telegram I left my breakfast behind to come and meet you; that I am dying of hunger; and that when my appetite claims satisfaction, I cannot bear to hear myself speak : whence this conclusion—after the first course I shall be at your service. And calm yourselves, for the far-famed Robinson Crusoe, who wrote a pretty little volume of about three hundred pages, with illustrations, met with no adventures that can in the least be compared to mine!"

" You were not wounded?"

"Nor killed : no, as you see. All the same, I will not tell you a word. Oh, I have surprises for you ! such surprises ! enough to make you gape with wonder for the rest of your lives, which, I hope, may be long."

They could not extract any further information from him. He had a curiously joyous look; and beneath each of his words they could discern a mysterious reticence; for although he declared that he would not speak, it was easy for the most unobservant person to guess that he was burning to tell them some great piece of news.

Twenty times or more he repeated the same phrases, with the Parisian accent which was the pride of his heart.

"You will be surprised ! you will be surprised, every one of you ! "

In fact he was a little too cheerful; and observing that Valville's face grew gloomy, he added—

"By the way, did your expedition through the woods succeed ? "

"No," said Charles, laconically, somewhat irritated by this tone of exaggerated gaiety.

"Ah, bah ! a bad thing ! what ! nothing at all ? and you never met the worthy Red Ralph ? "

"Ralph is dead," said Freedy.

This time Eusèbe looked grave.

"Well done," he said; "for, between ourselves, he was a rough customer."

"My dear Eusèbe," said Valville, rather drily, "you know that we are very glad to see you again safe and sound; but allow me to tell you that your merriment is somewhat out of place. You forget that my poor sister, Jeanne, has disappeared; and that . . ."

He could not complete his sentence; for Eusèbe bent forward as if he wished to hide the expression of his countenance, and interrupted him quickly—

"Ah! just so! you want to lecture Coco? Then I'll be off."

And he galloped away, spurring on his horse as he left them.

Freedy and Valville looked at each other. Had Eusèbe gone mad?

Yet, without confessing it, they felt some curiosity augmented by each moment's delay, to know what had happened, and the word 'surprise,' emphasized by Eusèbe, rang in their anxious ears.

They put their horses to a gallop and soon arrived at the town. Without stopping they turned into Canal Street, and drew bridle only when they had reached the Blanchemonts' house.

Scarcely had they dismounted when the hall doors were flung widely open.

A cry of surprise, indeed, escaped their lips; for the servants and negroes, dressed in holiday garb, were all drawn up to meet them, and the walls and doors were half hidden beneath decorations of leaves and flowers.

The steward opened the drawing-room door and drew back to let the newcomers pass in.

The room was empty.

"What is the matter?" cried Valville.

" This is the surprise !" exclaimed Eusèbe's voice.

And the young man reappeared, with his sister Alice, Madame Longpré, and all the Blanchemont family.

"Charles," said Alice to her lover, "you have been strong in bearing sorrow, can you also be strong in bearing joy ? "

Charles turned pale : all the blood seemed to leave his face.

"Ah, speak !" he cried ; "for mercy's sake, tell me what all this means."

Then the door of another room opened, and two young girls appeared, with arms entwined around each other's waists.   The first was Lucile.

But who was the other ?

"Jeanne ! my dearest Jeanne !" exclaimed Charles, and, rushing forward, he pressed his sister in his arms.

"Don't you think I have given you a surprise after all ? " cried Eusèbe.

Yes, it was Jeanne herself, alive and well.

Overwhelmed with emotion, Valville sank down upon a sofa, scarcely able to speak or stand.

"Yes, I am here," said Jeanne.   "And first of all, let me tell you, Charles, that the happiness of seeing each other again is due to . . . to . . . him ! "

'To him ?'   She meant Coco, the Parisian dandy.

And, in spite of all his assurance, Eusèbe turned as red as a turkey-cock, and murmured—

"It's true—a little ; but I must say that a good deal is owing to yourself, Mademoiselle."

"Come to the dining-room," said M. Blanchemont, "and there Jeanne and Eusèbe will tell us all."

Is there any sight more beautiful, or more touching, than that of the first family meal taken in common by the members of a family reunited after a long and bitter separation? How many events, how many fears and sorrows had torn the hearts of these men and women since last they met together.

And their stories! They had to be told and compared before they could seem possible, for their details were curiously intermixed and entangled.

Jeanne had suffered much; and yet, as she frankly owned, the man Red Ralph had retained some traces of noble feeling within him. He had threatened her a hundred times, but a word, a look, had been sufficient to quell him. He had given way to unbridled excesses of rage resembling madness, and again he had seemed to be afraid and ashamed of himself.

"And still," Jeanne added, "I was always doubtful whether his passions would not carry him too far. I lived in perpetual fear. Ah, those sleepless nights when I heard this man, who also did not sleep, prowling round my cave like a wild beast!

"At last I gathered, from a few words dropped in my hearing, that you were in pursuit of him. That day I gave myself up for lost. There was a frightful, terrible scene between us. Yet once more I conquered; but then he forced me away from Devil's Rock. I felt that he was no longer master of himself; I despaired, felt that I was lost, and resolved at all hazards to escape.

How I managed to quit the cave where he had placed me, how it was that they did not find me, I cannot tell. It seems like a miracle to me now!

"When I felt the free air blow upon my brow I think I went mad. I ran forward through the darkness—anywhere—knocking against the trees and slipping over the rocks. Once I lost my balance and should have fallen down a precipice but for a timely hand that seized and saved me—your brother's hand, Alice."

"Ah, my friend, my brother!" cried Valville, seizing Eusèbe's hand.

"All the same," said Eusèbe, "you were going to treat me in very peculiar manner just now, because I looked a little bit too cheerful."

"Forgive me."

"Perhaps . . . if you are good."

"But how did it happen, my dear Eusèbe," asked Freedy, "that chance led you so opportunely to Mademoiselle Jeanne's aid?"

"In this way," said Eusèbe. "I must tell you I had a grudge against the detective . . ."

"Against me?" said Ned Bark, laughing.

"Yes, indeed! You always looked as if you were laughing at me, as if I didn't make enough show; so I resolved to play you a trick in my own way."

"How?"

"In this way—I, Eusebius the Great, would find her whom you thought you could discover by yourselves; so I took my walking-stick and set off on a little tour in the neighbourhood. But I turned to the right and to the left, and I went straight on, and I soon lost myself completely. You may perhaps think that I was frightened. I had good reason to be so since I set foot on this land of Vespucius—I will not vex the shade of Christopher Columbus by mentioning his name. But I said to myself: 'I have learned that if one goes straight on one will always reach some place or other, even in America.' So off I set again—I don't know where. Between ourselves, I may mention that this country sadly lacks two things—newspapers and restaurants. I won't positively swear that I did not swallow a sort of live frog which I mistook for a fruit!

" I went on and on, with watchful eyes and wary footsteps. Night came. I swung myself up into a tree, after having addressed to any snakes that might be in the neighbourhood a touchingly-worded request that they would leave me alone. I was suddenly awakened by a rustling of branches. I looked and saw a black form, and I said to myself, ' There's a policeman. I'll ask him the way.' I slipped down from my tree, and —the black form made a false step and nearly fell. I picked it up, and it was—Mademoiselle! And really, I am quite pleased with what I have done !"

The brave lad laughed again. But his gaiety was somewhat forced, and a tear was standing in his eye.

" How did you get back to Louisiana ? "

" Ah, brother," said Jeanne, " M. Eusèbe cannot tell you himself that it would have been impossible for anyone to show more courage, more devotion, more patience than he did. When my strength failed he spoke to me of those I loved, and he provided for all my wants with marvellous skill . . ."

" I made you eat very nasty things sometimes," said Eusèbe.

"Monsieur Eusèbe," said the girl, fixing her big clear eyes on Eusèbe's face, "please do not interrupt me. I will say what I think, and that is, that you are the best of friends and the most courageous of men."

" Good ! I shall have the Monthyon prize for bravery —twelve hundred francs and a medal."

" No ; only the hearty thanks of a woman who will never forget that she owes her life to you. In short, we made our way to the St. John's River, where we found a vessel that brought us to Picolata. The way hither was easy. And that is how, dear Charles, we have the delight of seeing each other once again."

In spite of his modesty, Eusèbe was the hero of the day. Freedy almost envied him. Valville gave a short account of his adventures at Green House ; but when he told the manner of Red Ralph's death, Jeanne said :—

" Forgive him, he has expiated his crime."

Little yet remains for us to tell in order to bring the story to a close.

The friends—to which rank Ned Bark was elevated at once—soon recovered from the effects of their long and dreary expeditions.

Charles Valville married Alice Lodier. Two other marriages were celebrated on the same day.

One of them, as our readers will have foreseen, was that of Freedy with Lucile.

The other—but we have given it the title of the concluding ceremony too early—was really only the betrothal of Jeanne and Eusèbe.

Yes, of Eusèbe, who had renounced his peculiarly coloured trousers and waistcoat, and was beginning to grow more thoughtful, although he had not lost his inexhaustible fund of gaiety.

A journey followed this betrothal and the weddings.

They made a pilgrimage to Devil's Rock in Florida, where Jeanne and Alice, in company with those whom they loved, recalled their former sorrowful experiences of the place.

But the sun was shining on the rocks and torrents, and Nature was so beautiful that the friends could smile there, even while remembering the past.

One person remains whose end we ought to know.

When Ned Bark, true to his word, repaired to the house in which Phil Samster had been detained, he found nothing but a heap of ashes and cinders. In a fit of drunken frenzy the wretched man must have set fire to the building and perished in the flames.

The incendiary had met with a death worthy of himself.

Eusèbe's betrothal has ended in a marriage.

As it is given to no man to be perfect, he has again, since his arrival in Paris, attended faithfully all theatrical performances.

But it is right to say that Jeanne is always at his side, that he adores her, and that she has completed his education.

He has sobered down now, and wears no colours but grey and black !

THE END.

PRINTED BY BALLANTYNE, HANSON AND CO.
EDINBURGH AND LONDON